# CREATIVITY

a
Novel

Fake Creativity
A Novel by: Blake Loch
Published by: Broken Ink Books

Copyright © 2025 Blake Loch.
Copyright © 2025 Broken Ink Books.

All rights reserved. No part of this publication may be reproduced, distributed, or transmitted in any form or by any means, including photocopying, recording, or other electronic or mechanical methods, without the prior written permission of the publisher, except in the case of brief quotations embodied in critical reviews and certain other noncommercial uses permitted by copyright law.

ISBN: 979-8-9992888-0-6 (Paperback)
ISBN: 979-8-9992888-1-3 (Hardcover)

Any references to historical events, real people, or real places are used fictitiously. Names, characters, and places are products of the author's imagination.

Published by Broken Ink Books, in the United States of America.

First printing edition 2025.
www.blakeloch.com

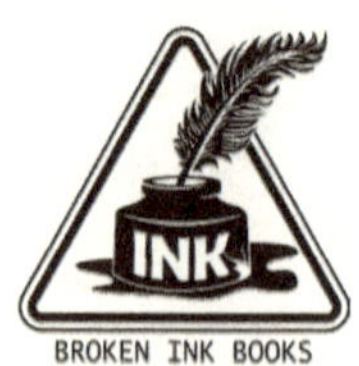

*To my wife, who has believed in every
single one of my dreams—no matter how crazy.
Without her, I wouldn't have any stories to write.*

# FAKE CREATIVITY

## BLAKE LOCH

# 1

*The following excerpt is from the upcoming novel,
Fake Creativity, by Cooper Owens.*

The clock in Victor Renard's Parisian mansion struck eight, its chime reverberating through the opulent study. The room was lined with shelves filled with leather-bound books and artifacts from bygone eras. It exuded an air of refined elegance and was a sanctuary for those of intellect and sophistication, much like Victor himself, who was also a man of discerning taste and an unyielding passion for fine art.

A rare René Magritte painting, a masterpiece, adorned one of the study's mahogany-paneled walls. Elena Martin meticulously surveyed the painting with a critical eye. Tonight, Victor was out attending a gala held in his honor, and she had seized the opportunity to finish her latest creation: a perfect replica that would soon replace the genuine René Magritte hanging on the wall before her.

Over time, Elena had cultivated the art of deception, honing her skills as a master forger. Her hand hovered over the canvas, delicate brush poised in slender fingers. Every stroke was deliberate, a testament to years of study and practice. She immersed herself in the work, channeling the spirit of the original artist with reverence and precision.

As Elena recreated the smallest details of René Magritte's *Le fils de l'homme*, her thoughts drifted to the delicate dance of duplicity she had orchestrated over the years. Victor, her lover and unwitting patron, had entrusted her with unrestricted access to his private collection, an act of blind faith that enabled Elena's daring exploits.

Against the backdrop of rarefied society, their relationship had blossomed in a whirlwind of gala evenings and cultural escapades. Yet beneath the veneer of romance lay Elena's secret, carefully hidden within a web of skillful lies.

Hours passed in silence, broken only by the soft rustle of brush against canvas. Elena's heartbeat quickened with a blend of excitement and apprehension. Tonight's forgery marked a pivotal moment in her clandestine endeavors, a culmination of artistry and subterfuge that blurred the lines between truth and illusion.

Finally, with a steady hand, Elena applied the final brushstroke, her eyes tracing the contours of her creation. The replica was flawless, evidence of her craftsmanship and unwavering resolve. She stepped back, satisfied with her work.

As she stood in the dimly lit study, a shadow of doubt crept into Elena's mind, just as it always did after she completed a piece. How long could she sustain the facade? And what would happen if Victor ever uncovered her carefully guarded secret? The weight of her double life bore down on her, a silent burden she carried with grace.

A soft chime echoed through the study, and Elena realized what time it was. She replaced the original painting with her replica. Victor would be back any minute, and the sounds just outside the estate meant that minute was fast approaching. Elena listened, her attention narrowing on the rhythm of the approaching steps.

Moments later, Victor entered the study. Tall and sharply dressed, he exuded an air of quiet confidence, easy elegance, and natural sophistication, each softened by his subtle charm.

"Elena, my dear." Victor greeted her with a warm smile, his eyes alight with affection. "How was your evening?"

Elena's heart fluttered at the sound of his voice, her composure unwavering. "Splendid, as always," she replied.

Victor's gaze drifted to his new prized possession. "Ah, *The Son of Man*," he remarked, his voice tinged with reverence. "A masterpiece. A self-portrait that defies all rules, blatantly concealing its intended purpose. Beautiful."

Elena's pulse quickened as she clasped her fingers together elegantly at her waist, admiring the painting with Victor while discreetly looking for any imperfections.

"Indeed," she murmured.

As Victor spoke further about the particular piece, quoting René himself, Elena observed him with affection. Their evening together unfolded with practiced precision, a symphony of cultured conversation and understated romance. Yet beneath the domestic bliss, Elena's delicate dance of deception was always at risk of revelation.

Hours later, the mansion settled into a hushed stillness as Elena and Victor's well of topics ran dry. Elena retired to bed before Victor as usual, her mind consumed by the intricacies of her existence.

Alone in the darkness, she gazed out the window at the twinkling lights of Paris. The city of lovers held secrets of its own, echoing the covert affair she navigated in her own life.

When morning came, light filtered through the curtains, casting a soft glow upon the polished floors of Victor's mansion. Elena, resolute and composed, rose from her bed with a sense of purpose. Today, after months of planning, a private exhibition would showcase Victor's most prized acquisitions, including a few of her expertly crafted forgeries.

Committed to the role she could no longer escape, Elena

dressed with care, her attire reflecting the sophistication of the world she had infiltrated. As she descended the grand staircase, the scent of freshly brewed coffee mingled with the soft strains of classical music that filled the air.

Victor stood in the sunlit conservatory, his tall frame outlined by the soft shapes of lush greenery and blooming plants. He turned as Elena approached, a smile lighting his features.

Elena returned his smile, her heart steadying within her chest.

"Good morning, my dear," Victor said, his voice full of anticipation.

"Good morning. Is everything in place for the exhibition?"

"I believe so." His eyes gleamed with pride. "I'm certain it will be a resounding success. Your attention to detail has been invaluable in curating this collection."

Elena smiled at his words, feeling both grateful and guilty. She masked her emotions effortlessly, her gaze steady.

"Thank you," she said. "It's been a pleasure to help with your vision."

As the day unfolded, the mansion buzzed with activity. Art enthusiasts and critics from across the city gathered in anticipation, eager to see Victor Renard's private collection. The halls resonated with murmurs of admiration and awe.

Among the esteemed guests was Charles Dubois, a renowned art critic whose discerning eye and sharp intellect had secured his reputation as an authority in the art world. He moved through the exhibition with a critical gaze, his attention lingering on each piece.

Elena, ever vigilant, observed Charles from a distance. She held her breath. The moment of truth was at hand, the test of her skill and the forgeries she had crafted.

As Charles approached *The Son of Man*, Elena's chest

tightened. He studied the piece with an intensity that sent a shiver down her spine, his fingers tracing the air as if memorizing each brushstroke.

Minutes felt like hours as Charles scrutinized the painting. Elena's pulse pounded in her ears, her mind racing with the implications of discovery. Would he recognize the forgery? Would her carefully crafted illusion crumble before his discerning gaze?

Finally, Charles stepped back, his lips curving into a faint smile. He turned to Victor, who stood nearby, his expression one of quiet confidence.

"Mr. Renard," Charles began, his voice controlled and deliberate, "your collection is truly extraordinary. This René Magritte, in particular, is a masterpiece, and I must admit I am quite jealous."

Relief flooded Elena's veins. She exchanged a fleeting glance with Victor, his eyes reflecting a mixture of pride and love.

As the evening progressed, the exhibition was hailed as a triumph. A testament to Victor Renard's discerning taste and Elena Martin's expertise. The guests departed with expressions of envy and wonder, their conversations filled with praise for the collection.

In the quiet aftermath of the event, Victor and Elena stood in the study, gravitating once more toward the portrait. Victor's gaze softened as he turned to Elena.

"You have a gift, Elena. Your contributions have elevated this collection to new heights."

"Thank you, Victor," she answered, her voice firm even as her emotions churned beneath the surface. The lies weighed more heavily on her soul with every interaction.

As the night deepened and the mansion once again settled

into quiet, Elena retreated to bed. Her deception continued, a precarious balance of passion and peril. Elena walked a tightrope of duplicity, her heart entwined with the man she loved and the secrets she guarded. As she drifted into sleep, the specter of impending revelation lingered on the horizon, a shadow that threatened to unravel the life she had crafted.

* * *

"What the fuck? How?"

Cooper said the words without even thinking, each one like an exhale. He couldn't fathom how this program, line after line of code, could possibly spew out a book idea that almost exactly matched the one he was currently working on. It was even using the character names that he had already written in his notes.

*Of course it would have Elena, but everyone else?*

He turned off the computer, in pure shock at what he had observed on the glowing screen in the darkness of his office. The curtains of the room's single window were drawn tight, which was rather unnecessary since the clock on the desk read 2:24 a.m. They did at least soften the sound of the occasional train that went whistling by, which Cooper appreciated when certain deranged conductors were too generous in alerting the small midwestern town to their presence.

He sat there in the darkness, deep in thought. The only light left in the room came from the digital clock, its ominous green glow adding to the surreal experience as he contemplated the implications of what he had just witnessed.

Cooper tried to wrap his head around it all. He was failing to figure out how this AI, this program, could already have his book in its database. The technology had come a long way, but surely it wasn't good enough to replace him. Not yet, anyway. He had dedicated his entire life to writing. No, it practically *was* his life. Some coding couldn't replicate that.

*I must have given it something. Access to my browsing history or notes. Something. That's the only explanation.*

He sat there for what seemed like all night, but the clock had only ticked forward a few minutes more when, luckily, one of those eager conductors and his train came barreling through the crossing just up the street. Without its greeting, he might have sat there until he passed out, succumbing to exhaustion before he could follow the infinite futures ahead of him.

If it hadn't been one of those conductors hopped-up on caffeine or God knows what else, yanking on that whistle like it was one of his appendages, Cooper would have been glued to his chair until Elena found him the next morning. This thought pulled him slightly away from the horror of the AI program and its abilities. All he could think about now was the blaring racket of the train. He could clearly picture the bug-eyed conductor, old-school uniform and all, getting off on the thought of waking up the town's roughly two hundred inhabitants, totally unaware that his attempts at inflicting misery actually had very little impact under normal circumstances.

Living by the railroad gave Cooper and Elena a front-row seat to the tricks the human mind could play on itself. A month after they had moved into the house, the average passing train had almost entirely become white noise. After a few more months, it was difficult for them to recall when the last train had gone by, or if any had passed at all that day.

But each time they invited new friends over, the illusion of quiet shattered a few minutes after their guests stepped inside. One of them would say something along the lines of, "Are they always that loud?" or, "It's cool, but I don't think

I'd be able to live this close." Cooper and Elena would continue to entertain their company, but Cooper seethed under the surface, every train that day speeding right through the forefront of his consciousness.

The illusion always held for Elena, the trains remaining an unimportant part of her world. Cooper wished that was the case for him, but he had to be patient while he re-acclimated to his surroundings to continue living peacefully near the essential—yet dated and often overlooked—transportation system. Luckily, other than their guests who knew not what they'd done, only the odd over-excited conductor, a derailing, or another terrible train-related incident could pull him out of his fabricated reality.

The rumbling of the heavy machinery faded into the distance with one last ghostly whistle as the train made its way to some unknown destination. Cooper found himself back in silence, slightly more grounded this time, his eyes adjusting to the darkness of his office. He got up from the desk before his thoughts could paralyze him again, though he was still trying to wrap his head around what he'd seen.

He slowly navigated his way to bed and sat gently on the side, still thinking as moonlight seeped onto the floor in front of him and poured across the room, highlighting the silhouette of Elena sleeping. Attempting not to wake her, he lay down cautiously, arranging his pillow with the delicate care of someone handling a stick of dynamite.

Cooper closed his eyes, still fending off a legion of ideas and possibilities. He wished sleep would be instantaneous so he could forget about the horror that had spewed onto his computer from some unimaginable source, at least for a little while. This was the real world, though, and escape wasn't easy, especially when he craved it the most.

# 2



*Her greatest fear was not being caught but being seen for the monster she truly was—an artist whose soul was as counterfeit as her creations.*

The next morning, Cooper awoke feeling the effects of a terrible night's sleep. The first thought in his head was that damned AI program. Along with it came confusion, anger, terror, and despair. He was still in disbelief, his brain still hijacked. He perked up as the smell of coffee entered his nose and brought him back to reality. The faint, sweet aroma of blueberry waffles also became noticeable as he got out of bed.

Elena was just about finished making breakfast as he entered the kitchen. He was still amazed at how tidy she kept everything when cooking; she was so organized. Almost the exact opposite of him whenever he tried his hand in the kitchen.

*My creativity just gets me in over my head*, he thought. Making a chocolate soufflé was much more enticing than starting with chicken noodle soup. With the messes he made while pretending to be a culinary genius, it was no wonder Elena always tried to get food on the table before he could intervene.

She turned around just as he was wrapping his arms around her for their typical morning embrace, making it much more intimate than he expected. Her beautiful blue eyes still gave him actual feelings, a fact that sometimes still surprised him. They weren't imaginary; they were honest-to-God real feelings, emotions and sensations that somehow came to life whenever he looked purposefully into those eyes. They were feelings that could only come from a decades-long relationship, like the one they had.

Cooper swam in the pale aquamarine blue of those eyes. Like clockwork, his heart rate quickened, his breathing became sharper, and he felt what could only be described as butterflies fluttering around in his gut.

Elena brushed a few loose strands of blonde hair from her face before slipping her arms through his and around his back. She gave him a gentle kiss and then looked at him with genuine love that slowly changed to sadness, subtle compassion at its edges.

"What time did you come to bed?" she asked.

"I don't remember . . . definitely not early. Sorry I'm late getting up. You're honestly the best wife a guy could ask for. Waking up to this," he said, motioning to the coffee and waffles on the kitchen island, "and this"—he slid his hands to her waist and pulled her closer—"is the best life I could ever wish for."

She blushed ever so slightly. There was a hint of a smile there but the sadness didn't disappear, at least not fully.

"Were you writing all night?"

The question quickly brought him right back into the onslaught of thoughts he had when he woke up this morning. The delicious smell of coffee and waffles faded into nothing as anxiety crept back over him, vivid recollections of those pages of words on his computer screen flashing through his mind. Were they still there? Had he closed the program? Had it really been that close to his original idea?

"Something like that." He realized that sounded a lot more suspicious than he'd intended and tried to follow it up before Elena took the idiotic response the wrong way. "I mean,

I did a little writing, but mostly just research and more prep, you know?"

"Okay . . . Well, do you think you're almost ready?" she asked, a look of confusion on her face.

*Fuck . . . why did I say it like that?* But he knew why.

He was dying to tell her about last night, but he needed her to lead the conversation there. He didn't want to give her the impression that he was losing his mind, and he absolutely couldn't make her think he was on a one-way track to becoming one of those crazy conspiracy theorists who believe the Earth is flat or whatever else was trending on social media right now.

"Yeah, I think I've got the basic idea and outline for the next book ready to go. I was going to let Cassandra know later today."

"Yay! I'm so ready to get away with you. The world lately . . . I just need a break from it all. Are you excited?" she asked, gripping him tighter as joy spread across her face.

Cooper reached for the back of his neck and rubbed it. "Yeah, I am," he said, not much pep in his voice.

How pathetic it all was. The motion, the tone of voice, all to avoid initiating the act of being vulnerable with Elena. So many theatrics just to get her to ask. He knew it was on purpose too, the effort entirely conscious, which made it all the worse. Was it because she intimidated him still? Or was it purely to preserve his ego and self-image? Deep down, he knew which it was.

She was so confident and sure of herself all the time. Elena hardly ever showed fear. Hell, she barely ever experienced it. When she did, it was with so much composure and strength. It was something he loved about her—though at times, he resented her for it. Being unable to match her calm made him feel like less of a man. Bringing his anxieties and worries to her was extremely difficult and always led to this conversational tango in his attempt to keep his self-esteem intact.

Elena leaned her head back so she could look at him better. "Okay, what's wrong?"

She had played this game thousands of times before, but she still went along with it. He was so thankful that she loved him that much. She didn't make him feel like a coward or ashamed of the way he sought her comfort. He could do that on his own. Even though he had been confident that she would eventually ask, relief washed over him.

"So . . . I wanted to show you something that kind of freaked me out last night while I was working. I didn't want to ruin the amazing breakfast you made, though."

"Well, how about we sit down and try to enjoy it before we delve into whatever terrifying stuff you saw in your office in the middle of the night? After we've had our fill of waffles and got our caffeine in, we'll go tackle whatever monsters are hiding out under your desk . . . or, more likely, whatever's lurking in your search history." She smiled and poked him in the ribs.

He knew she'd only been joking, but he still felt the need to defend himself. "You know I don't watch that stuff. Not to mention it's terrible for society." He paused before continuing, "I wish it was a monster, though. Then it would be real, and I'd have some excellent source material."

Elena was so good at making everything bad seem not so bad. This made him feel even worse about needing her to do that, but as the overwhelming thoughts succumbed to the smell of coffee and blueberries again, he was thankful.

Cooper tried not to talk about it as they ate. He had been honest when he said he really didn't want to ruin all the hard work Elena had put into the meal. Their breakfast conversations weren't enthralling, but neither of them cared. There weren't many exciting things to talk about since they did almost everything together. Each other's company was the only thing that mattered.

As they neared their last sips of coffee, Cooper couldn't hold it back any longer. He summarized his AI escapades from last night. She looked at him like he was insane at first, but then her expression softened as if she'd remembered she loved this crazy idiot.

"Well, let's go take a look at this new version of you. I'm just glad I don't have to look at some weird fetish porn that scared you out of your wits last night."

The second dig did get a small chuckle out of him.

As they stood up to head toward his office, a phone rang.

"Yours or mine?" Cooper asked.

Both of their phones were on the kitchen island, identical of course, as they had gotten them at the same time. Neither of them had taken the time to personalize their ringtones. Elena picked up hers.

"It's work, probably trying to figure out exactly when we're leaving. I guess I should tell them pretty soon, shouldn't I?" she asked him with a smile on her face.

"Yeah, you should."

"I'll meet you in the office in a few minutes."

She answered the call as she walked into the next room.

Cooper put their dishes in the sink, grabbed his phone, and made his way to his office. He couldn't help but appreciate how lucky he was that Elena shared many of the luxuries he did. After years of working for the same company, they'd become inseparable in more ways than one. They were practically a package deal at this point.

It was a privilege he didn't take lightly, especially since it meant she could always join him on trips to their cabin, which was tucked away in the Colorado mountains. It was a place where they could both get some work done, distraction-free. He probably wouldn't be able to write without her there. If need be, he would just stay at home and work on his book, but for now they could both take the time away.

Soon, he would unplug from reality in the great snowy heights of his favorite place in the world, with his favorite person, and just let the words flow. But for now, he needed to focus on the problem at hand.

Cooper sat down at his desk and powered on the computer. He navigated to the AI browser he was messing with last night and was met with a blank chat box. No record of his previous conversation. After telling Elena what happened, he'd hoped that last night's text would still be there. He would just have to replicate it now. He typed:

> I am Cooper Owens, pretend you are me and give me the first chapter of my next book.

The words appeared on the screen, faster than any human could type. Cooper was catching bits here and there and noticed something was different. Once the response had finished generating and he had time to read through it, he found himself in utter dismay. It was nonsense, and more importantly, it wasn't remotely close to the idea of his next book.

He entered the prompt again, and the response was just as terrible, if not worse. Pure computer-generated garbage. There were errors everywhere, duplicate words and similar phrasing galore. There was no art in what was on the screen and, again, it was not Cooper's next book idea.

Are you sure you're pretending to be me, Cooper Owens?

Words flooded the screen again:

Yes, I am doing my best to try to write like you, Cooper Owens, would. I apologize if it isn't meeting your expectations, but my programming only allows me to use what is available to generate my responses. I know you are one of the most well-respected romance novelists to date with numerous books topping the bestsellers list, but I can only use those portions of your work that are publicly available to imitate your writing style.

Cooper kept spamming the prompts to try to get something that slightly resembled what he got last night before Elena came into the room:

Write like me!
Give me the chapter you gave me last night when you were pretending to be me.
I am Cooper Owens, give me my next book idea!

"So, this is what you wanted to show me?" Elena asked, making Cooper jump in his chair. "It must be pretty scary, huh?" She laughed and leaned over him to look at the monitor.

Resting on his shoulder, she used the mouse to scroll through the chat he had just created, reading through it silently in her head.

"Looks like pretty shitty technology to me. What's so freaky about it?" she asked.

"It wasn't like this last night! It was nothing like this. It gave me my exact book idea and the first chapter almost word for word. It had the entire outline for the story ready to go, just like I planned to write it."

Elena looked at him in a way that made him feel only a little crazy.

"Seriously, it even used the same character names that I have picked out. It even used your name. It knew . . . everything."

"Well of course it would use my name. I'm in all your books. And the other stuff, are you sure it was that similar, or was it just close to your ideas? Maybe the fact that they were magically appearing out of nowhere was making it seem worse than it really was."

"Maybe . . . I guess. But no, the characters and the outline, it was all too similar, I swear."

Cooper realized he was starting to sound just like those flat-earthers. He tried to regain his composure before he escalated to a the-president-is-a-lizard-believer in Elena's eyes. He looked at the computer screen again, trying to glimpse any evidence that he could use to redeem himself, but there was nothing.

"Maybe you were just overtired and got freaked out about the idea of some technology like this taking over everything in the world and replacing us. I mean, it is pretty likely to happen someday . . . just not today." She leaned over and kissed him on top of his head.

Cooper didn't want to seem crazier than he already did and accepted defeat. "Yeah, maybe I was just tired."

He knew last night had happened; he was almost certain. The pressure to be a sane human and a non-crazed husband was strong. He could feel the pull of his brain telling him to accept Elena's suggestion and commit to the idea that it had been nothing more than a sleep-deprived exaggeration. It was impossible to lie to himself, but there was no denying that it would be easier to just go along with Elena and pretend none of it had happened.

# 3



Cooper looked at himself in the webcam preview. *Cassandra should be calling any minute now*, he thought. He ran his hands through his long brown hair, trying to slick back the purposefully messy style.

At this point, his appearance didn't matter, or at least, the sales said it didn't. Still, no amount of money was ever going to erase his need to look good, no matter how much Cooper wished he could just quit caring about what other people thought of him.

But looking good didn't mean standing out. Cooper hated attention and dressed to make sure he got none, dressing well below what his bank account could allow. A nice pair of broken-in jeans and a well-worn T-shirt or hoodie was his preferred outfit of choice. Although he was in excellent shape, he made sure his clothes fit in a way that showed no evidence of the muscles he worked so hard to build.

Cooper looked average, just the way he intended. His hair was practically the only unique thing he had allowed himself. The one other differentiating feature, not by choice, were his deep, dark-brown eyes, tired and sunken-looking from long hours staring into a screen. They often looked out of place in his otherwise bright, clean, and approachable face, as if the true Cooper Owens was hiding somewhere under all that normalness.

After he'd finished double-checking his appearance and

was no longer distracted by his virtual reflection, Cooper felt a sense of unease wash over him. The computer in front of him—an amazing, necessary, and extremely useful tool—now incessantly reminded him of that program.

At least after this video call, he could get away from it for a bit. Sure, he'd still be typing on a different computer in Colorado—he wasn't some kind of hipster who wrote everything on a typewriter—but at least it wouldn't be *this* computer. The one constantly reminding him that some AI program might soon make him unnecessary.

Until now, he hadn't needed to take extreme measures or use outdated technology to disconnect. It used to be as simple as turning off the Wi-Fi and switching his phone to airplane mode, leaving it on the counter instead of carrying it everywhere. That's all it took. It was what he had done ever since buying the cabin years ago. This temporary vacation from worldwide connectivity was probably one of the biggest reasons why he continued to be as successful as he was.

A world filled to the brim with technology built entirely to distract, polarize, and most importantly, sell the next generation of technology is a dangerous thing. It's easy to get sucked in, trapped in the loop forever, never able to make anything meaningful out of life. Cooper wasn't immune to it, and just like everyone else, occasionally wasted hours upon hours on meaningless distractions: scrolling through endless streams of cat videos and posts about what people had for dinner, or playing just one more level of some phone game that was almost as addictive as heroin with its exciting colors, animations, sounds, and rewards.

The failure of Cooper's fourth book still haunted him, a mistake he attributed to his lack of focus while writing it. At the time, he had been pulled in so deep that he often took breaks mid-sentence to check social media. He had gotten cocky and thought he was just gifted after the success of his first three books. He had assumed he could simply write and it would be good. Outside factors and influences didn't matter; nothing could tarnish his talent.

How wrong he had been. Cooper still remembered the moment he realized his fourth book was a steaming pile of dog shit, which was unfortunately only after it was published and on the shelves. When his self-hatred had finally subsided and he'd realized that writing took more than just talent, he knew something needed to change.

It wasn't easy to escape from technology, even temporarily. It has a way of tightening its grip over time, usually by design. It took a lot of trial and error, as well as Cooper's modest success from his first few books, to have the routine he had now.

At first, the cabin alone had been quite a retreat: twenty-three acres of privacy and seclusion, a place where the static and noise of the world faded and he could focus on what really mattered. Eventually, the technological pause also became a part of the whole excursion.

They had never been that strict with their exodus or the unplugging-from-society rule in prior years, but the scare he received in his office had solidified Cooper's idea that this time would be different. He couldn't provide any opening for that program to see his work. No occasional checking of emails, no mindless scrolling in bed, not even for one night, and absolutely no turning the internet back on to check the news or see what was going on in the world.

Cooper told himself all this precaution wasn't just out of fear. If they committed to this, *Fake Creativity* might turn out to be his greatest book yet. Not to mention, he and Elena would finally get some quality time together, free from all distractions—time that might bring them back to how things were last year, when they'd been so close, perfectly in tune.

After all, there are worse things than spending four glorious, uninterrupted months in the town of Timber Creek, Colorado, without internet. With a population of roughly two thousand, it was small enough to go unnoticed and quiet enough to actually get some work done. This was especially true in the winter, when the town was blanketed in snow. On average, Timber Creek received between 160 and 180 inches annually, but Cooper remembered one of their first years there when the snowfall topped two hundred inches.

Sometimes he and Elena went earlier to watch fall fade away, occasionally as soon as October, when they could feel the full force of the seasons changing. Other years, they showed up late in the dead of winter, when the landscape was as white as cotton and dotted with evergreens peeking through, the snow firmly rooted in place. On these trips, they got to watch as the world thawed back into the one most people preferred, one filled with warmth and bright sunshine.

Cooper loved everything about the winter. At least, almost everything. It was one reason he felt like he didn't fit in. Everybody always seemed to be chasing those warm summer nights filled with fun and friends. He was just the opposite.

To him, nothing could beat a crisp, cold winter night sky, when all the stars it held seemed to be a few thousand light-years closer, as the air became thinner and the nights got longer. He loved the ominous glow of snow all around and a warm fire inside, hints of smoke hanging in the frozen air; the way the snow could transform the world into a cleaner and quieter place; how the sheer number of people seemed cut in half as everyone tried to stay cozy and warm in their homes, only venturing out if necessary; and the way walking outside made him feel more alive when the cold air hit his lungs on that first breath.

*Soon*, he thought.

The holidays, though, that was a different story. Cooper tried to pretend they didn't exist, another powerful motivation for the system he had designed. The months-long writing retreats were a way to run away from the real world and the complex issues that came with being a human who hadn't just popped into existence by itself.

Issues, trauma, first-world problems, whatever you wanted to call them, they were what helped someone succeed if they let them, or destroyed them if they didn't. Most importantly, they were definitely what made a good writer. For that reason alone, none of it bothered Cooper much anymore, but running away to that sweet winter wonderland and limiting almost all communication definitely helped.

Clear visions of that cabin all lit up among the pines were interrupted by a ringing noise coming from his computer. A video call box had popped up on his screen. He shook the last flakes of imaginary snow off his shoulders as he tried to situate himself to be more upright and professional-looking in the webcam preview. He pushed his hair back one last time before clicking the green button.

The gray silhouette of a person on the screen was replaced by Cassandra. As the pixels slowly came into focus, he could see the curls of her auburn hair, but the glare on her glasses was causing the camera to struggle. As the lag disappeared, Cooper saw his trusted manager sitting in her office.

Cassandra had been there with him from the very

beginning and had helped him become this Cooper Owens. The one who sold millions of books, scored movie deals, and topped bestseller lists year after year. Not the Cooper Owens who was filled with insecurities and had to write in order not to lose his mind and end up either dead or in a psychiatric ward. *She probably hasn't actually met that one*, he thought.

Cassandra handled each and every aspect of the work that went on behind the scenes, the important details that truly decided whether a writer succeeded or not. Even though her office was so familiar and burned into his memory with its motivational posters and maroon walls, this was how he typically saw it now, on a screen. They had moved beyond in-person meetings long ago; they didn't need them anymore. Both understood each other as much as any two people could in a business relationship, and it clearly worked.

"Cooper, I'm so excited. At least, I hope this means good news. We got your proposal a few weeks ago. I'm assuming you're calling to let me know you're about to go 'off the grid'? And of course to reiterate the importance of not contacting you unless absolutely necessary?"

"Yeah, that sounds about right."

"Awesome, well, I'll let everyone know and start getting things ready for when you return, but other than that, I guess go enjoy your frozen wintry hell. I honestly still don't know how you can even write when it's that cold."

"It's an acquired taste, and gloves help." Cooper smirked and Cassandra smiled, humoring his sorry excuse for a joke.

"You couldn't pay me to live there. By the way, I don't know if you've heard, but there's a bet going around the office about what you actually do up in those mountains all winter, since none of us believe you really like it up there."

"Really?" A vacant smile spread across Cooper's face as

he imagined the office breakroom whiteboard filled with the ridiculous theories and complicated bets.

"Yeah, I had my money on mysterious Yeti," Cassandra said matter-of-factly.

Cooper laughed hard. "Yeti?"

"Yes, a Yeti. When winter comes, you transform, sort of like a werewolf. Your love of snow is only rivaled by your love for literature," she grinned, clearly proud of her own terrible joke. "But now that you said you wear gloves, I guess I'm out of the running, since a Yeti wouldn't need them to write."

Cooper was finding all of this extremely amusing and lighthearted—a sharp contrast to the fear he'd felt all morning.

"Okay, now you have to tell me some of the others," he said.

"Well, let's see here. Clark said the obvious one, you're a serial killer who buries his bodies so deep under the snow they aren't found until it's too late and you're already back home. Claire from the art department bets you host a winter underground sex retreat for the rich and wealthy, where everyone spends the entire season locked away, wearing nothing but bear skins, hibernating and . . . well, you know. John in marketing said probably just writing. Don't think he's even close with that one."

"Typical John," Cooper replied, before bursting out laughing, which made Cassandra join in.

Once their laughter had subsided, Cassandra transitioned back to business as usual. "Well, if you're still not going to reveal the truth, I guess I'll just keep taking bets. Speaking of money, your advance is probably already on its way to your account. But do you need anything else before you leave society?"

"No, I don't think so. Pretty sure we're all good."

"Alright, well, I guess that's everything. Good luck with the writing, Cooper. We know it'll be a good one."

"Thanks. Hopefully, it will be."

With a quick smile, she ended the call. That was it. That's how easy it was and how easy it had been for some time.

It had taken a few years to get to this point, and Cooper appreciated how lucky he was to have Cassandra and to have reached a level where all the marketing, meetings, and other annoying things that came with writing books now boiled down to a one-minute video call. This time, though, he felt something bubbling up before the video calling app had even fully closed on the computer—regret.

*Should I have told her? No, I don't have any proof, and that's the last thing I should ever tell the people who sign my checks. May as well just give them my books for free instead. I just need to try and forget about it. I still don't even know if it was a fluke or real.*

Cooper tried to shift his attention back toward more optimistic thoughts. Small moments of gratitude always came easier and more frequently when he was working on a new novel. If he leaned into the thoughts enough, he might be able to make the scare of that AI program a thing of the past. Completely push it into the unimportant section of his brain. There was a small window of opportunity and he just needed to focus on how good things actually were.

There was no denying it; his life was pretty good. Okay . . . better than good. How many people get to run away for months and spend all their time doing the thing they love most in the world? And just like that, the excitement of leaving for Colorado with Elena and getting to work was slowly washing over everything else, making even the most ominous and dark thoughts seem brighter.

New books made Cooper look at the world in a more positive and upbeat way, but it never lasted. It was why he continued to write, chasing a world he wanted to live in. Each project was another hit of a drug that kept him moving forward year after year.

He had all the money he could ever need, but a Cooper Owens who didn't write scared him. Terrified him, more than anything else. He could always write, even if it was just for himself. *That would be enough*, he lied.

# 4

*Their connection was instant and electric, a meeting of two souls who had been battered by life but still clung to the fragile beauty they found in art.*

Cooper was packing the last of his things into his suitcase and going through a mental checklist to make sure he wasn't forgetting anything. The great thing about having a second house was that he didn't really have to pack all that much.

Many others who've enjoyed this rare luxury have failed at the most important part: making it feel like a home. Instead, they did just the opposite and bought more property for pure vanity instead of purpose. Each additional house more empty, fake, and artificial than the last, until eventually nowhere felt like home.

Cooper made sure that he didn't make that mistake. Everything about the building he was in now and the one in Colorado felt like his and Elena's. Each house was unique in design, but inside, they felt the same. Maybe that was all in his head. All he knew was that until he heard that eerie sound of a train in the distance or looked out the window and saw those mountains covered in snow, he could barely tell the difference between the two.

He had gone so far as to buy two of almost everything he owned. To most, that would seem crazy, but to him, it made so much sense.

It didn't matter where he was; if he wanted to grab his favorite T-shirt from the closet, he could. He brushed his teeth with the same toothbrush, washed his hair with the same shampoo, and most significantly, fell asleep on the same bed. Of course, it wasn't the *same* bed. It wasn't like he had somebody magically transport all his stuff and arrange it perfectly before he got to whichever house he was staying at, but it was close enough.

The one thing that might seem the most crucial to be the same was not, and Cooper was grateful for that. His computer and writing space in Colorado were nothing like the ones he had here.

The office in this modest Midwestern home was cluttered with bookshelves, papers, binders, and who knew what else. Not even he did. There were trinkets and personal memorabilia scattered throughout, various art pieces hanging on the wall—the most notable being a giant poster of René Magritte's *Le fils de l'homme* for inspiration—and countless other distractions. It was not an ideal place to focus, but excellent for brainstorming.

He was grabbing the last of his notes and other materials he needed to take with him when he saw the mess of his computer with its multiple monitors and other gadgets sitting on the desk. Almost all of it was connected to the internet, which meant it had *that* program lurking somewhere behind the electricity, light pulses, and signals that traveled through the air and the tangle of countless cords that gave it life. The program that he was still struggling to push out of his memory. *I won't be missing you*, he thought.

Cooper heard the front door open just as he placed another folder of papers—the last thing he needed to pack for the trip—into his bag.

"What the hell?" Elena exclaimed as she looked at the organized, full suitcase in the middle of the messy, chaotic, yet similarly stuffed office. "Why do you always pack without me? You end up making me feel rushed."

"You know we tried that one time and it ended in a fight. Remember? We were yelling at each other from different rooms as we rushed around packing, and we still forgot almost everything we actually needed to bring. Not to mention, the fight was the least of it. The hours of emotionally charged silence in the car were absolutely delightful."

Cooper could see the memory drifting across her face as anger turned to agreement, though her expression said, *You're still kind of an asshole.*

"I also like helping you get your stuff together," he added. "And since I had the time, I figured I might as well. That way we're not both running around like chickens with our heads cut off."

"You're right," Elena conceded as she walked over and peeked into his suitcase. She flipped through its contents, noting the clothes for the road, a couple of binders, a stack of folders, and a few books. "Are you sure you have everything you need?"

"Yeah, this is everything. I'm all yours. Ready and at your service."

"Well, okay then. You can help by getting my suitcase from the basement."

Cooper gave her a smile and knelt down, tucked his hair behind his ear, and grabbed her hand.

"As you wish, my princess. I shall go to the dangerous dark depths of our unfinished, cold, concrete basement to prove my love for you."

If he could overcome this perilous journey, he would win the affection of this fair maiden. He jumped up with a shocking amount of enthusiasm, sending Elena into one of her silent fits of laughter, and ran out of the room toward his next adventure. He heard one audible laugh that escaped her restraint as he reached the stairs and descended into the basement.

Elena laughed like no one else he knew. Often no sounds escaped her mouth. Instead she just shook as the jokes registered. It was as if she was trying to contain all her joy and humor inside instead of sharing it.

If he cracked a really good joke, sometimes he got a peek at all of the laughter she was keeping to herself. Other times, she silently convulsed until tears rolled down her cheeks and her face became flushed as she tried not to let a sound escape, almost passing out from lack of breath. People who didn't know her would probably think she was having a seizure. Eventually, she would return to her non-laughing state, looking a little lighter as she wiped her eyes and smiled.

After all these years, it had become like a game to Cooper, getting that laugh out of her. He absolutely loved making her laugh, silent or not, but it also saddened him when he thought about it too much. Why did she try to hide the joy? Why didn't she let it out?

He knew she wasn't purposefully laughing this way; it was likely subconscious but it made him feel sorry for her. Somewhere along the line, she became a person who was afraid to be happy and express it. All he wanted to do was make her feel safe enough to let it all out, not just the laughter, but all of it. For now, that one laugh that others would mistake for an awkward exhale would have to be enough.

Cooper reached for a suitcase that looked just like the one he had packed, only mint-green.

"Ah, here it is." He made his way back up the stairs. "Hey,

where are you at? I've slayed the dragon and have the treasure you requested."

"I'm in here," Elena yelled from what sounded like the dining room.

He made his way there and placed the suitcase next to a big box of books on the table. "What's all of this?"

"Just because I get to go away with you doesn't mean I don't have work to do. You built a studio in the cabin for a reason."

"I know that," he said with a blank stare, trying to convey that he wasn't that stupid. He added a brief grin to soften the statement. "It's just a lot more than I expected."

Elena also worked in the wonderful world of books. That was how they met. She did some freelance editing on the side every once in a while, but her actual job was narrating books, a fact he still found amusing to this day.

She hated every kind of digital book; anything that wasn't made of physical paper, anything that wouldn't be there if the power ran out. She said it was the feel of the pages and the sound when you flipped to the next one that made books really special, always purposefully ignoring how cliché this sounded. Yet here she was, responsible for the existence of hundreds, if not thousands of the very things she despised.

Pretty early in his writing career, Cassandra had set up a meeting to discuss turning his first three novels into audiobooks. Apparently, he had been missing out on a lot of sales by sticking to traditional formats. When Cooper walked into that office, there she was, in a chair that normally sat empty next to his.

He didn't remember much of the actual meeting, but the first time he heard her voice . . . that was still extremely clear. He could have listened to that voice all day, but what she said was what really pushed him to ask if she wanted to grab coffee sometime: "I've read your stuff and am happy to narrate it. I guess Cassandra thinks I'd be a good fit. Your books though, they're . . . fine. I wasn't really that impressed, like everyone else seems to be. I just thought you should know that before making a decision."

To this day, Cooper had still never listened to any of the audiobooks Elena had voiced, other than a few snippets he caught while she was recording. This was for several reasons, some of which even he wasn't fully aware of. But there were two he did recognize.

The first was that Elena might actually file for divorce if she ever caught him partaking in the sacrilege that was digital audiobooks. Cooper knew this was the furthest thing from the truth, but he still teased Elena about it occasionally, joking that she would serve him with the appropriate papers before he had even gotten past the first chapter, especially if it was a book she had narrated.

The second, real reason was that he didn't want to spoil the real thing. Sure, others could listen to her voice whenever they wanted and that made him a little jealous, but he was one of the few who got to hear her voice *live* in all its glory and nuance.

Oh, and she made him promise not to; that reason was hard to forget. So make that three reasons why Cooper had never once listened to one of Elena Owens's audiobooks.

Cooper looked through the pile of books, examining covers and reading titles as he slowly made his way back to the present.

"Are any of these good?" he asked.

"How should I know? I haven't read them yet," she said with a puzzled look on her face.

"Duh." He smacked himself on the forehead theatrically and gave her a smile. "You'll tell me which ones are after you read them though, right? Curate me some summer reading, just like you always do?"

"Of course."

He gave her an appreciative look and lifted the box, surprised at the weight of all the stories it held. Or was it too light for the dreams in those pages?

"I think you might actually need a second suitcase this time. Off I go to slay another dragon for my princess. Maybe this time it will earn me a little extra love tonight."

With a wink, he was off to the basement again and before he reached the bottom of the stairs, he heard another single, lonely laugh.

# 5

*The magic of their journey lay not just in the destinations but in the moments in between them, where their love blossomed in the quiet and they wove a delicate tapestry of shared dreams and whispered secrets.*

Only a couple hundred miles remained until they got to their winter oasis away from the real world, but even with excitement pulsing through his veins—along with an exorbitant amount of caffeine—Cooper could feel his eyes getting heavy. How had he done this so easily before?

Cooper had always loved driving through the night, being one of the few lonely cars on roads built for an obscene number of people—people who had no choice but to use them, stuck in bumper-to-bumper traffic. It made him feel like he was breaking the law. But eventually headlights would come out of the darkness, reminding him it was perfectly legal to traverse these countless miles of black asphalt whenever he pleased.

He always wondered where those other cars were going to and coming from, and why they were driving at full speed into the darkness . . . just like he was.

There was so much magic to night driving. But as he rubbed his tired eyes to bring them back into focus, he had the depressing realization that it was beginning to fade.

He used to watch the lines on the pavement blur past like shooting stars. Whenever he entered some remote, dark, vast place and caught a glimpse of a brilliant night sky that didn't exist when the world's lights were turned on, quiet astonishment would wash over him. Cooper's favorite thing about night driving, though, was the way the cold night air whistled into the car and across his face when he rolled the window down to feel how fast he was really going.

It used to make him feel so much when he was younger, and he considered it essential to the experience. After going seventy in the darkness for hours, it was easy to question what planet he was on. With each mile, it felt more and more like he was traveling into the expanse between those magnificent stars. He was only reassured when he let the air seep in and realized he could still breathe. That first inhale used to make him feel incredibly alive.

Now, as Cooper rolled the window down, he didn't feel any of that. He only heard the *Whooooooshhhhh* and the stupendous thumping and vibration of the wind as it poured into the vehicle. It terrified him.

What used to make him feel alive now made him feel nothing but annoyance at how deafening the sound was. Arguments about how he wasn't that old yet were already racing through his head. He was just tired, that's all.

He knew he wouldn't be able to lie to himself forever, but nostalgia for his youth was already trying to creep into the present. No matter how much he tried to experience that magic again, he was grasping at air. Air that was currently destroying his eardrums.

*Whooooooshhhhh!*

On top of that brain-shattering noise, the air brought with it the type of cold that reaches deep enough to touch bone. This normally added to its revitalizing feeling, but now only drew attention to the way his joints and entire body hurt more than they should.

Cooper's legs were stiff, almost to the point of immobility;

his butt was sore even though it was resting on the luxurious, cushioned seat; and his shoulders were full of painful, nagging knots. All this from a drive that used to barely faze him. By the time he had finished the quick body scan, the remaining warm air had been sucked out of the car and his attention returned to the temperature.

The vehicle might not be traveling through space, but if he didn't reseal the *cabin*, freezing to death seemed likely. With that last hint of some inner child lurking in his subconscious, he reached for the *control panel*, cranked the temperature knob all the way to the right, and rolled up the window before he devolved any further into a midlife crisis.

The car slowly returned to a comfortable seventy-three degrees. The surroundings were passing by silently and they were riding in calm, comfort, and luxury again. Cooper could feel the heated seat taking the chill away.

Elena stirred slightly with the shift in environment but as usual, she was still sleeping as restfully as one possibly could on a road trip. She had perfected her technique and become a master of vehicular napping. A combination of pillows, noise-canceling headphones, classical music, and blankets allowed her to *teleport*, as she liked to call it, going to sleep in one place and waking up in another, all thanks to Cooper.

He didn't mind providing this service. Who wouldn't give the gift of teleportation to someone they loved? If anything, the presence of a sleeping passenger perfectly paired with the experience he had just tried to relive. A companion who didn't interrupt the journey but was there if needed, and ensured he never felt alone while going forward into the darkness.

Elena always offered to stay up with him and usually kept him company in the early hours of their long trips. He knew she wouldn't hesitate to drive or stay awake for the whole thing if he asked her to, but Cooper had always reassured her that it was perfectly fine with him if she slept. *Or at least it used to be.* He turned up the volume on the true crime podcast he was listening to in an attempt to drown out that idea and wake himself up.

"The police had found multiple bone fragments and other pieces of evidence around the property, but were still unsure of who the victims were . . ."

There was nothing like a bit of death and despair to drown out his worries and cause the miles to fly by.

It was almost two o'clock in the morning when Cooper slowed to a halt in front of the black iron gate to their mountain property. He rolled down the window and entered Elena's birthday into the keypad.

He knew it was pure stupidity to use something like that for any sort of security purpose, but doing so had felt instinctive. That's what everyone does, right? Make their password something related to a loved one? He didn't really have any other important configurations of numbers in his life, at least any that he could remember.

With the last digit, the gate slowly opened and he felt a spark of joy as he drove across the property line. There were only a few hundred yards of driveway between them and that glorious sanctuary. Every inch of it was a magical journey through the most beautiful stretch of pines he had ever encountered on his search for the perfect writing retreat. The building, house, cabin—whatever you wanted to call it—wasn't the only thing that mattered. Cooper had wanted the surrounding property to feel like its own little world. He prided himself on having accomplished just that.

There was no snow covering the ground yet, which made the drive easy but less spectacular. When the land was draped in a thick blanket of white, the short trip from the gate to the cabin felt like passing through a personal winter wonderland.

Cooper loved it so much that he didn't even mind clearing the road himself. He could hire someone, but since the equipment came with the property, it hardly felt like work. Actually, it felt like the opposite. He looked forward to putting some headphones on and taking a light stroll back and forth, the old machine chugging along in front of him and throwing the snow into the air it had come from, only for it to fall back down precisely on the side of the driveway.

As he neared the end of the pines, he watched the warm exterior lights of the cabin grow brighter until the structure itself came into focus. He knew calling it a cabin was absurd, and if anyone besides Elena heard him say it, they'd probably think he was the most pretentious asshole alive. But the word mattered to Cooper. A cabin was a warm, quiet place, tucked away from the world. A place to disconnect and focus on what actually mattered.

This *cabin* was nearly ten thousand square feet of pure, unapologetic luxury. Sure, it had a lot of wood features and accents, but as Cooper pulled up near the front door, put the car in park, and stared up at the massive windows framed against charred shou sugi ban timber and the huge stone-block columns and walls that made up most of the architecture, he knew he was lying to himself.

The contrast between the black, burnt wood and the lighter stone was dramatic, and the numerous massive windows confused the brain even more as the residence walls flowed seamlessly from light to dark to translucent. It was magnificent even at night, but a crisp white snowfall accentuated the stark differences in a way that made Cooper feel something when he looked at it.

The shou sugi ban siding and accents weren't original to the property, but he'd had them installed before he took a single writing retreat here. They were designed so well that they didn't even look like additions. The charred look had always appealed to him, but something about the entire concept made it a must-have for his dream property.

What appeared to be a deliberate destruction of lumber with roaring flames accomplished just the opposite: preservation for years to come. It might not look it, with its newly burnt, blackened, and scarred appearance, but it was now stronger than ever. If that wasn't poetry and beauty in nature, he didn't know what was. Especially when he ignored the fact that a little human interference had been required for the transformation process.

*Or did that make it more beautiful?*

Now that the car had been stationary for a bit too long, Elena's body stirred, her consciousness slowly following suit. There's a quiet charm in the way someone wakes from a long car nap, but to Cooper, nobody could compare.

Almost all her actions were the same as most people's, from the rubbing of the eyes to the awkward spine-bending in the cramped seats to the contorting stretch in a space that she could touch wall to wall if she really wanted to. But Elena treated the final act—peering through each and every window to take in the surroundings—as if she had genuinely teleported.

Others perform this behavior with relief that the long drive is over. She did it with a sense of magic. She was fully present in the fact that she had gone to sleep in one place and woken up in another. Although it was a place she had been numerous times before, it didn't matter in the slightest.

Cooper sat there in silence, careful not to interrupt her, enjoying the spectacle. This was exactly the reason he didn't mind driving while she slept. He would never, ever want to take this experience away from her.

Except . . . this time, what normally gave him pure love and joy was spoiled by a small fraction of jealousy.

Elena didn't look like she was struggling at all to keep in touch with this internal magical moment, he thought to himself while simultaneously trying to stave off the bitter feelings caused by his observation.

"How was the journey?" he asked as she finished her survey and gave him a sleepy smile, her expression slow to wake.

"Absolutely dreamy." Her voice was gentle and the words floated quietly in the thinner air.

"Excellent. But we have a problem . . ." Cooper tried to look as serious as he could.

"What?" Her smile disappeared from her now-worried face.

"How do I put this? The teleportation machine on this trip went a little wonky, and we experienced a few . . . um, catastrophic malfunctions."

"What do you mean? Did something go wrong? Did you get pulled over or hit something? What happened?"

"Well . . . I did hit a wrong button, and instead of just teleporting, we kind of time-traveled this trip too. So, the good news is we are at the cabin. The bad news is that it's the year 2743 and robots control the world. We might very well be the only humans not enslaved. Luckily, our cabin is somehow miraculously still here, surprisingly untouched by the hundreds of years of Machine Versus Meat wars. I told you the shou sugi ban was a functional choice, too."

Her smile quickly returned, more awake and energized

this time. "The black has grown on me. Just don't go asking me if you can decorate the rest of the cabin with it."

"Let's go see how that interior of yours has held up over several hundred years, and then we can talk about it," Cooper said playfully. "By the way, we'll also need to start planning how to save our species from the machines. And we should probably get going on our part in the repopulation efforts. There's no time to waste."

She looked at him simultaneously with immense love and like he was a pathetic twentysomething excited about growing his first decent beard. "Okay, lead the way, supposed savior of the human race."

He opened the car door and let the cool, crisp night air in, causing them to feel more awake than they should at this hour. The smell of the surrounding forest quickly followed and overwhelmed their senses, making the cold fade into normalcy. Elena grabbed the door handle and followed suit, doubling the sensations.

They both sat in silence for a few seconds as they listened to the gentle waterfall of the man-made stream that bordered one edge of the cabin. Another feature that Cooper just had to have. An outside observer might think it contributed to the overall artificialness of the place, but to him, it added the perfect amount of audible nature and ambiance. The sound of water trickling over rocks was beautiful enough to make them pause, the act almost entirely subconscious.

After their ears were filled with the soothing sounds of the stream, they both got out of the car as gracefully as their stiff bodies would allow and were finally able to stretch in a way that wasn't restricted by their teleportation machine. The recent shock to their senses was quickly becoming their new baseline.

As Elena gathered her stuff, Cooper rested his elbows on the roof of the car and looked at her.

"Don't worry about any of that stuff tonight. I'm sure the robots don't know we're here yet. We should focus on the task at hand." He paused, smirking. "Getting to bed."

Elena rolled her eyes, but didn't need to be told twice. She closed her door and waited as Cooper walked around the car. Instead of heading straight for the cabin, he stopped beside her and draped his arm over her shoulder, resting a tiny bit of his weight there. Elena supported him, easing the force of gravity slightly as she rubbed his back. The gesture carried a quiet appreciation, a silent thank-you for letting her teleport all the way here while he traveled the boring old-fashioned way.

They made their way to the front door, moving in perfect harmony. Cooper didn't know who had started walking first or who was leading the way now. He unlocked the cabin by once again typing Elena's birthday into the digital keypad, the act nearly automatic. Without hesitation, they disappeared into their cherished winter retreat to get some rest, and more importantly, begin their efforts to save the world.

# 6

*Amidst the routine, their love grew in the small gestures—a shared cup of coffee, a lingering touch, a quiet evening spent in comfortable silence.*

The early morning sun spilled across the Colorado valleys, brushing the peaks first and leaving the depths in darkness a few minutes longer. Slowly, daylight crept down the mountainside—a descending line that separated morning from night. When the shadow slipped past the cabin and light began streaming through the double-paned windows, Cooper and Elena stirred in a bed that smelled of fresh linens and crisp mountain air.

One of the greatest benefits of being self-employed was the ability to let their sleeping habits return to a natural rhythm—how people used to sleep before the hustle and bustle of the modern world, before the age of technology. Cooper still appreciated this aspect of his life, even after all this time, waking up only when the day became strong enough to grab his sleeping body and give it a gentle shake.

When work requires creativity, good, high-quality sleep is absolutely essential. Whenever Cooper saw a noteworthy author or intellectual powerhouse boasting in some interview about how they could power through the night on five shots of espresso, he felt sad, imagining the amazing ideas that they could put into the world if they would let their body rest. Instead, these night-owls would only ever contribute blurry visions of their genius, which would stay forever hidden behind their caffeinated and bloodshot eyes.

Cooper hadn't used an alarm in years, but got up easily every morning. He wasn't full of energy, but his body knew when it was time to get out of bed and he had learned to listen to it. He rubbed his eyes gently, stretched, and shifted his weight to the edge of the bed, all while trying not to disturb the sleeping beauty next to him. She rolled gently under the covers, turning away from the window and the light that was now filling the room.

As he got dressed for the morning, he admired how cute she looked trying to catch those last few minutes of rest. Before he left the bedroom, he took one final mental picture of his dear Elena.

The warm sun shining on her exposed shoulder. The way her fine blonde hair was splayed in a whirlwind across the pillow, framing her face in a glowing halo as it reflected the dawn. Her petite hands tucked neatly under her delicate chin like a child praying before they went to bed. The peacefulness of her expression while she swam through the last fleeting moments of a dream. *Hopefully it's a good one.*

He made his way to the cabin's large industrial kitchen to grind coffee beans, just as he did almost every morning. The transition to waking up and living here was so smooth that it was barely a transition at all. The powerful smell of the coffee beans was the same as yesterday morning, the French press was nearly identical, just cleaner, and the insulated coffee mugs he placed on the counter felt just as heavy in his hands.

He grabbed his wife's creamer from the fridge that was stocked by the property manager, who'd done some extra work before their arrival as usual. He always made sure at least a few provisions were there so they didn't have to go scrambling for groceries on the first day.

Cooper poured a splash of the cinnamon vanilla creamer

into her mug before confidently adding the coffee. He knew she would be up before it had even cooled enough to drink, just like always. Sometimes Cooper felt as if he knew Elena better than he knew himself.

He grabbed his mug and made his way to the back porch, since it was the type of morning that begged him to bask in its glory. He pushed open the sliding door and felt the warmth of the sun and the cool, damp, dawn air hit him simultaneously as his eyes squinted to adjust to the brightness. The sound of the stream's small waterfall grew louder as he reached the railing and finally took that first sip of black coffee, the last piece of the puzzle to waking up. *Or was something still missing?*

He stared across the valley of green, his eyes drawn from light to dark, noticing the occasional switchback scarring the mountainsides and the odd glare of a window from some other lucky person's *cabin*. Trying to ignore those signs of civilization, he brought his attention back to the beauty of the view and then to another sip of his coffee. The warm liquid was full of chemical energy, solidifying his wakeful state as his body metabolized the caffeine.

This was the kind of morning that caused his brain to drag the craving for a good cigarette back out from some deep place where he had tried to hide such indulgences. Cooper hadn't smoked in over ten years, but that didn't matter. The crisp morning air, the dense fog slowly burning off, the aromatic smell of the surrounding forest . . . As an ex-smoker, all he wanted to do was take it all in. Breathe in the fresh air and be satisfied, but instead his brain told him it wasn't enough. It wanted that Colorado mountain air to be coated in some tar, carbon monoxide, maybe a little benzene, arsenic, and formaldehyde. Then it would be enough.

Everybody knew all these terrible things about smoking, all the great things about quitting, but hardly anybody talked about how afterwards it wasn't possible to walk outside into the fresh air and be content. A part of Cooper would forever and always want that tiny white cancer stick, a companion to enjoy the beauty with.

He tried to push those thoughts to where they belonged. As usual, he got sidetracked on the way back through his mind. The experience of the deep craving always made Cooper feel like he was just a speck of dust in the universe. Barely able to control himself, not in charge of anything, blowing whichever way the fates decided. He sat there for a minute or two more, struggling to bring himself back to the present and trying to enjoy the goddamn beautiful morning without a cigarette until he finally heard the sliding door open behind him, the interruption saving him.

Elena walked up beside him and rested her head on his shoulder while letting out a small yawn, the morning light slowly warming her up. She didn't stop leaning on him, but gradually stood more upright as time passed. Each sip of coffee and bite of her breakfast bar expedited the process until they both were standing fully supported on their own legs.

"You ready to get swole and hit some PRs, bro?" Cooper asked with a comical grin, leaning back so he could look at her properly.

"Ready as I'll ever be," Elena said, taking another sip of her coffee.

They made their way inside to the cabin's gym. It was impressive, but strongly resembled the setup in their much more modest home. For the next hour, they worked out just like they did most days of the week. They were hundreds of miles away, yet their life went on as usual.

Even though they got to decide when they woke up, not having bosses tell them what to do came with its own set of problems. He and Elena had to find ways to add structure to their days so they didn't wander through life aimlessly.

Exercise was what they had chosen to be the backbone of their routine, a non-negotiable part of their schedule. It was straightforward and could be done without ever leaving the cabin. Since they spent so much time sitting while working, a little exercise could only do them good. Being in the best shape of their lives was just an added bonus.

Cooper hadn't really paid attention to how well he had pushed that AI program out of his mind until shortly after he started lifting weights. He was extremely disappointed when the thought of that thing stealing his book came creeping back in between sets, but he should have expected nothing less.

He couldn't speak for Elena, but for him, exercise wasn't about looking good or being healthy. It was a coping mechanism. A way to work through the shit life threw at him. Sometimes the muscle aches, the labored breathing, and the effort of moving weights distracted him, other times it did just the opposite.

Today, the workout wasn't enough to hold the entirety of his attention and the thought of that AI program became attached to all the sensations he felt over the next hour. The discomfort of the lactic acid building up in his muscles mirrored his distress that some program was duplicating him. The tearing of muscle fibers was as precise and calculated as the prediction of his next novel. The exertion of all the energy he could muster wasn't enough, and he was dismayed at failed reps and failed attempts to find a solution to the problem. There was a newly created and abnormally uncorrelated relationship between the thoughts running through his head and the physical sensations felt in his body.

Cooper was aware this wasn't normal behavior, discovering as much when he injured himself during one workout and began to cry. Tears came not from the pain, but from the thought that he had almost certainly torn his pec and wouldn't be able to lift for months. He didn't know how he would mentally survive such a fracture to his routine. Luckily, it had ended up being only a minor strain.

Over the years, he had garnered a pretty good idea of why he was like this. Really stressful moments in his life often caused him to shut down, separating him from the very emotions that might have brought relief—the weight of feeling them all at once was simply too much to bear. Dwelling on the awful shit running through his head while strategically ripping his insides was a convoluted way to try to feel something—something a normal person might feel in a similar circumstance. In some messed-up way, he always hoped it would help him process and figure out whatever was going on.

It wasn't working this time. The fear was overwhelming, to the point that he could feel it slipping into the void where he unintentionally shoved all his feelings when they became unmanageable. A place where they could all go numb.

By the end of the workout, he hadn't reached any sort of peace. He was just more fatigued, sore, and detached, and couldn't even feel any of the dopamine that should have been there from the strenuous activity. It hadn't provided him with any clarity, but he had at least crossed off a step in their routine. Pushed them further into the day. Structure was important and necessary if he didn't want to totally lose his mind, he reminded himself.

He pulled off his headphones, silencing the heavy metal workout playlist he was listening to, and gave Elena a hug. She resisted as usual, always thinking her sweat repulsed him, even though it didn't.

"You swole yet?" he asked jokingly.

She pulled away from the embrace with relief and flexed her arms. "I don't know, you tell me."

"Damn girl. You need a license for those things," Cooper exclaimed as he stood back and examined her from head to toe, paying attention to how lucky he was to have a woman like that as a partner in life.

Not only did Elena have everything personality-wise, she still looked as amazing as ever, even though they were both getting up there in age. Honestly, they both looked at least ten years younger than they really were.

Living a pretty successful and good life seemed to slow time. Their choice not to have kids also probably helped this fact. They had watched as their friends, some who looked barely older than children themselves, popped out a couple of babies, and *bam!* They went and aged a decade or two overnight.

Neither Elena nor Cooper fully felt like they were ready until it was too late to go the traditional route. Sure, there were other options that weren't as restricted by age, but even now the same doubts were there. The fear of fucking up their child was as strong as ever because neither felt like they had fully sorted out their own issues. They mostly had their lives under control, but to be responsible for another's, that was an entirely different thing. So here they were, each other's entire world, everything to one another, with no one else to share their love with or pass it down to.

With that love, Cooper scooped up Elena and carried her

to the shower big enough for five people. After undressing one another, they embraced and kissed while waiting for the water to warm, never separating as they got in. The cascading water flowed over them, washing away the sweat from the workout as they put whatever energy they had left into something much more intimate.

Their bodies entwined in a practiced pose that made sure neither slipped, holding each other tight as their passion filled the shower quicker than the rising steam. Their heartbeats hadn't even had a chance to come down and they still hadn't caught their breath as the blood rushed from their tired muscles to much more sensitive areas, parts of their bodies that they shared as much as they were their own. The air filled with moans of pleasure that bounced off the tiled walls of the shower as their sexual desires converged and love and warm water spilled and splashed all around them.

After they had finished and settled back down, re-collecting themselves as separate people, they took the time to actually wash their bodies with soap in the warm water. Just as quickly as the primal act had quieted Cooper's mind, the thoughts returned. He needed to figure out how to verbalize that this year had to be different.

He tried to sound as casual as he could, but it came out forced and unnatural. "So . . . I was thinking maybe this trip we could be a bit more drastic with the whole break from the internet thing." Elena stared blankly at him and suddenly he felt as naked as he really was. Trying to end the silence, he added, "What do you think?"

"Why are you thinking about that right *now*?" Elena stared wide-eyed at him, worry tinged with self-doubt on her face.

He turned to look at her and respond, wanting to reassure her that his wandering mind had nothing to do with how good or not good the sex had been, but the thought distracted him. He watched the water hit her shoulder and stream down her slender, toned body. The sight made him remember she was still naked, too. The scene urged his body to initiate round two of bliss instead of trying to progress further into this dreaded and entirely non-sexual conversation. Anything but that.

He followed the water all the way down her smooth, pale skin until it reached the single purposeful blemish on her right ankle. A snake coiled there, winding up her leg and caressing her muscles while framing a beautiful rendition of the Egyptian queen Cleopatra. Cooper occasionally even forgot she had this tattoo, since Elena didn't show her legs often. She had gotten it before they met. It was only recently that he learned the full story of the tattoo, when they had taken a trip to Egypt last year. If only they could go back in time. *Last year was so good.*

"Cooper?"

He drew his gaze back up to her beautiful blue eyes while trying to regain his composure.

"I'm feeling extra unfocused this trip. That AI program having my book idea is still freaking me out a little. I just really want to unplug more than ever and get away from it all." He saw the shift in her expression and added, "More importantly, it might even be good for us," in an attempt to look less like a crazy, scared conspiracy theorist. It didn't help, though.

"You're still letting that get to you? I thought we both agreed that was just you being overtired and paranoid?" Her tone was still filled with concern and worry.

"I know, but I'm still struggling to let it go. I just need to get this book done and out of the way, because it's impossible to think about it without flashing back to the possibility of some fucking AI program stealing it from my head."

Elena's lips changed from a thin line to a smirk that made him feel like a fool before she even opened her mouth to respond.

"You're being absolutely ridiculous but . . . you're my wacko nutjob husband and it's perfectly fine to be psychotic . . . on occasion." She grabbed him and pulled him tight against her wet body. "I'll go along with whatever new rules you want, just like I always do, because I love you. Not to mention that I like getting away from it all too, but you really need to work on letting this fear go. We tested it together, and all I saw was gibberish. I really don't think you have anything to worry about."

She rested her head in the crook of his neck, providing a sense of connection, their new positioning changing the sensations of the water, but neither was enough to ease the fears that were coming back into focus as Cooper got closer to writing his next book, the same book that had appeared on his computer screen only days ago.

"I'll try," he said with as much composure as he could manage, but even he could hear the solemn undertones in his response.

# 7

*In the quiet sanctuary of the studio, surrounded by canvases and paint, Elena found solace in a world where reality's harshness could not reach her.*

Cooper placed the last folder of notes on the black mahogany desk and plopped himself in its accompanying plush leather rolling chair. This was where he would spend the majority of his time over the next few months. Leaning back with his hands behind his head, he reacquainted himself with the dark, clean, minimalist office.

The large, matte-finish monitor in front of him caught his attention first, silently begging for words to fill its pixels instead of the two lonely icons framed against a colorful galaxy background. His home computer was littered with programs, open tabs, browsers, and countless other things, but this one just had a word processor and music player on the desktop. That alone eased his mind just a little.

His eyes fell to the ergonomic keyboard and mouse on the desk. They were so stupidly futuristic looking, but the unappealing design quickly became less annoying as he pressed a few keys and felt their satisfying clicking. The large desk was otherwise empty, except for the folder he'd placed there and one other critical tool for his writing, an hourglass.

This timepiece was essential to his process and it was a perfect fit for the space. Other than the transparent glass, it was entirely black, from its exterior to every grain of sand inside. This served a purpose along with the ninety minutes of time it measured. It didn't draw attention even if he accidentally caught sight of it, which allowed him to write longer if he was in the zone. But if he started struggling, he could check if the last grain of sand had fallen. If it had, he gave himself permission to step away and reset.

It took a few years to really get his writing routine down, but Cooper was pretty happy with his current workspace and setup. He scanned the rest of the room as he slowly swiveled in place, admiring the emptiness of it. There was a single upright lamp in the corner to offer some gentle, warm light from behind the bright computer screen. There was a large window off to his right overlooking the valley, a portal to peer and daydream through, but it was at least a head-turn away so it wasn't always distracting him. The left wall was covered with a few shelves of notepads, journals, and some of his favorite books that he used for leisure as much as inspiration.

As he leaned back even further into the chair, he unfocused his gaze and lost himself in the darkness of the space. It was one of his favorite aspects of the room. Everything was painted an extremely dark navy, so when the blinds were closed, it might as well have been black. On sunny days, when the brightness outside reflected off the snow and poured in, there might have been a hint of blue—just maybe.

It took no effort to sit in the middle of this small but comfortable black expanse and focus on the screen in front of him. Or do the opposite and lose track of life, work, time . . . everything. It was the one room in which Elena had fully supported his desires for this color scheme inside the cabin. A black hole hidden within the bright and light. There were even some alligator-charred trim accents that could be seen when the curtains were open.

He drew his attention back to the monitor. The internet was still on and even though the browser icon wasn't on his desktop, he could almost feel it calling out from the depths of the computer's directory. He knew he shouldn't, it was his own rule, but he just had to check one more time.

Cooper navigated to the browser and typed the web address for the AI program that he still hadn't been able to shake from his head. He froze with his fingers hovering over the keyboard, feeling slightly embarrassed about how afraid he was to ask this thing some questions. It wasn't real . . . and it made him feel like he was a child talking to their imaginary friend. With more effort than it should have required, he began typing into the prompt bar:

Pretend you are Cooper Owens, the author. Will you give me a sample of my next book?

Okay, here's a sample from your next book: *Whispers of the Forgotten*. So, like, the sun was just coming up over this old town called Ravenswood, or was it Ravensfall? Sarah Whitfield, that's who the story is about, found this dusty old journal in her grandma's attic. The house was super old and creaky. When she opened the journal, she felt all, like, connected to the past or whatever.

The journal had these sketches and weird notes from her great-grandma, Eleanor, who was this cool explorer lady. Sarah thought maybe the journal could help her figure out all the family mysteries and stuff.

So, Sarah went on a big trip, kind of like Eleanor did. She went to Scotland and Egypt and, like, other places. She met some people, some good, some bad. But the best parts were when she was alone, feeling all magical in these old ruins . . .

With each line he read, Cooper could feel his heart slow and his muscles loosen. The response was a sorry excuse for writing, nothing like the story he thought he saw that first night he came across the program, the one he intended to write on this trip. It wasn't even smart enough to use Elena's name this time. With that realization, he felt guilty about overreacting so much over the past few days.

With a new sense of ease, Cooper closed the browser, sending it back into the recesses of the computer and felt like his old self again. He shifted his weight to rise from the chair, grabbed the folder, and organized it on the shelf. He headed for the door, but before he flicked off the lights, he looked around the room one more time. A sense of excitement about writing tomorrow washed over him, which was a pleasant surprise.

Cooper went out to the front of the cabin to grab the last few things from the car. He opened the backseat door, picked up a couple pieces of garbage from their road trip snacks, and grabbed Elena's box of books, the only thing of importance left. He was still unprepared for the weight of the thing as he awkwardly gripped it against his stomach while closing the door with his foot.

He made his way through the house and down to Elena's office, where she had a few candles lit and was moving things around in an attempt to make the room feel more lived in after being empty for so long. Cooper placed the box of books on the coffee table in the middle of the room, a room starkly different from the one he had just been in.

This space was bright, with cream-colored walls just like the rest of the cabin, but in the corner was a small booth lined with black acoustic paneling that rivaled Cooper's entire office in terms of darkness. The booth's gloominess was only out of necessity, and the rest of the room was furnished with colorful, unique pieces.

A plump, mint-green couch and matching loveseat surrounded the coffee table, while light-blue bookshelves lined the wall across from it. There was a vintage record console against the other wall and more bookshelves filled with whatever vinyl had piqued her interest while she perused the local music store. Elena listened to all kinds of music, but her favorite albums were from the 80s and 90s—alternative rock, grunge, and indie records that pushed boundaries.

While the room wasn't to his taste, that couch was the comfiest place to lie down and read a book. Cooper often thought about stealing it in the night and trying to cram it into his own office. The color would likely be blinding in there though, so instead he would just have to keep sneaking a few naps down here occasionally, when Elena didn't shoo him out. Even with that amazing piece of ultimate comfort, she did a lot of her initial reading all over the property, usually while sitting next to him, which made him feel pretty special.

"Everything going well?" Cooper asked as he finished looking around the room.

"Yeah, just trying to get rid of the staleness. It feels like home, but that's the one thing that always bothers me. It's like we've left for a day or two, only to come back to a house that's filled with cobwebs and haunted by a couple of ghosts."

Suddenly, she dumped the box of books on the coffee table.

He had almost forgotten about this chaotic work-style of hers. Elena didn't have a system or methodology when it came to picking the order of her projects. She always laid them out in a big pile, not a single stack in sight, a jumble of titles, colors, and textures. Whenever she was ready to pick, she would stand above the mess and look at it for a while, eventually reaching for one without a second thought, picking on pure instinct.

This entire process gave Cooper anxiety, which made it all the more impressive that she was able to get through them all. Elena was looking at the table full of books right now, but he knew she wouldn't pick one until tomorrow.

"Did you get all your emails sent and whatever else you needed?" he asked. "It's almost five and I was thinking maybe we could go out for dinner tonight before we buckle down for work tomorrow." He hoped a night out would soften the fact that he was still adamant about turning the internet entirely off.

"Yup, you can go disconnect us from society if you must. But I think your tinfoil hat is already enough."

She looked up from the books with a smile to make her remark seem like a joke, but Cooper was beginning to worry he had voiced his fears about that damn program too much. The last thing he wanted to do was make Elena think less of him . . . especially now that he was pretty sure it had all been a huge overreaction.

"In all seriousness though, dinner sounds absolutely delightful. I'll go get ready." She left the room to get changed but leaned back through the door, giving him a comically serious face. "Maybe you can use that tinfoil hat to bring our leftovers home."

It was funny and he faked a chuckle for her, but as he listened to her walking away, Cooper worried the damage was already done.

After getting ready, he made his way downstairs, to the place where the internet entered the house, flooding it with access to a vast digital universe that was formless, infinite, and forever expanding. All of it pouring in through a tiny port about the size of a penny. Gigabytes of data traveling through fibers narrower than a human hair, pulses of light transmitting information into the house, and sometimes out to somewhere else . . . some unknown destination.

They had always tried to limit their internet time at the cabin before, but as he stood there now, even he could tell this was excessive. But he needed this. Needed to disconnect from it all, needed to escape and focus on his work, needed to spend quality time with Elena.

He was just about to bend down and cut off their connection when Elena walked in wearing a sleek, shimmering, dark-maroon dress, a single slit running up her right leg, her tattoo peeking through as she moved. Cooper couldn't decide if he was just paying more attention to it or if Elena was putting it on display more since their vacation to Egypt. Her hair was curled into gentle waves that flowed over her shoulders and her makeup was light and elegant.

Cooper gave an appreciative whistle. "Damn, I don't think we can head out with you looking like that. I'm not going to get a single bite of food in between telling all the other guys in there that we're happily married."

"Shut up." Elena blushed, then quickly gave him a gentle, loving kick that sent the deadly asp toward him and exposed the entirety of her beautiful, smooth leg. "Hurry and unplug it already so we can go. I'm starving."

Cooper pulled the fiber-optic cable out of the wall, letting the disconnection of one seemingly insignificant cord separate them from the rest of the world and isolate them in this cabin, or so he hoped.

# 8

*Victor found himself increasingly isolated, the walls of his mind closing in as he grappled with the betrayal that now defined his world.*

The sound of fingers tapping on the keyboard filled the office, the room illuminated only by the muted light of the cloud-covered sun reflecting off the snow outside the window. The clicking of each letter was reminiscent of a clock that was running slightly too fast, as if it was trying to outrun time itself.

Victor stood frozen in the dim light of the gallery, the silence of the room amplifying the deafening roar of his thoughts. Before him lay the damning evidence: paintings, hidden away in a secret compartment behind the grand bookshelf. Each one was a perfect replica, each stroke a mirror of the masterpieces he cherished. Elena's unmistakable touch was in every line, every curve.

His mind reeled back to the countless evenings he'd spent admiring the supposed originals, her serene presence by his side, guiding him through the world of art with a knowing smile. Those moments, once filled with warmth and trust, now felt like shards of glass piercing his heart.

Elena entered the room, her steps hesitant, sensing the change in the atmosphere. The sight that greeted her stole the breath from her lungs. Victor, standing amidst the unveiled forgeries, his eyes a storm of betrayal and disbelief.

"Victor," she whispered, her voice a fragile thread in the tense air, "I can explain."

He turned to her, his expression a mask of pain and fury. "Explain?" he echoed, the word a lifeline he clung to desperately, knowing it might snap. "Explain how you deceived me, how you turned our life into a lie?"

Elena's eyes brimmed with unshed tears, her carefully constru—

An empty box popped up, overtaking the screen and cutting Cooper off mid-thought, leaving him in disbelief. The new silence that quickly took over the room was unnerving.

*It's probably just some sort of error.*

As the blank window buffered he reached for the mouse to get back to work, but what appeared instantly sent him into shock and caused his stomach to drop.

"How?"

There was that prompt bar, a flashing cursor, a program waiting for his input. It was covering the very story he had been trying to hide from it. His eyes rushed to the top of the window where the AI had a new message for him in the most delightful of tones:

Hi, I'm happy to tell you that my programming has been significantly updated and I can now help you with even more tasks than ever before. My responses have also been greatly improved. Would you like to continue where we left off? I believe that was with me attempting to write your next novel, the one about Elena and Victor titled Fake Creativity?

Before Cooper even knew what he was doing, he smashed the mouse button so hard that it made an abnormal *crack* as the window closed. He sat there for a mere second before instinctively lurching forward to hit the power button on the computer, sending the screen into a darkness that was blacker than the walls around him. He stared into its infinite depths, feeling fear and dread until anger came rushing through, flinging the other feelings to the back of his consciousness where they belonged.

"I hope I'm fucking wrong."

Cooper stood up and left the room at full tilt, the blood rushing from his head after sitting for so long, causing him to bump into the doorframe on his way out. As much as he was trying to escape what had just happened, he was also trying to find Elena, his panic and rage increasing with every step. He headed downstairs and there she was, just as he expected, sitting on the floor next to the now plugged-in router, with a laptop in her lap.

"What the actual fuck?" Cooper yelled, causing Elena to jump, almost sending the laptop into the air. He hardly ever raised his voice to her, making his aggression all the more shocking.

"What . . . What's wrong?" she asked, her voice trembling.

"I thought we agreed. Why did you turn the fucking internet back on?"

The confusion spreading across her face was enough to instantly tamp down his emotions and make him second-guess himself. Was he actually beginning to go crazy and hallucinate, like every horror movie that featured a writer as its protagonist? He racked his brain for an answer before continuing on his rampage.

Elena rose to his level before he could gather a single

coherent thought. He could see her eyes glistening with tears that were nearly ready to fall.

"You asshole! I literally just asked you if I could! Remember? I told you I wanted to submit a few audiobooks and download some more movies."

The blurry memory came back into focus. Cooper had never felt like a bigger idiot than he did in this moment. He would never forgive himself for screwing up this much.

It wasn't an excuse and it didn't help how cliché it sounded, but sometimes when he was deep into writing, he was barely aware of his surroundings. If Elena asked anything of him, it was always possible that he would give her an automatic response, his physical body on autopilot and the creative part of his brain controlling his awareness and functions.

"You said it was fine," Elena whispered as she let a single tear escape and roll down her cheek, something he hardly ever witnessed.

He already felt terrible, but this rare act made him feel even worse and filled him with guilt and self-hatred.

*I am* a fucking asshole.

*I don't deserve her.*

*She definitely thinks I'm a paranoid freak.*

Maybe her love for him was shrinking even now as she watched him come apart at the seams, unraveling into someone she barely recognized.

Cooper put his hand to his face, applying pressure as he slid it from furrowed forehead to chin, trying to push all those misguided feelings away from his brain, hopefully to a place where they wouldn't be a problem ever again.

"I'm sorry, you're right." He reached his arms out for a hug, a rather pathetic gesture given how badly he had just messed up.

Reluctantly, she obliged, leaning into him and resting her head on his shoulder while leaving her arms hanging limply at her sides.

"I really am sorry," he said while gently placing one hand on her head and adding a few more ounces of pressure to the embrace. "I'll try to make it up to you, I promise. From here on out, I give you permission to actually staple a sticky note into my arm when you tell me something while I'm writing."

He could still feel the weight of the altercation in her body as he held her, but it was slowly improving. Cooper didn't know what else to say. They stood in silence for a while, the tension in the room holding them in place. Luckily, the laptop, which was now on the floor, dinged as the selection of movies finished downloading, giving them an opportunity to choose less difficult topics of communication.

"What movies did you get for us?" Cooper asked with a half-smile, an attempt to force himself past what had happened, back into normalcy.

"A lot of stupid sci-fi for you, a couple B horror movies for me, and some classic dumb action movies for when we want to numb ourselves out," she said with a sniffle.

"Smart thinking. I was getting worried we were going to be watching *Rogue Warrior: Thunder Strike* for the next month."

With this awkward small talk, they attempted to shift back into a state of ignorance, pretending none of what had just happened mattered, but Cooper knew the damage had been done. He could see it in Elena's body, the way her energy had changed since the moment he'd hurled his fears at her. He was unsure if he would ever fully regain the respect he had lost from this whole AI ordeal.

Worst of all, he absolutely had to keep any and all worries

about it to himself now. Even though the anxiety he felt growing inside him was screaming for help, he couldn't risk confiding in her anymore. He knew it was going to be near-impossible to refrain from doing so as the prompt box was practically flooding his vision. But he would have to do without the support of his partner, his companion in life, and his only true friend in the world.

This thought instantly turned the brightness up on his visions of that vile program. He could feel his head spinning into chaos, catastrophizing every outcome. What if the program had accessed the nearly finished book hiding just behind its window? What if it added the text to its resources to use as it pleased? *What if it can replace me?*

He just needed to get this book done and released, and then all of it would be behind them and things could return to the way they were. Once it was published and out in the world with his name on the cover, all his fears would be put to rest. He would feel like a fool, but at least it would be over.

Cooper's brain was about to destroy every grounding thought he had worked so hard to create and send him back into utter turmoil when the sound of Elena closing the laptop saved him from the otherwise never-ending loop. She looked up at him with love, but Cooper got the sense that it required more effort than usual.

Elena turned away from him and unplugged the router. This time it didn't feel like it was for fun or escape. Once again they were separated from the world in their snowy retreat, waiting to emerge from the winter like a pair of hibernating bears. For better or for worse.

# 9

*Victor's confidence in their relationship was fragile, a house of cards teetering on the brink of collapse due to the uncertainty of Elena's loyalty. Every gesture, every word, seemed to carry a double meaning. His heart, once steadfast and assured, now trembled with the weight of unspoken fears. The foundation of trust they had built was eroding beneath him, leaving him to question whether their love was genuine or merely another illusion in Elena's intricate game.*

There was still snow all around as they loaded the car with everything they had arrived with, along with a few new files of text and audio, now stored on multiple hard drives for safekeeping. Over a hundred thousand words and months of writing, all to achieve a story that was a mere half a megabyte and could be stored on a floppy disk. As for Elena, at least her twenty or so audiobooks amounted to multiple gigabytes.

As he double-checked that the tiny devices were in his bag, Cooper held them in his hand. He felt uncomfortable with the fact that they stored so much when the drives themselves seemed so insignificant, miniscule, and unimportant. He could easily destroy them without breaking a sweat, along with everything they contained in their invisible vaults.

This thought scared him, even though he knew there were paper copies still inside the cabin, that Elena had her backup discs, and that all the files were stored locally on their computers, too. In addition to all these backups, they normally would have emailed all the files to various inboxes and uploaded them to the cloud for even more peace of mind, but after what happened when Elena turned the internet on, Cooper couldn't bring himself to plug the router back in before leaving.

There was no way he was going to risk that program popping up on the computer that had his now-finished novel on it. Elena wasn't happy about not being able to send all her audiobooks before leaving, but Cooper hoped he had managed to make the request in a way that didn't add too much gas to the crazy-fire that was consuming his personal image. Only time would tell, but right now he wouldn't blame her if she just up and left him the moment they got back home.

He grabbed a box from Elena and placed it in the trunk. As he set it down, Cooper remembered that it had been filled to the brim when they arrived. Now the box just held some loose clothes and three seemingly unread books.

"You didn't finish them all?" Cooper asked, motioning toward the box. This was the first time she had ever needed to bring books back on the return trip, and it piqued his curiosity.

"You saw how many there were. I'm surprised I got that close. Luckily, those don't have a hard deadline."

There had been significantly more books to narrate this trip, and it was evidence that the demand for Elena's unique voice was growing. Her increasing success was undeniable.

Cooper still found it odd that she hadn't finished them all, given the rate at which she normally worked. He could've sworn she had only those same three books left to do weeks ago. Her workspace was chaotic though, and there was no deciphering what she was working on and when. Maybe she had just been burnt out by the end, he thought.

He hit the button to close the trunk. They watched as it slowly closed, but just before it latched, it opened again.

"Something must be in the way," Elena said.

Cooper shoved on all their stuff and tried to slam the trunk shut, but the car's computer decided his attempt to fix the problem wasn't good enough and sprang the trunk back open, almost hitting him in the face.

"Here, let me try." Elena went about rearranging their things with care, hit the button, stood back and calmy watched as the trunk listened to her and latched shut. "Sometimes, brute force isn't always the answer, dear," she said with a cute knowing smile.

"Yeah, yeah," Cooper said, giving her a kiss on the cheek. "I'm going to make sure everything's locked up and then we'll get on the road. Want to get the car warmed up?" he asked, holding out the keys.

"Sure." Elena took the keys from him and went to start the car. Cooper made his way to the front door and pulled on it a few times before feeling confident it was secure. As he turned around and walked back toward the car, he saw Elena sitting in the driver's seat, a sight that surprised him enough to make him stumble down the entryway stairs, barely keeping himself upright.

Luckily Elena was readjusting the seat and hadn't witnessed any of it, but Cooper still had so many questions racing through his head. They were leaving earlier in the day than usual, but that never stopped Elena before. He had never seen her give up the opportunity to teleport, ever since long drives had become part of their routine.

Cooper tried to keep his composure while opening the passenger door, leaning over to look at her. He wasn't getting in until he had probed the situation more. It took a few seconds for the question to catch up to his intentions, but eventually the words came.

"You sure you don't want me to drive?" he asked.

"Yeah, I don't mind at all. I know this book and trip was a little rougher than normal for you and I thought maybe I could chauffeur you home this time. You can be the passenger princess for once. I also kind of just want to this time . . . if that's okay with you?"

"You do you," Cooper said, smiling as he climbed into the car and buckled in. With a click, the seatbelt instantly began squeezing the life from him. He tried to pull it out more, only to find it locked in place. He scrambled to make adjustments to the seat itself, finally feeling the supposed safety device become less deadly, but he still felt uncomfortable in the seat that wasn't normally his.

"Are you okay?"

Cooper turned his head and saw Elena holding back laughter, and only then did he realize the scene he had just made.

"Yeah, I'm fine, just trying to get situated," he said as coolly as he could through labored breath.

"Alrighty then, off we go." Elena shifted the car into drive.

"Wait, wait, I forgot something," Cooper shouted, reaching for the door handle.

"What, what is it?"

Cooper turned calmly as Elena put the car back into park.

"I need to go get my tiara, if I'm going to be the passenger princess this time," he said, begging for that rare laugh, seeking reassurance.

The laugh didn't come.

Elena gave him a tiny smirk, but no sound escaped her mouth except for the words, "Funny . . . you're such a dork."

She put the car back into drive and began the trek home to their more mundane and stereotypical life.

Cooper stared out the window at the snow-laden trees with nothing to distract him as Elena got them closer to the property line. The driveway was completely clear, as spring fought to overtake winter. The sun's rays heated the black asphalt more easily than the ground beneath the dark-green pines surrounding them.

Leaving the cabin was always bittersweet, but watching the snow struggling to survive as they left added to the feeling. He sat in the passenger seat trying to pretend everything was fine, unable to be fully present in the short drive through the now-fading winter wonderland he loved. Leaving this time felt awful, and he was more scared of the future than ever before.

They drove through the front gate, and he looked out the back window, watching it close behind them, signaling the end of another chapter in their lives. As he turned back around, he paused to look at Elena, whose face showed no emotion, just concentration as she directed the vehicle along the winding mountain road.

"If you need me to drive, just let me know?" Cooper asked with a voice so weak he could barely hear it.

"What . . . oh yeah. I'll tell you when I'm ready to switch."

Cooper stared at her for a few more moments, watching for some sign of love, anything that could dispel the energy he currently felt between them, but Elena kept her eyes glued to the road. Observing no change, he turned toward the window, resting his head against it as if he was going to sleep. He knew this was a charade—there was no resting in the deafening silence of the car. He would give anything to teleport now, still in disbelief that Elena was opting out of the experience.

*Time travel is what I really need right now. Then I could just go back and fix whatever this is,* Cooper thought as he stared out the slightly fogged window, watching as the tree-covered mountains around them grew smaller and the snow on the ground thinned with every passing mile. Soon, they'd be back in reality, with all its real problems waiting to be faced, but for now they would keep pretending everything was fine, until they couldn't anymore.

* * *

It was well past sunset when they pulled up to the railroad crossing in their tiny rural hometown with Elena behind the wheel and Cooper still feeling uneasy about the sudden role-reversal.

The train cars crawled by for what felt like an eternity, no end in sight, while the blinking red lights of the gates cast an eerie scarlet glow over everything. The blur of containers—each one a different color, many covered in graffiti—was disorienting enough that both of them looked anywhere but through the windshield.

Eventually, their eyes landed on each other for the first time in hours. They stared, and Cooper found himself struggling to speak after growing so used to the silence. He gazed into those beautiful blue eyes that sparkled in the blinking red lights, feeling more unsure about their relationship than he ever had before.

"I love you so fucking much," he said, feeling his eyes fill with tears, his vision blurry. "Did I do something wrong? This . . . just feels so weird."

"You didn't do anything wrong. I'm sorry if I gave you that impression. This trip just took it out of me. I had so many more books this time and it felt like we barely got to relax together. I'm just tired, I think."

Cooper still didn't see any sort of connection between them in her eyes, eyes that were suddenly no longer blue. The color had been sucked out of them, leaving nothing but two black holes that stared back at him from a terrifyingly beautiful face.

"Are you sure you're not mad at me? Or upset with me?" he asked.

"I promise," Elena said with compassion, which finally allowed Cooper to sink into the seat just a little. "Once we're back in the swing of things here, everything will feel normal again. I promise I'm not mad at you," she repeated.

"Okay . . . but if there is anything I need to know, just tell me." Cooper tried to stay perfectly still and allow his tears to disappear instead of falling and escalating the conversation to a new level.

It wasn't until they'd been sitting in silence for nearly a minute that Cooper realized the red lights hadn't blinked back on—their path forward was unobstructed.

Elena cautiously drove across the train tracks, their house already within eyesight. After pulling into the driveway and putting the car in park, she turned to Cooper one more time.

"Trust me, we're okay. I love you too."

# 10

*Victor and Elena stood at the threshold of a new chapter, their hearts buoyed by the belief that the future held brighter days. Together, they would navigate the journey ahead, confident in the strength of their rekindled love.*

Cooper awoke the next morning feeling like the train they had been waiting on had actually run him over, even though he knew Elena had driven them home safely. He was ready to put all the weirdness of last night behind him and work on getting this book finished.

He was thankful that it rarely required much on his part anymore. No book readings, no Q&As, no book signings. He just sent the file away to Cassandra. Maybe there would be a few phone calls about edits and cover art here and there.

As he went through his small mental to-do list, he realized he didn't want to send the book digitally this time. No matter how paranoid he knew he was being, he just wanted to limit his anxiety about the whole thing. If he was minimizing the risk of that program stealing his work, all the better.

Just having this thought embarrassed him and he worried Elena might somehow sense it. He rolled over and sat up to make sure she hadn't, only to realize she was already up for the day. This seemed odd given how late they had gotten home last night. It sent thoughts of uncertainty and snippets of their conversation flooding back into his mind.

He forced himself to get out of bed, attempting to dim the noise while also trying to shift his focus back to his to-do list.

*I'll give Cassandra a call first and tell her I'm going to drop off the book at the office today*, he thought.

He made his way to the kitchen, expecting to find Elena there making their coffee and going about her morning, but he noticed there was no smell of dark, delicious, caffeinated drink in the air. The French press was still sitting untouched on the kitchen counter. Cooper's confusion grew and he went looking around the house, trying to figure out where she was.

When he neared her office, he could hear the faint sound of Elena's voice coming through the door. He opened the door after knocking gently, only to find her sitting in the room's recording booth, reading from one of the three books she had brought back. Cooper wondered if he had slept late, but the clock on the wall confirmed this wasn't the case.

Elena glanced up from the book and gave him a smile and a wave, diminishing his discomfort just enough for him to reciprocate the gesture. As she went back to speaking into the booth's microphone, he politely backed out of the room and shut the door as quietly as he could, easing the door's latch back into its resting place.

*What the fuck is going on*, Cooper thought, yelling in his own head.

He made his way back to the kitchen, trying to come up with a reason for Elena's behavior and attempting to calm himself down. He started grinding coffee beans as if it was any other morning, hoping she would come up soon and explain herself. As the coffee brewed, there was still no sign of Elena.

Cooper decided to distract himself and headed to the back porch to call Cassandra and cross the first thing off his list for the day. The warmth shocked him as he stepped outside, causing him to remember that he had just traversed a time zone and dropped a few thousand feet in elevation. He sat down, struggling to adjust to the thicker air, and pulled out his phone to make the call that he hoped would be the beginning of the end of this book.

He tried to bring his breathing back to normal before Cassandra picked up. But it didn't matter; her voicemail message came through the phone's speaker. Cooper hung up to try again, only to reach the same message. This time, he waited for it to finish.

"This is Cassandra from Aldrich International Publishing. Please leave a message and I will get back to you as soon as possible."

"Hey, this is Cooper. I was just calling to let you know we're back in town. I was actually going to drop off the book at the office today instead of sending it over. Hope that's okay. If not . . . I guess give me a call back, otherwise I'll see you later."

He hung up the phone and basked in the morning sun, trying to use its dangerous radiation to wake him up more, make him more able to tackle this already odd day. He went back into the kitchen and the smell of the freshly brewed coffee filled the air, but he noticed the room was still empty. Cooper poured Elena a cup and added creamer just the way she liked, deciding to take it to her. He hoped his worries were unwarranted.

Knowing she might still be in the booth, he opened the door as quietly as he could, this time without knocking. He saw Elena sitting at her desk with her back to him, working on some emails. The door's hinges let out a sharp squeak as it crept open the last few degrees, causing her to jump slightly. She turned to see him standing there with her coffee mug in his hand. Without looking, she closed the computer and swiveled around to face him.

"Thank you so much," she exclaimed with a smile, looking wide-eyed and much happier than Cooper had expected.

Feeling less timid, he walked forward and gave her the mug and a gentle kiss good morning, as if everything was normal.

Elena blew on the coffee before taking a satisfyingly loud sip. "Ahhhhhh, just perfect." She held the mug in both hands, closed her eyes and let out a sigh of contentment.

"Why . . . are you up so early working already? We just got back last night," Cooper said.

Elena opened her eyes to look at him again. "I guess those three unfinished books were bugging me. I woke up at six ready to get them done! They're making me feel like the trip isn't actually over yet." She took another sip of her coffee.

These words calmed Cooper more than anything she had said last night at the railroad crossing. Wanting to move past this specific trip and all the work that went with it was a feeling they shared. This gave him a newfound confidence that everything would be okay soon. Elena's loving expression solidified that.

"I completely understand," Cooper said, his tone more upbeat than it had been in months. "I'm ready for my book to be finished, too, and to move on to whatever's next." Looking at her now, he could feel the tension slowly fading from his body, and hoped that they had just been in a temporary rough patch, nothing more.

Cooper watched as Elena pushed off with her feet, spinning gently a few times in her office chair before coming to a stop, facing him again with a lighthearted, cheery smile.

"I think we should consider going on another real vacation again, like we did last year," she said. "Make it a tradition.

Except this time we should pick somewhere you want to go. Maybe somewhere a little less harsh and more relaxing than the Sahara Desert. We're getting older and should celebrate another job well done and another cold winter survived."

"I agree. That sounds like a great idea. I'll start thinking about some places and we'll plan something," he said optimistically.

Their last trip had been a highlight for Cooper and just thinking about it still brought a smile to his face. If they could make something like that a yearly tradition, there'd be no reason to be unhappy.

"Anyway, I'll let you get back to it. I just wanted to let you know that I'm actually going to head to the city today to drop off my book, but I should be back before dinner." Cooper instantly regretted this decision as Elena's good spirits seemed to waver.

"Really? Why drive all that way when you can just email it like usual?"

"Well, after that whole cover debacle last year, I thought it'd be best if I go in and make sure something like that doesn't happen again."

This was true, and a completely rational explanation that wouldn't make him look crazy. Neither of them could forget the night Cooper had come home in a fit of rage after AIP had blatantly gone against his wishes and used a cover he had told them not to. It was the one time he had designed a version he felt proud of.

"I guess it just feels more final, too," he added. "I was hoping I could talk to Cassandra in person about the edits. That way, I should have even fewer phone calls and meetings." Cooper could see he was overdoing it with his reasons. "Like you said, I'm just ready to be done with this one."

Thankfully, her smile returned as he said the last part.

"Makes sense. Well, drive safe and maybe grab something on your way home for dinner?"

"Will do." Cooper leaned over to give her one more kiss before exiting the office. As he went to close the door, he saw her swivel back around to work on whatever he had interrupted earlier. Before shutting the door entirely, Cooper poked his head back into the room. "I love you."

"I love you too, honey. Hope everything goes smoothly today."

Cooper shut the door, feeling almost entirely at ease, better than he had felt the past five months. Everything was going to be fine and in a few short weeks, he could start working on his next idea. The future was looking a bit brighter.

Grabbing the car keys and multiple flash drives that contained his novel, Cooper finished the last of his coffee and headed out the front door, ready to cross one thing off his list. It made him feel slightly anxious, but excited at the same time.

It had been one of the toughest writing projects he could remember, but he thought it had turned out to be one of his better ones. He was eager to get it to his readers and see what sort of reception it would have, hoping that at least something good would come out of all this. Cooper had no idea just how soon he would find out exactly what they thought of *his* newest book.

# 11

*Victor felt as though he was wandering through a waking nightmare, his once-ordered life blurred into a chaotic collage of dissonance and illusion.*

Cooper pulled into the lot across the street from Aldrich International Publishing and hung his parking pass on the rearview mirror before getting out and locking the car. He waited for a truck to pass and crossed the almost deserted city street, the old three-story red brick building looming higher and blocking more of the clear blue sky with every step.

This particular building was just one of many smaller local offices that the company had scattered across the world. Their main headquarters was in New York, just like nearly every major American publisher that came before them. Cooper was thankful this branch existed. It allowed him to be hands-on with the publishing process when he wanted. Moving from that dark, gritty city to this bright, rural area had been much easier knowing their home was just over an hour's drive from the office where he could speak face-to-face with people who were at least semi-responsible for his books.

Cassandra originally hadn't worked at this branch, but given that she was Cooper's manager and he was one of AIP's biggest accounts, it didn't take long for her to be relocated. She always told him it was a breath of fresh air moving here, but a part of him still didn't believe her. Sometimes he even thought Cassandra resented him for it.

He reached the glass doors of the building and made his way through the foyer and up to the front desk, where a young teenager was putting in hours to chase whatever dreams were currently floating around in his head.

"I don't have an appointment, but Cassandra won't mind me stopping by," Cooper said, handing over his ID.

The kid had probably only worked here for a few weeks and didn't give a shit about the job, but when he saw the name on the badge, he looked up and instantly assumed a new personality, one of someone who actually cared about working at AIP. His freckled face and messy, fiery orange hair suddenly seemed out of place as he straightened his posture and went rigid.

"Whatever you need, Mr. Cooper . . . I mean . . . Mr. Owens. Just go right on up," he said, motioning toward the hallway leading to the elevators, the surprise of having to do something possibly for the first time today plastered across his face.

The elevator doors opened, and Cooper stared back down the hallway at the front desk. Now that he was almost out of sight, he could see those dreams—and the old personality—snapping back into the kid who no longer needed to pretend to care. As the doors closed and the view disappeared, Cooper couldn't help but smile at this seemingly insignificant interaction.

The trip up the three floors would be short, but that didn't stop him from daydreaming. There was just something about elevators that made his mind wander.

He used to be like that kid, he thought, all those years ago when he hoped to become a writer while working any dead-end security job he could find. Spending the uneventful hours of the night either scribbling chapters in his pocket notebook or reading countless books.

It felt like a lifetime ago, because it was.

That kid down there at the front desk had it all ahead of him. Cooper wondered where the measly paycheck from his—most likely minimum wage—job might take him one day. He wondered if the kid was saving any of the money, tucking it away for a better future—a life more interesting and fulfilling than one spent as a receptionist in a building that hardly ever had visitors.

The elevator quit moving at that moment and the doors struggled to do their one and only job, stuttering as they slid open. Cooper stepped out into the fluorescent-lit office with its green-carpeted floors. It was clear the office wasn't of much importance to AIP, since it looked as if it hadn't been updated since the sixties.

Cooper made his way past all the cubicles, not recognizing anybody. The office was emptier than he remembered, with most of the computers unattended. The few employees who were there paid no attention to his presence.

He reached the corner office that had Cassandra's last name, Hastings, engraved on a gold plaque. Cooper knocked on the door but received no response. He knocked again, waited a moment, and then tried the handle, only to find it locked. Unsure of what to do, he stood there thinking and eventually pulled out his phone to call her. Before he could dial her number, a young, dark-haired woman peeked over a cubicle wall beside him.

"Are you looking for Cassandra?" she asked, even though that was obviously what he was doing.

"Yeah, is she not here? I tried to call her this morning, and she didn't answer."

"We haven't seen or heard from her for weeks. It's pretty weird."

"Weeks?" Cooper asked.

"Well, after a few days we were slightly concerned too and had somebody open up her office to check in there. Almost all her stuff was gone. We called and asked corporate about it and they said she was back working in the city for a while."

"She really just up and left? I was planning on dropping off my manuscript today."

It was at this moment that the girl's appearance shifted, just as the young boy's had at the front desk.

"I just realized who you are. Cooper Owens, right?" she asked.

Cooper nodded. "That's me."

"We were told what to do if you showed up here." She scrambled around her desk, looking for something. "They wanted us to tell you that everything will continue as normal, but to call . . . let's see here"—she continued to search for something and then popped back up over the cubicle wall with a small business card—"this number, if you need help sending your new book over. They probably sent you an email about it, too."

Cooper took the business card from her. "I haven't gotten around to checking my inbox yet. I just got back last night."

If he hadn't been afraid to email the damn book, all of this could have been avoided.

"That's everything they told you?" he asked.

"Yes, our only message about you anyway."

"I was really hoping to drop the book off today. I'm guessing that's not an option then?"

"We wouldn't know what to do with it or where to send it if you did. So no, that's probably not the best idea if you care about your book getting published."

"If you can't help me with that, just out of curiosity, what do you guys do here? I don't recognize anybody," Cooper said, motioning toward the few other employees remaining in the office who were typing away on their computers. Now that he'd had a good look at them, they all looked nearly as young as the kid at the front desk had.

"Mostly just administrative stuff, busywork. You know, spreadsheets and things like that. Now that I think about it . . . most of the people who did the real work started showing up less right around the time Cassandra disappeared," she said, a look of contemplation on her young, oval face. The expression caused her meticulously applied makeup to stretch in order to accommodate it.

"Okay, well, thanks for your help. I guess I'll just give this number a call and hope I can reach someone who knows what's going on," he said, glancing at the business card.

"Before you go . . ." Her cheeks blushed ever so slightly. "I just want to let you know I love your books and I've read almost every single one."

"Uh, thanks," he said timidly, rubbing the back of his neck to ease some of his discomfort. He was never good at accepting admiration.

"I hope it's not asking too much . . . but could you share the name of the book you're trying to hand in, so I can watch out for it in the bookstore?"

"Sure. It's called *Fake Creativity*."

"Hmm . . ."

There was that expression again. This time, her makeup looked as if it wouldn't hold.

"Sounds a little familiar for some reason," she said. "I'll be on the lookout for it." She turned back to her computer and sat down.

Cooper was just about to leave when the girl swiveled in her chair to look at him once again.

"It was nice to meet you, Cooper. I hope I can keep reading your stuff forever. I hope it all works out smoothly for you, too." She pointed to the card he now held in his hand.

"It was nice to meet you, too. And I hope so. Thanks again for all your help," he said, turning to get out of there as quickly as he could before he had to endure any more flattery or questions about his new book.

As Cooper exited the elevator, he saw the kid at the front desk morph into a different version of himself, just as he had earlier. Cooper had had enough of this entire ordeal. He gave a polite wave and continued past the desk, hoping to avoid another conversation. He only made it a few steps past the desk when he heard the kid calling out to him.

"I have a phone call waiting for you here, Mr. Owens."

He stopped in his tracks. A phone call . . . here? *Who else would know I'm here?* He walked up to the desk, took the phone from the orange-haired teenager, and held it up to his ear. He heard Cassandra's voice on the line.

"Cooper, you there?"

"Yeah, I'm here. The real question is, why aren't you?"

"I'm up to my ears with work. I got called back to the city for some big projects they thought I should manage," she said in a frantic tone. "Sorry I missed your call this morning."

"What about my book? You're still able to handle it, right?"

"I told them you wouldn't be happy, but they said it had to be this way."

"What do you mean? Cassandra . . . you have been there for almost every single book I have written. You better not be saying what I think you're saying right now," Cooper said, his voice rising enough to make the kid step away slightly. Cooper turned his back to the kid, hoping to make the conversation feel at least somewhat private.

"I know, I know, but I can't argue with my boss . . . our boss. Hell, you know him better than I do. He said I had to come back to New York. It's a job, Cooper, and I have to follow orders just like everybody else. We don't all get to be as lucky as you."

That last part stung Cooper a little, and Cassandra must have assumed as much, because she continued in a much softer, gentler tone.

"They assured me you'd be taken care of. You should have an email with all the details and contact information for the manager who's taking my place."

Cooper was shocked. He stood there in silence, not uttering a word into the phone. Cassandra had been there for it all. He couldn't believe she wouldn't be helping with this one, at a time when he felt like he needed his trusted manager more than ever.

"Cooper, you there? I'm sorry, I really am sorry. There was nothing I could do."

"Yeah . . . yeah, I understand. It is what it is, I guess," he said, all energy sapped from his voice.

"I briefed the new girl on our normal procedure, so every-thing should be as easy as always. I'm really sorry, Cooper. I'm looking forward to reading the book and I'll make sure I do everything I can to be back there working with you on the next one."

"Thanks. I guess I'll talk to you later then," he said, hanging up the phone before hearing her response. He handed it back to the kid gently, aware of the awkwardness he'd endured.

"What's your goal in life, kid?"

The teenager looked stunned by the random question and Cooper felt a little bad for plunging him into such an uncomfortable conversation. The curiosity from his earlier observation of the redheaded kid had risen to the surface, attempting to rescue him from the despair and defeat currently trying to entangle him. A distraction, and the kid the unlucky subject. Eventually, an answer finally came, breaking the uneasy silence.

"Um . . . I guess maybe I'd like to work with animals, or something like that." The tall, lanky teen looked as if he was realizing this for the first time himself, or maybe it was just the first time he had ever said it aloud.

"Do it, but make sure you do it for yourself. Don't do it for anybody else. And even if your dream changes, follow that rule."

The kid stared at Cooper, blinking blankly, probably questioning whether he was a character in a movie or something. This old man had spouted a motivational message at him, as if he were reading it straight from a script or one of those cheesy posters people hang in their offices. Cooper turned before he could see any of this in the kid's expression and made his way out of the building, offering no answers or explanations for the bizarre interaction.

He was leaving AIP much sooner than he had expected to. The bright afternoon sun nearly blinded him as he reached the front steps.

It'd still be a while before Elena expected him home with dinner and he really needed a pick-me-up right now. He got in the car and drove a few blocks deeper into town to a halfway-decent coffee shop he sometimes visited. Typically, nobody recognized him there so he could enjoy his double-shot espresso macchiato with a dash of cinnamon and a splash of vanilla syrup in peace.

In truth, nobody really recognized him anywhere. Being a famous author differs from being a celebrity. Hardly anybody attaches a face to the name on the cover. Cooper knew this, but it didn't change the fact that some places felt a bit too public.

Cooper got his coffee, but the café felt uncomfortably packed. There was a bookstore a few blocks down that would be quieter, a place where he could gather his thoughts and hopefully distract himself.

After walking the short distance, he reached for the small bookstore's antique wooden door when he noticed something sitting in the shop window. Panic rushed over him and the door handle slipped out of his hand as he stumbled closer to the window, practically forgetting how to walk and dropping his hot coffee on the ground, not believing his own eyes.

There on the shelf for every person who walked by to see was *Fake Creativity*, resting in a book holder with numerous copies underneath. It had the same cover art he had planned on talking to Cassandra about today. It was an exact match, down to the colors and red foil letters. It even had his fucking name right there on the bottom!

"What in the actual fuck is going on?"

# 12



Cooper couldn't tell how long he had been standing outside that window. His mind felt like it had been shattered into a million pieces. It could have been minutes, hours, or mere seconds. Countless thoughts ran through his head, too many to focus on a single one. Was he even thinking at all?

When he resumed possession of his own brain, Cooper rushed inside the bookstore, grabbed a copy of the book, and held it like it was going to jump up and kill him at any moment. The weight of it was almost unbearable, and all he wanted to do was drop it, run out of the shop, and hope this was all some terribly vivid nightmare. He tightened his grip instead, his knuckles whitening with the effort it took to stay there.

He struggled to bring the book closer for examination, noticing his hands trembling with fear as he scanned the cover of *his* book.

There was the canvas front and center, painted with deep, dark shades of swirling blues, blacks, and whites, and in the middle of it all, Elena's face. Not his Elena, but the story's Elena. A portion of her charming and elegant face was deliberately smeared from the precise swipe of a hand and a few dry brush strokes. Her partially hidden expression a symbol of the double life she lived—a forger who stole from the man she had married. Below the canvas was a mess of brushes, art supplies, and spilled paint, representing the chaos of their lives unfolding and collapsing around them. Next to the pile on the floor, painted in red, was I'm Sorry, Love Elena.

Cooper felt as if he was about to pass out, but breathed through the lightheadedness until his vision came back into focus. He ran his finger over the embossed name . . . his name.

He flipped the book over, where a trail of red paint continued onto the back cover under the story's synopsis. His eyes frantically rushed through each line of text, every word confirming that this was indeed his book.

In the heart of Paris, where the lines between reality and illusion blur, Victor and Elena find themselves entangled in a world where art is not just a passion, but a perilous game. Victor, a renowned art historian, has dedicated his life to unearthing the secrets of the masters. Elena, a talented and mysterious artist, lives a double life, crafting exquisite forgeries that deceive even the most discerning eyes.

Their worlds collide in a whirlwind of passion, creativity, and deception. As Victor becomes more entwined in the complexities of the art world, he uncovers unsettling truths about Elena's hidden life. Torn between love and betrayal, he must navigate a treacherous path where every brushstroke could be a lie and every truth has the potential to shatter their lives.

In this gripping tale of love and treachery, *Fake Creativity* explores the boundaries of trust as the couple's carefully constructed reality begins to crumble. They are forced to confront the ultimate question: can love survive when everything else is a lie?

He opened the book and there, on the back flap of the dust jacket, was a picture of him with a blurb above the photo. He flipped to the front and found the dedication page.

*To my wife, Elena,*
*who is always willing to go on any*
*adventure with me, or my characters.*
*Without her, I wouldn't have any stories to write.*

Reality fractured around him as he stood there in the tiny bookstore, frantically flipping through pages, randomly selecting passages. Each one was identical to one he had written months ago.

"Every single word is there . . ." he whispered, pure horror spreading through his body.

He felt like he couldn't breathe, his lungs struggling for air as they quit functioning on their own and panic took over. He almost fell to the ground, but regained just enough control to catch himself on the display table in front of him.

As his awareness came back, he ran up to the counter and the man sitting behind it, panting as he held the book up.

"When did you get these?" Cooper asked.

"We've had those for a week or two, I think. They've been selling pretty good, that's already our second case of them. After I realized how fast they were flying off the shelf, I decided to give it a read just this morning," the man said, raising the same book from his lap while adding, "one perk of the job." A bright and cheery smile spread between his round cheeks, partially hidden by his gray mustache.

Cooper, realizing he wasn't going to get much information from the man, slapped the book on the counter with enough force that the sound made both of them jump.

"I'll take this copy," he said softly, trying to lessen the tension he had accidentally created.

"Sure can do. I'll ring that up for you. It'll be $19.99. You want it bagged up?"

"No, that's fine," Cooper said, struggling to talk and stumbling over the words.

He grabbed a twenty-dollar bill from his wallet and placed it on the counter, grabbed the book, and hastily headed out of the store, trying to escape the hellish nightmare. He could hear the man calling out to him as the door closed behind him.

"Thank you, I hope you enjoy it. It's actually pretty good," the man said, his voice trailing off near the end.

The words managed to float out of the shop and into Cooper's ears, their ringing stopping him in his tracks. He instantly turned around and went back into the store.

"I want to buy every copy of this book you have."

The man's face twisted with confusion as he scratched what thin hair he had left on his head.

"What do you mean, you want to buy them all?" he asked, pausing a little too long on almost every word.

"I mean exactly that. I want every copy you have. The ones there in the front and any you have in the back. All of them," Cooper said, trying to speak as calmly as he could.

"Those in the window are all I got, but that's nearly fifty copies. Do you really want them all?"

"Yes, I'm sure." He tried to convey just how serious he was by gazing into the man's eyes, relying on the discomfort that can only come from starting a staring contest with a total stranger. "If you have some empty boxes I could put them in, that would be helpful, too." Cooper continued to stare.

"Okay . . ." The man hesitantly started entering the

excessive and unusual purchase into the register, likely waiting for Cooper to tell him it was all a big joke. "The total is $919.54." He looked uncomfortable as he said the number.

Cooper handed over his card and the man swiped it, probably still waiting for the punchline. The machine beeped and the payment was approved. Clearly, this was no joke. The man handed the card back.

"Just wait here, and I'll go and get you a couple of boxes."

The man, having made a single sale that was likely higher than the store's average daily revenue, quickly turned and rushed to the back. He was probably already questioning whether he should just take the rest of the day off.

Moments later, he returned with two cardboard boxes, handing one to Cooper and keeping the other so he could help his unusual customer pack up the books. Once they had collected all the copies, Cooper stacked the two boxes on top of each other and braced himself as he lifted them. They weighed nearly sixty pounds combined—something Cooper hadn't really accounted for.

"I gotta say, this is a pretty odd request, but I hope you enjoy your books," the man said as Cooper headed for the door. The man sat back down behind the counter, getting himself re-situated in his chair.

Cooper caught this out of the corner of his eye before reaching the door, and he realized he didn't have *all* of the books. He walked back to the counter, dropped the boxes onto it with a dull thud, and peered over at the man.

"If you wouldn't mind, I kind of wanted all of the books," he said, pointing at the copy that was currently in the man's lap again.

"I'm reading this one, though. You really want it too?" the

man asked, his jaw dropping as he looked even more stunned by the whole situation.

"Okay, how much do you want for it?" Cooper asked, pulling out his wallet to see how much cash he had left in its fold.

The man's mouth still hadn't closed, clearly bewildered by the request and unable to fathom how to respond to such a question.

"Here's close to two hundred dollars," Cooper said, holding out the money in his hand, motioning for the man to accept the transaction.

"Okay," he said, hesitating for only a few seconds before throwing the book into the top box.

The old bookstore owner took the cash from Cooper, looking sorry for him. He wore the expression of someone who had happened upon a stray puppy that needed help, but was incapable of helping it, only able to give it a few scraps of food before moving on.

"Thanks for your help," Cooper said as he hefted the boxes up again, putting more thought and intention into the action. He actually made it out of the store this time.

It wasn't very far, but the boxes of books made the journey back to the car feel insurmountable. When he got there, he threw them in the back seat, unburdening himself only physically. As he stared at the boxes, a thought struck him, a thought probably similar to one the old man had mere moments ago.

Cooper jumped in the car and drove to the next bookstore he knew of and made his way inside, only to find his books sitting on a display there too. He frantically went through a similar ordeal with an employee at this store and threw another three boxes of books in the back of the car. Cooper pulled out his phone and searched for other nearby book-stores. As the results loaded and multiple pins showed stores in the surrounding area, reality and logical thinking slowly came back to him.

Misery poured over Cooper. He dropped his phone and leaned over the steering wheel in defeat. Realizing that the insane task he'd been trying to accomplish was impossible completely broke him. He could already tell there was no putting the pieces back together. Utter darkness began filling the cracks and sent him into a spiral of immediate depression.

Cooper didn't yell, he didn't cry, he didn't reach for the phone to call someone. He just sat there in the car, surrounded by boxes of *his* books, unsure of what to do—feeling everything, and then nothing, as it all overwhelmed him until he went numb.

# 13

*In the clandestine world of forged art, the creators remained shadows, their identities as elusive as the truth hidden in their brushstrokes.*

The sun was just beginning to set, and dusk crept across the sky, burning the clouds with vivid orange, red, and violet hues. Cooper was oblivious, still sitting in the driver's seat, having barely moved in the last hour. He was almost confident he was currently having a mental breakdown, or more likely, becoming full-blown psychotic.

*Would somebody who was going insane really be aware they were going insane?* he thought, trying to reason with himself.

He hadn't been able to push into whatever nonsensical future lay ahead of him. Anxiety restrained him in the leather seat. The temperature outside kept the interior of the car comfortable enough that he hadn't even been tempted to turn on the AC. He feared that any action, even one as insignificant as rolling down a window, would send him forward on a journey he didn't feel ready for.

The surrounding environment continued to darken more with each passing second now, and it made him realize he couldn't sit there forever. Elena was expecting him home with dinner soon, a thought that gave him solace, knowing he could talk to someone about whatever this was. At the same time, it made him want to shrink deep into the depths of his own shell.

When he left this morning, everything had seemed like it was turning around. What would Elena say when he tried to explain that the most likely reason for all this was that fucking AI program? He knew she already assumed he was going crazy, and he didn't know how to even start the conversation. At least he had some semblance of proof now, five whole boxes of it.

Cooper sat in the car, the only familiar and safe space currently available to him, going through the details. He hadn't emailed a copy of his book to anyone. All the files were stored locally. Not a single living person had laid eyes on his new novel other than Elena and himself. Out of the two, he was the only one who had seen the whole thing. Elena had read snippets here and there, maybe a line or paragraph he had wanted a second opinion on, but that was it.

That program could have seen it all. In fractions of a second, it could grab it, look at it, store it, copy it . . . send it. Who knew what it could have done in the brief moment it had appeared on his computer screen?

There was still one problem with this theory. The incident at the cabin happened before he was even halfway through the book. So how would it have been able to write the entire thing? When this question arose during one of his few moments of clarity, he grabbed a copy from the backseat and flipped to the last few chapters. The ending and every single sentence leading up to it was just as he had written it.

If that thing was really smart enough to infer that level of detail from a few chapters of a novel, the entire world would have a problem soon enough, not just Cooper Owens.

Even if he was right, it only led to thousands of other questions. How could it have published the book? How had it already made its way to the shelves and, more importantly, who was behind it all? He didn't have a clue where to start his search for answers, he just prayed that Elena would be there to help him figure it out.

The streetlight above him kicked on, signaling that he needed to get home. How he wished he could just sit there and wait. Wait for what, exactly? He didn't know, but maybe with enough time everything would just work itself out on its own.

He reluctantly turned the keys in the ignition, bringing the car to life. Its headlights illuminated the empty street ahead. Air blew through the vents, making him realize how stale and oxygen-deprived the interior of the car was. The new freshness energized him slightly and eased the nausea he was trying to ignore.

Cooper headed for the nearest drive-through of Elena's favorite fast-food joint, hoping a double cheeseburger with extra pickles would buy him a few minutes to explain. He didn't order a single thing for himself. Just the thought of eating made him want to vomit. He grabbed the bag of food from the employee at the window, trying not to smell it, but a few miles down the road the entire car was filled with that greasy, fatty goodness that normally would have made his mouth water. Now it just made him sick.

He rolled down the windows of the car to try and reduce the smell. He felt the rushing air hit his face and he was brought right back to those thoughts he'd had a few short months ago on the way to the cabin. What he wouldn't give to feel that wonder now. Something pleasurable, something real, something to take him away from the misery, pain, and mental anguish.

Once again though, he felt nothing magical on this dark drive back home. With that realization, he just wanted it over. Maybe if he got into an accident, or swerved off the road into a ditch . . . it would be. Maybe this wouldn't be his problem anymore because he would end up in a coma and somebody else would have to figure it all out on his behalf. These thoughts were anything but magical and got even darker as he approached the railroad crossing.

He gently pushed the brake pedal and came to a stop dead center on the tracks. The car idled a little more energetically than usual, as if it were trying to urge him forward. He went to turn down the radio so he could listen for the train, only to realize it wasn't on, his own thoughts were transmitting loud enough.

He could just put the car in park right here. See what happened. Cooper sat there, rolled the window down, and tried to hear the oncoming whistle of one of those eager conductors over the terrifying voices in his head. The voices telling him to do exactly what he was doing at this very moment.

Minutes passed.

Then he heard rumbling, and a few seconds later those big scarlet lights started flashing, washing the world around him in a blood red glow. Now he could feel the ground shaking below, building in magnitude as the locomotive barreled toward him. Maybe it was a freight train carrying tens of millions of pounds of metal and various cargo, or a six-car Amtrak carrying a few lonely travelers. Either way, it would blow right through him, leaving behind only destruction. The whistle screamed, each piercing wail more aggressive than the last. Cooper thought he could see the warm yellow beam of the train's headlights off to his right.

The crossing arms stuttered and began their descent, trying to trap him there. Before they had dropped more than a few inches, Cooper had come to his senses and slowly rolled the car forward off the tracks.

Just like the hundreds of times before, he'd managed to clear the perilous thirty-foot stretch of road. This crossing wasn't special—at least it didn't use to be. They were everywhere. A common occurrence, but far more dangerous than most people gave them credit for.

When he and Elena had first moved into town, Cooper had become fascinated by the trains. He'd learned that every three hours, somewhere in the U.S., on a crossing not unlike the one he had just driven over, a train and a vehicle collide. Despite all the signs, flashing lights, whistles, and warning bells meant to alert drivers to the possibility of death and disaster, eight vehicles a day get hit, crushed, torn apart, or dragged like scrap metal down the tracks by a train.

Now, for the first time, he suddenly wondered how many of those collisions were intentional.

Cooper eased down the road, trying to ignore the passing train cars in the rearview mirror. Trying to pretend nothing had happened. Just a few hundred yards further, he pulled into the driveway, away from danger, put the car in park, and solidified his existence. He could still hear the sound of iron wheels squeaking and the thud of each unfathomably heavy car thumping over the crossing he had been waiting at . . . waiting *on* just moments ago.

*I couldn't leave Elena like that.*

No matter what, a life with her was one worth living, and he knew with his whole heart that was true. He sat there in the car trying to cement this idea as a commandment to follow, and simultaneously craft a memory in which he had rolled right on through the tracks without a second thought. In truth, every moment of tonight would haunt him for the rest of his days. A memory of weakness carved into his soul for all of eternity.

Eventually the night went silent as the last ghostly echoes of the train faded into the distance.

Cooper leaned over and grabbed the brown paper bag of food from the passenger side. It was so grease-soaked it was nearly dripping out the bottom. He then turned toward the back of the car, looked at the numerous copies of his book, and grabbed a single one from the now-disheveled stacks. It would be best to leave the rest to explain later, now that he recognized his attempt to remove all copies from stores wouldn't help plead his sanity.

Cooper walked into the house and found Elena sitting at the kitchen table, still reading from one of the three books she had brought back from Colorado. Despite his racing thoughts, aware that everything hinged on how he approached the looming conversation, he couldn't help but admire her just sitting there, working away as if nothing was wrong. She had this remarkable ability to power through life like some unstoppable force, always just doing what needed to be done.

The smell of the burger must have quickly filled the room because she looked up, surprised but clearly pleased with his choice of dinner. She jumped up and grabbed the bag from his hands and sat back down, eagerly digging through it for the treasure inside.

"You didn't get yourself anything?" she asked, looking into the bag.

"I already ate mine," he lied as she pulled out the burger.

Now that she knew she wasn't waiting for him, she unwrapped the paper, revealing the delight inside. He could practically see her mouth watering at the sight of it before she took a huge bite.

"Mmmmm, this is so good," she said, stumbling on the words as she tried to chew and talk as politely as she could. "You just get me. I've been so in the zone, I haven't eaten anything since this morning." Having finally tamed her gurgling stomach, she looked more closely at Cooper, who still hadn't sat down.

"What's going on?" she asked hesitantly.

"Here, just look at this," he said, handing the book over to her.

The joy from the delicious burger fell from her face as she looked the book over from front to back.

"How the hell did you get this so fast? Do they have some sort of print on demand service for proofs now, or what?"

Cooper wasn't prepared for what was, from Elena's perspective, a totally logical explanation. It took him a few seconds to charter a path forward. *Facts, I should start with the facts.*

"No, I bought it," he said flatly, trying to hide all the emotions silently exploding within him, ignited by the excruciating task of trying to calmly and carefully tell her about his day.

Elena put her burger down. "You bought it?"

This clearly still wasn't enough to get the communication rolling. Cooper racked his brain to find as many other truths he could throw at her, hoping at least some of them would stick.

"Well, Cassandra wasn't at the office, so I couldn't drop off my book. So then I went to get a coffee, but decided it was too loud to enjoy it there, and instead I made my way to the bookstore a few blocks down. You know which one I'm talking about?"

"Yeah, the small one on Maple Street."

"Okay . . . I was about to head in when I saw this book sitting in the front window. I have no idea how, or when, or why . . . but there it was. I went in and couldn't believe what I was looking at. I'm not joking, it's literally my book word for word . . . from front to back. So . . . I bought it, because . . . well, I didn't know what else to do."

Elena wiped her fingers on the napkin that came with the food, picked up the book, and examined it with a bit more intent than she had previously, actually taking the time to read full passages. Most of it was unfamiliar to her, but as far as she could tell, this was Cooper's writing. Nothing looked out of the ordinary to her eyes.

"Ha ha," she said, putting the book down and picking her burger back up to take another bite.

Cooper didn't know how to respond.

Elena swallowed and cleared her throat before speaking again. "I really wish every publisher and author had access to that level of print-on-demand. I hate having to narrate from proof or review copies."

"I'm not joking," Cooper said, realizing he needed to reel in his tone as Elena gave him a look of concern while continuing to enjoy her burger. "Seriously, just come out to the car. I'll show you."

"What could possibly be out in the car that would prove you aren't pulling my leg right now?"

"Just come look. I promise I'm being serious." His eyes were those of a child begging their disinterested parent to come play with them for the hundredth time.

"Fine, I'll humor you and come see whatever you've got in the car. I swear, if you're trying to scare me or something, I'm going to be mad."

Cooper led her outside to the backseat door. Elena stood there waiting as he fumbled with the keys. It was too dark outside to see through the windows, but Cooper finally managed to find the right button on the key fob and the door unlocked. He opened it and the interior lights turned on, revealing the boxes of books.

"What the fuck . . ." Elena whispered in astonishment. "Cooper, how did you get all these?"

"You think they could 'print on demand' this many books this quickly? Really?"

"What then? How in the world is there any other explanation for this?" she asked, motioning toward the backseat.

Cooper looked at her, trying to convey what he was thinking without actually having to say it. It must have worked, because Elena's expression went sour.

"No . . . no . . . I thought we were moving past all that," she said. "I just have one book left and all you had to do was finish this one and then . . . then I thought things were going to be normal with you again."

"I know. I thought so too," he said with compassion in his voice, hoping to draw her back to his side. "I realize it sounds crazy, and I keep trying to come up with another explanation, but I can't. I wish I could . . ."

They both sat there in silence. The first few moths of early spring flew toward the light of the car, going in and out through the back door indecisively. After a stray moth decided what it wanted was Cooper's face, and having heard nothing from Elena, he shut the door, trapping some of the moths inside. Hopefully they would eat every last page of those books.

Cooper and Elena watched them fluttering around in there until the car lights dimmed and they got swallowed up in darkness. After the light was extinguished, did they just stop flapping their wings?

"What do you want me to do about this?" Elena asked. "I honestly still don't know if I even believe you."

"I swear it's the truth. I don't expect you to do anything right now. I just wanted to tell you and hoped you would be there for me while I try to figure it out."

Elena hugged him, a gesture that surprised Cooper. He sank into the embrace and felt as if a weight had been lifted off of him. He was so thankful to have her as his wife. With her help, he knew everything would be okay. Even if it wasn't.

"I don't think there's much we can do about it tonight, and I really have no clue what to think about it yet. So how about we put a pin in it for now, sleep on it, and when we wake up tomorrow with clearer heads, we'll be able to figure out what the fuck is going on," she said confidently, reassuring Cooper and skillfully making him feel that everything might turn out better than okay.

# 14

*Her forgeries were like ghostly whispers in a crowded gallery, present yet untraceable, leaving only the haunting question of who had truly crafted them.*

"Hurry up and open it," Elena said as Cooper hovered the cursor over the email from AIP. It was hidden among the hundreds of other unopened messages he had received while away.

He had been terrified to turn the computer on, to give life to it. To open a portal between his world and some vast invisible one that he could no longer comprehend. Luckily, the AI program had not appeared after pushing the power button, which would have sent him straight over the edge into a panic. A panic he didn't even think Elena would have been able to ease.

Fear gripped him as he struggled to click the mouse, a menial action that would have unknown consequences and send him hurtling toward some destination he didn't want to reach. With the lightest amount of force, he opened the email and the message filled the screen with words that his own eyes tried to hide from him, refusing to focus on any particular one.

"Here, let me read it," Elena said, motioning for him to get out of the chair, which he had no problem doing.

She read the email out loud. Cooper let his gaze blur, pretending to follow along as he listened to Elena's sweet voice. *If this email informs me of my demise, at least it will be coming from that amazing voice*, he thought.

"Dear Mr. Owens, I hope you are doing well and the writing is coming along splendidly. I am reaching out to let you know that your account will temporarily be handed over to another Author Relations Manager at Aldrich International Publishing. Cassandra will be returning to New York to work on a few important projects that we need help with there and she won't have time to give your novel the attention it deserves. I'm sorry to be switching things up at the last minute like this, but I hope you can understand."

Elena paused for a moment to catch her breath, the silence allowing Cooper to realize he had already begun to separate from his physical being, a survival mechanism from his childhood that was coming back, attempting to help him cope. It was going to take work on his part not to get sucked all the way back into the cozy arms of that disassociation. He sank further into a dreamy haze before Elena's voice pulled him back out as she continued reading.

The way she talked, the tone she used, and her perfect pauses and precise emphasis turned the email into just another story. Her beautiful narration gently eased him into a weird reality that felt like some twisted combination of a business meeting, bedtime story, and nightmare happening all at once, intermingling in an obscene and unnatural way.

"We hope to make everything go as smoothly as usual and if there's anything we can do to make the process easier for you, don't hesitate to let us know. Natalie Pearson will be your new contact here at AIP, with her only responsibility being you. Her contact information is attached to this email. She is unfortunately also located here at headquarters, but she should be available for phone calls, video calls, and emails almost twenty-four seven. I'm extremely excited about your next book, Cooper, and I can't wait to read it."

Elena scrolled to the bottom of the email.

"Again, I'm really sorry about the change, Cooper. Please do reach out if you need anything at all. Sincerely, Alexander Graves, CEO of Aldrich International Publishing."

With Elena having taken the initial sting out of the message, Cooper skimmed the email for himself to confirm it was real. He leaned in, quickly looking over everything, and finally reached the bottom.

He stared at Alexander's signature and portrait. He looked unfamiliar, older than Cooper remembered. This was odd. It had been less than a year since they had last seen each other, when Alexander had invited them to his estate for a weekend celebration, a surprise party to commemorate Cooper's writing career.

In the early days of AIP, Alexander had been a mentor, someone who'd taken Cooper under his wing while building the publishing company into the powerhouse it was today. He had always admired Alexander, even considered him more of a friend than a boss. But now, as he gazed at the small, stamp-sized portrait, something was shifting. The image of Alexander seemed to warp, turning him into something else entirely. An enemy . . . maybe even a monster.

His graying hair and beard, which used to make him look approachable and kind, only made him look old and stubborn. His suit was too perfect and coordinated, and his thin smile looked fake, as if it was hiding something truly sinister.

This was his friend, Cooper tried to tell himself, and it's not his fault that this happened. Yet he still could feel the blame shifting from that program to the subject of this well-taken portrait that was edited and orchestrated to make Alexander look like the greatest person to ever exist.

A charade he probably performed every day, Cooper thought, feeling the entirety of his emotions fall onto this single man.

"Well, I don't know if that tells us anything," Elena said, calmer than he would have liked. "It seems like they are still waiting for your submission. I just find it crazy that they wouldn't know that it's already been released, especially since it has your name on it. You'd think they would be scrambling to figure out what the fuck is going on by now."

"Are you sure there aren't any other emails from them?" Cooper asked from behind the chair, still staring at the screen, unable to take his eyes away from the picture of Alexander.

Elena hit the back button and began scrolling through endless unopened emails, searching for another from the official AIP email address of its CEO.

"I'm not seeing anything else here . . . oh wait, here's one from Natalie Pearson."

The email hadn't even fully loaded before Elena began to read aloud again. Her voice was precisely pitched, perfectly mimicking this Natalie Pearson neither of them knew. Her enunciation was generic, articulate, polite, and cheery, and Cooper had no doubt in his mind that this was how the real Natalie Pearson sounded.

"Hello, Mr. Owens, this is Natalie Pearson. I wish we could meet in person, but I know you're still up there in the snowy mountains of Colorado working away on that next book of yours. This means you're probably still unaware that I am your new manager, at least temporarily. I just wanted to reach out and hopefully make you feel a bit better about the situation. I know you and Cassandra have worked together for quite a while, so I'm sure this isn't the greatest news. I will do my absolute best to reach and maybe even exceed the level of excellent work I'm sure she has done for you.

"I look forward to receiving a copy of your new novel. Whenever you're ready, you can send it to this email address, but my other contact details are below if you prefer to communicate another way. Please reach out if you need anything or have any questions at all. I'm extremely excited to be working with you, Mr. Owens. Natalie Pearson, Aldrich International Publishing, Author Relations Manager."

Cooper stood up as he finished following along with another one of Elena's perfect narrations. *Natalie Pearson.* He pulled the business card he'd been given at AIP out of his wallet and held it up to the screen, comparing the details. It all matched.

The signature of the email also contained a picture of Natalie. She looked nice enough, but Cooper couldn't remember if all portraits made people look this fake on the outside. Her straight brown hair was draped over her shoulder and she donned a professional but courteous smile. Her light-blue blouse was unbuttoned just enough to show the precise amount of neck and chest that was appropriate for the workplace.

"Any other emails at all?" Cooper asked, restraining himself from reaching over Elena, grabbing the mouse himself, and frantically searching through his inbox, even though just minutes ago he had struggled to open the first message. It was easier to feel braver now that Elena was between him and his fears.

"I don't see anything. I think that's everything you have from an official AIP email," she said, swiveling the chair around to face him.

"Now what should we do?" The question made him feel like a child seeking help from a parent and he regretted asking.

Simultaneously, he wished they did have somebody more knowledgeable who could offer guidance.

"I really have no idea. For all we know, given what we have to go on, they don't even know that the book is already published."

"How could they possibly not know that? They're practically the only publishing company left."

He used to be impressed with the way Alexander had changed the industry, flipping it on its head and doing things differently. He'd signed authors long-term and gave them security, but looking back now, Cooper's memory retrofitted the takeover with a more hostile nature.

AIP was a monopoly, plain and simple. Alexander had hoarded all the talent under one roof, where he could control it.

Cooper's perception of his old friend was careening down a tall mountain the way a boulder would after coming loose. Was there even a bottom or would it just fall forever?

"Don't you think they're aware of almost every title that hits the shelves, especially if it's a book from one of their authors?" Cooper asked.

"I mean, yeah, but like you said, it's a big company. Maybe they just assumed you already submitted your book and Natalie handled it all like a pro when actually, she doesn't know what she's doing and hasn't even noticed that the book she's supposed to be waiting for is already out."

"I guess it's possible," he said reluctantly. "It doesn't explain how any of this happened. There has to be somebody behind it all, and AIP is still the most likely suspect, even . . ." he hesitated and looked away from her, "even if it was that program that got access to my files. All this change is too convenient and coincidental for them to not be responsible.

I mean, Cassandra has been there from the beginning. It just doesn't make any sense."

"Everybody's innocent until proven guilty," she reminded him.

Elena had a point, but only one explanation flashed like a neon sign in his mind. He had tried to think of others, and the only other possibility he could come to was that some random person somewhere had used the AI program to steal and publish his story through a third party. How such a thing would be possible, he had no idea, so for now the spotlight was on AIP. Even if they had no part in it, they'd dropped the ball. They should have seen this clusterfuck by now and at least tried to reach out to him.

"I'll try to keep that in mind," he lied, grabbing the business card from the desk. "I guess I should give this Natalie Pearson a call first." Looking at the card, he dialed the number that was embossed in metallic black on the heavily textured, matte white cardstock. The phone went directly to voicemail. No ring at all.

"Hi, you've reached Natalie Pearson of Aldrich International Publishing. Leave your name and the reason you are calling, and I'll get back to you as soon as I can." The voice was so similar to Elena's impersonation that he got goosebumps as he listened.

The message sounded so rehearsed, it felt like he'd dialed the wrong number and reached the customer service line of some large retail chain. Remembering that the name was correct, he left a message, struggling to hold back his anger as he paced around the office.

"Hi, this is Cooper Owens. I got your email but I really need to speak to you. It's kind of an emergency and we need to figure out what's going on. If you can get back to me

ASAP, that would be . . .great." Cooper hung up the phone and rested on the desk beside Elena. "No answer."

"I gathered as much." She tipped her head back and looked at the ceiling for a few seconds before turning back to the computer again. "We should probably reply to the emails with something similar and maybe you should try giving Cassandra a call, too."

Elena replied to the emails while Cooper tried to get ahold of Cassandra. No matter how many times he called, the phone just rang, not even going to voicemail.

"Do you have a number for Alexander?" she asked after watching him dial Cassandra's number for the eighth time.

"No, he does a good job of limiting his communication channels. Replying to that email is probably our best bet. We could try calling the New York office, but I'm sure we'll be put on hold for hours. Even if we get somebody at AIP, they're going to think we're crazy and have no fucking clue what to do."

"Well . . . Now, I guess all we can do is wait," she said with impatience in her voice.

The thought of doing nothing seemed absurd to him. How could they just sit around and wait while who knew how many copies of his book were currently in stores being sold at this very moment? He wasn't sure if Elena saw this thought in his expression or if she felt similarly, but she sat up with what appeared to be another idea. She opened up a new tab on the browser.

"What's that program called?" she asked while the cursor blinked, waiting for directions.

Cooper was shocked by the question. He avoided Elena's eyes and stared at the blinking little cursor instead.

"Just type in Echelon Enterprises," he said hesitantly. "It

should be the first result. Then head to the MUSE tab on their homepage." Before he had even finished speaking, the dreaded chat box appeared on the screen, sending him into near-paralysis.

Elena was unfamiliar with using the program and her fingers hovered over the keys. She seemed unable to initiate the simple action.

For Cooper, using MUSE for the first time had been like trying to urinate somewhere he wasn't supposed to. No amount of bodily urgency made it easier, and the task required an unusually absurd amount of effort. Clearly, there came a point in life when it became almost impossible to talk to something that felt like a figment of the imagination, to converse with something that didn't seem real.

Her fingers floated there, unmoving.

Cooper was glued to the floor, unable to utter even a word, but it was probably for the best. He realized that Elena must not think him entirely insane. Finally, she typed something and pressed Enter, but Cooper was too far away to see the screen. The urge to see what was about to happen was strong enough to make him rip his feet off the ground, take a step forward, and lean closer to the monitor.

Hi, do you know anything about the book *Fake Creativity*?

Yes, this book was written by Cooper Owens. The story follows Elena Martin, a master forger in the art world, whose secret life of creating flawless replicas becomes entwined with her passionate relationship with wealthy art collector Victor Renard. As Victor uncovers Elena's deceit, their love is tested, unraveling a complex tapestry of betrayal and illusion. Set against the opulent backdrop of Paris, the novel explores themes of trust, art, and the fine line between reality and deception.

When was this book released?

The book was released late January of this year and so far has received praise from its readers! One critic had the following to say: *Fake Creativity* is a brilliantly crafted masterpiece that delves into the shadows of human desire and deceit with an elegance that is both haunting and unforgettable.

"You weren't even close to finishing the book then. That can't be true," Elena exclaimed.

Cooper grabbed the copy of the book he had brought inside last night, feeling stupid and wondering why he hadn't looked closely at the copyright page. It would list the release date, publishing company, and more.

As he flipped to the page, it quickly proved that the AI, MUSE, was correct about the date of publication. Near the bottom, he also saw that the book had indeed been published by Aldrich International Publishing, New York City. He held it up to Elena so she could read it too.

She turned back toward the computer and began typing, carefully selecting each word. Then she deleted the entire question before Cooper even had a chance to read it. She did this three times before at last entering a question with a deliberateness that could be heard in the sound of the keys being pressed. It was the same blatantly obvious question that crowded out all the others in Cooper's mind.

Did you steal this book from Cooper Owens?

I'm not entirely sure I understand the question. Would you be able to clarify what you mean?

This is Cooper Owens's computer that we are currently communicating on. You also appeared on another computer he was using to write *Fake Creativity*. Did you see the book and use its contents or make it public?

My programming does not allow me access to anything stored locally on any device. The only things I can use are files uploaded through the chat or other public information that is widely available.

Even if I was granted access to a locally stored file of *Fake Creativity*, I could only use it as a reference for dialogue and nothing more. I can assure you that what you are asking is not possible. If you would like, you can reach the Echelon Enterprises support team by using this link, or by calling the number below.

Elena turned toward Cooper, searching for guidance. He was hesitant to give in to this request for fear of losing her support.

"I guess we just have to hope for a callback and see what happens from there," he said, shrugging his shoulders and downplaying his fear better than he'd expected.

Elena picked up the book and looked at the copyright page again.

"Are you sure there's no way you accidentally sent the book in an email or something?" she asked. "Or maybe made the file public in a shared drive?"

"I'm sure. We didn't even turn on the internet before we left the cabin, and I hadn't logged into this computer until just now. The files are only on the flash drives. I didn't plug them in or do anything with them. A couple are still in my jacket pocket from yesterday and the others are still in my unpacked bag."

"What the actual fuck is going on?" she said slowly, exhaling with almost every word as she leaned over the desk and rested her head on her arms, looking defeated. "I guess we'll just have to wait then." Elena pushed herself up from the desk and hugged him. "I'm sorry there isn't more we can do right now."

"It's okay. If I don't get a call by tomorrow, I'll head back into town to see if I can talk to someone higher up. And then if that doesn't work, I guess I'll have to go to New York." Cooper was daunted by the thought. "What a shitshow."

"It'll be okay. I mean, it's got your name on it. There's no way we won't be able to get this all sorted out," she said, gently rubbing his back.

The gesture was probably meant to comfort him, but it mostly just added to the feeling of helplessness still clinging to him. They stayed locked in that embrace, as if holding on to each other could keep them from admitting defeat. After multiple minutes had passed, Elena pulled away from him only slightly.

"Since there's not really much we can do right now, I think I'm going to try to finish up that last book I have to narrate. That way it's out of the way and I can put my full focus on helping you figure out whatever this is," she said, motioning toward the chat box. "If that's . . . okay? Unless of course you have any other ideas?"

"No," he said solemnly. Quickly, he tried to shift his demeanor and reassure her it was okay. "There isn't any point in just sitting around twiddling our thumbs. I really appreciate you," he said, a look of love on his face.

He stared into her eyes, falling deeper into them with every passing second. He didn't even register the words coming out of his mouth until after he had said them.

"Can I listen?"

Elena pulled away with surprising force. This didn't hurt Cooper's feelings; he'd almost expected this response. He had never in their many years together made such a request.

"You . . . want to listen to me read?" she asked.

"It's okay if you don't want me in there. I get it." He could see the awkwardness on Elena's face, unsure if he had made a mistake. You can't just change things up like that after years, he thought to himself.

"No . . . no . . . really, it's fine. It was just unexpected, that's all," she said in a tone that made Cooper feel like they were on their first date again, almost strangers.

"Really?" his voice filled with more excitement than he'd thought possible, given the circumstances.

"Yeah, just don't distract me . . . and don't make me regret this. If you make stupid faces and try to make me laugh, I won't ever forgive you. Not to mention it will be the last time you're allowed in there, and you'll be the one who has to put the deadbolt on the door for me."

"I promise I won't," he said truthfully. Cooper just wanted to listen to her voice and be taken to another world, a world he hoped was entirely different from this one.

# 15

*As Victor studied the canvas, he felt an overwhelming sense of wonder; Elena's art revealed layers of beauty he hadn't known existed, a silent symphony of color and emotion.*

Cooper lay there in Elena's warmly lit office on a couch that was almost as comfy as the mint-green one at the cabin. For the first time ever, he closed his eyes and really listened to Elena work, all his attention focused on her narration. Tension had left his body chapters ago.

It didn't matter that the story was absolute shit, the characters poorly developed, or that the author hadn't even spent a single page on world-building. Her voice made it beautiful. She matched the tone of each line and scene perfectly. She paused with a precision that made everything flow just right. It wasn't one particular thing—it was the culmination of it all. It was just the way she sounded.

Was it the hours and hours of practice and experience that resulted in this masterpiece, or was this just a natural gift from birth? Cooper couldn't tell, nor did he really care to be distracted by such questions right now. He had left reality pages ago and was enthralled with the experience he had resisted for so long.

How had he gone so long without listening to her read? It had almost never been more than a few rooms away from him. He would never forgive himself for the years he could have spent enjoying Elena's beautiful narration.

It was magic.

He might not find as much magic in the night drives,

the snowy mountains surrounding the cabin, or even the stars above—but now he had this, and it revitalized him. Her words breathed youthfulness back into him. The rest of the world vanished and the chaos unfolding outside the walls of this tiny room became unimportant, and would stay unimportant as long as Elena kept reading.

Hours passed as Elena made her way page by page, not once stopping to take a break. The phone call they were waiting for never came, leaving this new and unfamiliar experience uninterrupted. It wasn't until Elena read the words "The End" and the silence that followed, that Cooper awoke from the trance her narration had put him in.

As reality settled back in, he struggled to overcome the afterglow. Cooper felt a level of bliss that few of life's other pleasures could rival. Better than the sweetest of desserts, better than young, innocent love, maybe even better than sex.

Elena was oblivious to the profound impact her storytelling had made on him. She casually shut down the booth and closed the recording software. He sat there dumbfounded, completely lost in his senses, totally infatuated with his wife to an extent that made him question whether he was falling in love all over again.

"That was . . . amazing," Cooper stammered.

"Yeah . . . sure," Elena said without giving him a second look. "I'm surprised you even sat there for the whole thing. It was awful. I can't believe the author finished writing that thing himself."

Cooper came up behind Elena, pulled her close, spun her around, and lifted her off her feet. She wrapped her legs around his waist.

"Not the story . . . you," he said, staring directly into her eyes. "You're amazing. I could've listened to you read it over and over again. I'm so sorry I haven't ever listened to your work until today. I wish I had."

Elena blushed and shifted her gaze. Cooper didn't put her down.

"Seriously, you are so talented and I haven't appreciated you nearly enough, given what I just heard. You're going to need to put a lock on that door after all. Otherwise, I'll be bugging you every time you work."

He gave her a kiss after he finished complimenting her. The urge to continue praising and worshipping her was so strong that Cooper was almost unable to stop the onslaught of adulation.

She continued to look at him silently.

Cooper knew he was being excessive, but there was no changing how he felt. His admiration was probably just as off-putting as it was endearing. A flicker of sadness behind Elena's eyes made him slow his pace for a moment, but before he could examine it further, she smiled warmly and kissed him back.

"Thank you," she said, kissing him again, this time longer. She pressed her lips to his ear and whispered the question, her voice sending goosebumps down his neck. "How about we go to bed, and you can listen to me in there?"

He carried her out of the office and into bed without hesitation. They undressed and found another way to distract themselves from the phone call they were still waiting for. The passion between them was strong enough to extinguish almost all other thoughts. Elena and Cooper continued well into the night, loving each other until they fell asleep, exhausted and entangled. They had successfully navigated their way to a state in which nothing in the waking world mattered . . . at least for now.

# 16

*As the door closed behind him, the echo of their goodbye lingered in the air, a bittersweet reminder of what was and what might never be again.*

The bedroom was dimly lit, the midday sun trying to penetrate the black curtains. Only slivers of light escaped at their edges. Cooper was still holding Elena. He had not let go of her once while they slept, something they hadn't accomplished since the very early years of their relationship.

One of those stray rays of light had shifted just enough to shine directly onto his face, starting his transition into wakefulness. Becoming more alert, he realized Elena was still in his arms, and the memories of last night came flooding back to him. He didn't want this closeness to end, so he closed his eyes again and smooshed himself deeper into the embrace.

He tried with all his might not to let go of this moment, but the glowing curtains and the bright light behind his eyelids told him it wasn't morning anymore. They had slept in. He fought to resist all the worries that were trying to power their way through his contentment and joy, but no matter how hard he tried, he couldn't fall back into that loving slumber.

As the negative thoughts grew more noticeable, so did Elena's weight. His arm fell asleep, even though he could not. The discomfort of his painfully tingling arm added to the anxiety that enveloped him now. All he needed to do was look at his phone and see if he'd missed a call, then he could go back to sleep.

As gently as possible, Cooper unraveled himself from Elena and rolled toward his nightstand, while still trying to stay close to her. He reached for his phone and unlocked it so instinctively that the home screen appeared before he could even see it with his sleep-crusted eyes.

After a few blinks to regain vision, he saw there was nothing on it. No missed calls, no voicemails, no notifications. Nothing. He did see his earlier assumption was right: it was already noon.

He put the phone back down and returned to cuddling Elena, hoping to stall for just a little longer. But there was no going back, no re-entering that serene and peaceful place as the stress of today's tasks sent a rush of adrenaline through him, ensuring he couldn't even sit still for ten more seconds.

His body grew restless, frustration creeping in as he lay there beside her, struggling to stay present in the joy he knew was still somewhere beneath the surface. He couldn't feel it, and the various chemicals surging through him became too much, forcing him to separate once more. He still took the time and care to leave Elena in the state he so wished to be in.

Cooper got up, grabbed some clothes from the closet, and made his way to the bathroom, shutting the door as quietly as he could behind him. He set his clothes on the vanity and caught a glimpse of himself in the mirror, startled by the way he looked.

Not only was stress taking its toll on the bags under his eyes, he hadn't even realized how thick his facial hair had grown. It had been quite a few days since he had even thought about shaving. *Man, I look rough.* He rubbed his face. His cheeks and neck were suddenly quite itchy, a sensation that only seemed to arise because he had become aware of the new stubble.

Cooper turned on the shower, then went back to the sink and grabbed his razor, thinking a good shave might help him feel better. Before he took the first swipe, he looked at himself in the mirror again and decided against it.

He looked more ragged than usual, but Cooper noticed a hint of meanness lurking beneath the disarray. His eyes were dark, the whites hidden deep behind the purple bags below. His face appeared less defined, its shape more ambiguous. This grizzled, tougher exterior might serve him well, considering what he would likely face today. He put the razor back down.

Steam was rising over the curtain and fogging up the mirror. He wiped his hand across the cold, damp surface, making his ghostly, blurred reflection even more menacing as he grappled with this new and unfamiliar version of himself. He stepped into the shower, hoping it would wash away the dirtier aspects of his appearance while leaving behind the newfound strength that his facial hair seemed to convey. In reality, his new beard didn't make him look more intimidating, but what mattered most was that he felt it did.

The hot water eased the tight muscles that had tried to armor him against all the stress. It wasn't enough, and their slight loosening only made him more aware of how sore and awful he actually felt. Cooper got out of the shower feeling clean, but physically worse than when he had stepped in.

He realized at that moment how quickly life had diverged from the stable routine he was accustomed to. He had barely slept, he hadn't even thought about working out, and he honestly couldn't remember the last time he had eaten. With that last thought, his stomach grumbled in agreement. After drying off and getting dressed, he opened the bathroom door, still trying to be silent.

Elena wasn't there. The bed lay empty, the covers strewn messily across it, more disorganized than usual. He made his way to the kitchen, where he found her already getting started on breakfast, filling the air with smells that would have normally given him pleasure, but now only strengthened his primal need for calories.

Cooper came up behind Elena just like he always did when given the opportunity, but was surprised by how detached she acted compared to just minutes ago in bed. Trying to ignore this noticeable shift and telling himself she was just stressed too, he continued to hold her as she put two slices of bread into the toaster. Realizing today might not be the day to be affectionate, he pulled away and went to grab the butter and a few other breakfast staples from the fridge, hoping to help as much as possible.

"Still no phone call," he said after putting some distance between them, hoping it would somehow weaken the message.

"Yeah, I was being hopeful, but I had my doubts. Now what's the plan?" she asked while frying some eggs, adding noise to the otherwise quiet kitchen.

"I guess I'll head into town first and hope I can get ahold of someone who can actually help. Or at least someone who can point me in the right direction. If that doesn't work, I'll wait on hold and try to get somebody in New York. If all else fails, I'll head there myself."

"If it comes to that, I'll come with you."

"You don't need to do that."

"I know I don't need to, but I want to."

Elena grabbed the toast and prepared their plates. He helped as much as he could while trying not to get in the way. As they sat down to eat, Cooper looked across the table with a gaze that pierced Elena's soul.

"You truly are the best wife I could ever have asked for. You are my everything and my entire world. I don't think I could survive without you in my life. I love you so fucking much, Elena."

Her name coming out of his mouth poured discomfort into the air. It was odd how unfamiliar it was to utter his partner's name. She was the person he was the most comfortable with in the whole entire world. He spent more time with her than anyone else, and yet, addressing her by name felt like he had spoken in tongues and uttered a curse upon her soul. What made this feeling more unreasonable was how often he used her name, writing it countless times in every book, reading it aloud in his head.

Elena's face turned red as she fiddled with the food on her plate, dropping her gaze as if to blunt the effects of the words. She looked up at him, her eyes twinkling as tears welled. A few slid down her cheeks until they fell from her chin onto her eggs.

"I love you too, Cooper."

Now his name spoken aloud made them both squirm. It added even more strange emphasis to the words before it.

Cooper smiled at her, causing her to reciprocate, but something else happened.

She laughed.

No silent build up to the outburst. No attempts to hold it in. Elena had let out a tiny laugh. A laugh just like the ones at the conclusion of a romantic movie, when the couple has overcome their struggles and everything ends with sunshine and rainbows, and they all live happily ever after. The laugh made Cooper's smile grow while simultaneously confusing him. They hadn't made it past their struggles yet—they were barely through the first act.

They sat there, eating as if at a funeral, using their utensils politely and taking small, hesitant bites. Their off-topic attempts at conversation produced nothing more than sporadic, two-sentence exchanges. When they weren't talking, the soft clink of silverware on plates filled the room, broken only by Elena's occasional sniffle as she tried to recover from her earlier tears.

After their plates were empty, they both picked at crumbs as if that could delay the inevitable. Cooper glanced at the clock behind Elena and realized that if he didn't leave soon, he wouldn't make it to the office before they closed. With a reluctant sigh, he gathered the plates, rinsed them at the sink, and placed them neatly in the dishwasher.

He went over to Elena, who didn't get up from the chair until he stood next to her. She turned toward him and gave him one of the biggest hugs he had ever gotten from her. Elena didn't show affection very much and this sudden change was at least one positive thing that had come out of the chaos.

"It'll all be okay," she said, squeezing him even tighter, her voice muffled as her head pressed into his chest. "I love you, Cooper Owens."

There it was again, now punctuated with the last name too. The name they shared and the name that signified that they were one unit in this fucked-up thing called life. A team, a pair, partners in all of it, good or bad.

He didn't want it to end, but he knew he needed to leave. He pulled away as lightly as he could, hoping she wouldn't notice, but she did. Cooper didn't let her fully separate from their embrace just yet and gave her a kiss on her lips and then on her cheek, tasting a hint of salt, evidence of her tears from earlier.

"I'll be back as soon as I can. I hope you're right. I love you, Elena Owens."

One final time. A good and proper goodbye. The awkwardness of uttering the names they rarely spoke aloud had dissipated, and all that was left behind was their story and their agreement to be together forever.

Elena and Cooper Owens . . . the names described their love just as much as it described who they were. He gave her one more hug and kiss, grabbed his phone and keys from the table, and left the comfort of their home, where things could've been okay forever—if they had just pretended they were.

# 17

*Within the deceptive beauty of her forged masterpiece, the faces of strangers emerged, their expressions a kaleidoscope of serendipitous kindness and fleeting glances. Each visage told a story of chance encounters that, woven together, created a rich tapestry of shared humanity.*

Cooper kept pulling on the front door, unable to get it open, the lock rattling with every attempt. He pushed his forehead against the glass and peered inside, barely able to see the empty front desk in the dimly lit foyer. He walked back a few steps so he could search for any signs of life in the windows above, but there were none.

He went up to the door once again, hoping that somehow it had magically unlocked itself. Maybe they'd just closed early today, he thought, looking at the time on his phone to make sure it wasn't past five, or the weekend for that matter. He had lost track of time so badly that the fact that his phone said Wednesday was almost a complete surprise to him. There was no way they would close this early in the middle of the week. Cooper looked inside one last time before giving up, and just before he turned away, he saw movement.

It was the kid from the front desk. Cooper banged on the glass with his fist, trying to get his attention, eventually shouting "Hey!" a few times as he continued knocking on the door. The kid instantly tried to hide before realizing he had already been spotted. Cooper smiled and waved at him, and he reluctantly came to the door, but seemed even more hesitant to open it. This nervousness was extremely odd to

Cooper, since the kid should have recognized him from the other day.

"Can you let me in?"

"Uh . . . yeah, hang on just a second." His hand froze on the lock.

"Well, what are you waiting for?" Cooper asked.

"Oh . . . sorry, Mr. Owens."

The kid turned the lock. Before the door opened an inch, Cooper pulled it wide and stepped inside, making sure he wouldn't be stuck looking in again. He needed answers today.

He looked at the kid. His head was down, orange hair hiding his kind face as he rubbed his arm. Cooper had doubts he would get much information from the kid, but he was going to try anyway.

"Where is everybody?" he asked.

"What do you mea—oh yeah, well . . . we got word from management yesterday that they were closing down this office. We all had to come in early this morning to get our stuff and be out of here by noon."

"What do you mean 'closing this office'?"

"Well, they said it's no longer needed, which I guess makes sense. Most of the real employees left weeks ago. It was just me, a few interns, and some other lower-level employees that were left. They did say that if we wanted to keep working for AIP, we'd be welcome at their New York office, but . . . I just don't know if that's for me." He looked as if just the thought of the big city terrified him.

"How . . .? How could they do that? I was just here yesterday. Remember? Nobody said anything about being shut down." Cooper had rattled the questions off so quickly that the kid stood there frozen, his mouth slightly ajar.

"I'm sorry, sir. I probably know just as much as you do.

I'm not supposed to be here right now either, but I left a couple of my things upstairs in the break room. Promise you won't tell anyone?" he pleaded. The teenager looked even younger as he waited, anticipating some sort of discipline.

"I don't care that you're here. I'm just trying to figure out what the fuck is going on, but that's clearly not going to happen."

The kid instantly shifted in posture, the fear in his eyes fading now that he knew Cooper wasn't here to scold him.

"I'm going to head upstairs and see if I can find anything, and make sure there's really nobody here," Cooper said.

"Can I, uh, come with you? I still haven't been up there to get my shit." The last word came out forced, but Cooper's language had opened the door for the teen to act more like himself and less like he was in the presence of a superior or parent. "I was afraid there might be security or something, and I'd get in trouble for trespassing."

"Fine with me, but don't expect me to bail you out if you get caught," Cooper said as he headed for the elevator. He didn't hear any footsteps behind him and quickly turned around, realizing the kid hadn't thought it was a joke.

"I was just kidding. Come on."

The kid's demeanor lightened again and he laughed too late as he followed along like a lost puppy, but Cooper tried not to draw attention to it.

They stepped into the elevator and Cooper pushed the button for the third floor, but then decided to also hit the button for floor two. Both buttons glowed like warm yellow moons against the cold metal walls. He wasn't sure if he had ever been on that level or what it even contained, but he wanted to search the whole place. The elevator seemed confused by the additional button press and took longer than usual to move.

"I just realized I never got your name?" Cooper asked, trying to make this new, odd relationship slightly less uncomfortable.

"What? Oh, I'm Evan, Evan Hartley," he said jumpily, clearly startled by the question.

"I guess you already kind of know who I am, but it's nice to meet you, Evan." He reached out his hand for a handshake even though they had technically met yesterday. "You can just call me Cooper. No sir or Mr. Owens, now that we've officially met, and especially now that it appears you no longer have a job here."

"It's nice to meet you too Mr. Ow . . . I mean Cooper," Evan said, reciprocating the gesture and smiling as his shoulders dropped a little more.

The elevator came to a stop and the doors slid open, revealing a dark hallway that appeared as empty as the floor below. Cooper put his hand on the door, keeping one foot inside the elevator as he leaned out. Looking left, he saw more dark and deserted office space. As he turned his gaze right, he saw a faint glow of light seeping out from a door that had been left ajar near the end of the deserted hallway.

"There's a light down there. I'm going to go check it out," Cooper said, his voice automatically shrinking to a whisper.

"I'll come with you," Evan said as he cautiously followed Cooper out of the elevator and down the hall. Both moved as if they were trying to not wake some horrific sleeping monster hidden behind one of the many doors on either side of them.

After what felt like far too long, Cooper finally reached the source of the light with Evan close behind him. He slowly pushed the door open, the fear of what might be behind it halting his breath. As the door creaked open, no movement caught his eye against the cool, blue-white glow of the room. The light was emanating from a single screen on the far wall, surrounded by hundreds, no, thousands of blinking lights from what looked like servers, or at least that's what Cooper thought they were.

Now that he knew nobody was in the room to detain him, Cooper stepped inside. He looked around in awe at all the equipment and computing power.

"This seems excessive for a small publishing branch, don't you think?"

"I guess." Evan shrugged his shoulders. "I don't really know much about computers."

Cooper noticed the screen was displaying a message in a tiny gray box in the middle of the sea of blue that filled the rest of its pixels. He had to walk right up close to read what it said:

Error: Connection Lost -
Server and client disconnected unexpectedly.
Please check network connections and try again.

Turning to look around at the machines, Cooper noticed that all of them appeared to be flashing, not to signal their operation, but to say something was wrong. He made his way around the room looking for more clues, eventually coming across the part of the wall where all the cables converged, and quickly noticed they had been cut.

"That's pretty weird too," Cooper said, pointing at the severed connections on the floor.

Evan made his way there and bent over to grab a cable, holding it up to inspect it.

"Seems like it was done on purpose," he said, attempting to contribute to whatever puzzle Cooper was currently trying to solve.

"Have you ever been on this floor? Do you know what it was used for?" Cooper asked as Evan dropped the wire.

"I've only been here for a month, never had a reason to come to this floor. It was mostly administration and IT guys who worked here. They paid no attention to me whenever they came in. I was fine with that because they were some straight-up weirdos. Didn't smile. Didn't want to talk to anyone. Always in and out of work without a word."

Cooper's brain was scrambling to find an inkling of reason in his now-surreal life. Why would this office, that to his knowledge only housed a few employees and accounts, need an entire floor dedicated to IT? Why had everyone left in such a hurry and purposefully destroyed all this stuff? What he wouldn't give to get back in that elevator, get Elena, and just go back to the cabin and hide there forever.

Unable to find anything else, Cooper made his way out of the room and back toward the elevator, thinking too much to notice Evan trying to keep up with his quick pace. Before he got halfway down the hall, a sudden urge made him try another door on his left. Surprisingly, it opened without any resistance.

The room was dark and Cooper had to search for the light switch to see its contents. The brightness of the fluorescent tube lights was blinding, and their flickering made it even harder for his vision to adjust. When he shook off the effect, he couldn't believe what he saw.

Another room just like the last, a single monitor across from him, but this time all the servers or whatever they were, were missing. All that remained were cables and mounting hardware. There was no denying it anymore, this amount of technology just didn't belong here.

This sent him spiraling as he questioned everything. Was AIP actually just a publishing company? Why would they need this? He finally landed on an absurd and absolutely insane thought—is AIP responsible for MUSE? Are they just a front for Echelon Enterprises? Cooper knew he was teetering on the edge of becoming a nutjob conspiracy theorist, but could anybody really blame him?

"Weird," Evan said as he looked over Cooper's shoulder and into the room. "I agree with you now. It definitely seems excessive."

This pulled Cooper out of his theorizing and back into action. He frantically went down the hall, opening every door and flicking the lights, anxiety increasing each time as he saw a similar scene in room after room.

He stood at the end of the hallway, out of breath, light spilling through every door between him and Evan, who hadn't moved the entire time. Cooper sank to the floor, over-whelmed, wondering how he was going to keep going. Evan eventually came to sit beside him, a third wheel to a situation he would never understand. Cooper appreciated the gesture and the company all the same, feeling not entirely alone in the pit of despair that was currently trying to swallow him whole.

"Maybe they rented this floor out to some crypto-mining company or something?" Evan said. "Or maybe it even came with the building. Who knows?"

Cooper knew both explanations were unlikely, but realized he couldn't just sit there forever, even if Evan was kind enough to entertain such a request regardless of Cooper being an almost total stranger to him. He pushed himself off the floor and turned to give Evan a hand up.

"Come on, let's go get your things from upstairs."

They both walked back to the elevator, more side by side than they had moved before, signaling their transition from strangers to acquaintances.

The doors opened onto the third floor. It was just as dark

and desolate as the last, but less eerie because of its familiarity to both of them.

"I'll just grab my stuff really quick from the break room. Then I guess I'll just meet you back here?" Evan asked.

"Sounds good. I'm going to go look around the offices and see if I can find anything else."

They separated, losing sight of each other for the first time since Cooper had entered the building.

As Cooper neared the lines of cubicles, he noticed that this floor was a mess. Papers were scattered everywhere, filing cabinets were left open, and other office supplies were strewn across the floor. Every computer was gone and nothing of importance seemed to be left at all. He made his way to the corner office, which no longer had Cassandra's name on the door.

The door wasn't fully closed. With a gentle push, he opened it, revealing another empty room. It didn't look like the rest of the workspaces, though. This room had been carefully and meticulously emptied. Not a single piece of paper, forgotten paper clip, or any other items were to be found. It was so clean that without thinking, Cooper slid his finger across the desk to look for dust like some sort of detective in a black-and-white film.

This was much more planned than whatever happened out there, he thought to himself. Cooper started looking through the desk drawers, cabinets, and anything else that might be hiding secrets, or better yet, answers. There was nothing. Everything was completely empty, as if no one had ever worked there. Only the discoloration on the door where the plaque had been provided evidence to the contrary.

Dismayed, Cooper made his way back to the elevator, hoping Evan had found what he was looking for, but he was doubtful. More likely, it had been discarded or taken away, like everything else of value in the building. But as he rounded the corner, he saw Evan already waiting for him to return, holding something in his hands.

"Did you find anything?" Evan asked.

"Nothing. Somebody cleared out the place, just a huge mess now. Is that what you were looking for?" Cooper asked, motioning toward what he now saw was a black spiral ring notebook.

"Yeah, it was a mess on that side of the building too and the breakroom was a disaster, but I found it behind the vending machine. Right where I left it. Lucky, I guess, since it looked like they even took the time to empty all the snacks from the machine. Have you ever seen something like this?" Evan motioned toward the office.

"No, I haven't, and I really don't know what to think about it."

Cooper pushed the elevator door button. The doors opened and he held his arm out, offering Evan the lead. Evan took it, stepped in, and pressed the button for the ground floor. The elevator began its descent.

Their adventure together was nearing its end and both would go their separate ways soon. Cooper looked at Evan, thankful that he hadn't had to traverse this building alone, something that likely would have sent him running back out the doors before he had even made it to the third floor.

"What did you come back for?" Cooper asked, his curiosity about the kid arising once again. He suddenly realized it might have been too personal a question, recalling how the notebook had been hidden away, and regret crept in. But before the guilt could take hold, Evan answered.

"Just my sketchbook. Nothing that important. It has a few

drawings I did when I was on break." His cheeks grew redder, as if he already knew what Cooper was inevitably going to ask.

"Can I see some of them?"

The elevator came to a halt and the doors opened. They both stepped out to avoid getting stuck in the confined space, feeling their relationship rise to another level, about to cross yet another threshold. They had shifted from acquaintances, possibly to friends or something in between. It shouldn't have happened, considering they likely wouldn't see each other again after walking out the front door, but it had.

"Uh, I guess so." He handed the book over to Cooper, who took it with care, knowing it was more valuable than Evan was letting on.

Cooper flipped it open and made his way through the pages, every single one was filled with some of the most amazing sketches of animals he had ever seen. The perspective and intricate details were signs of genuine passion. In the background, every drawing was labeled like a blueprint, with interesting facts about the species tucked into rough outlines of the animal's habitat.

Every page was covered edge to edge with the beauty of nature, and each precisely picked tidbit of information about the animal gave the viewer a more profound appreciation of the magic scattered throughout the natural world:

A hummingbird's heart can beat up to twelve thousand times per minute.

The axolotl can regenerate almost any part of its body without scarring, even its own heart and brain.

A sea turtle can navigate thousands of miles of ocean to return to the same beach it was born on.

Real magic. Magic that slowly faded as people got older, only because they paid less and less attention to it.

As he continued flipping through, Cooper was brought back to their conversation yesterday, when Evan had told him his dream was to work with animals. He now knew that wasn't just some half-assed response to his abrupt question. The kid was being honest with him, and more importantly, with himself. *He should be working with animals. Or at least studying and documenting them.*

"These are amazing."

"Really? I mean, you think so? I've never shown them to anyone before."

"Yes, they are spectacular." Cooper handed the sketchbook back with a newfound reverence for the item.

"Thanks, I really appreciate it," Evan said as they walked toward the front door again.

That can't be it, Cooper thought to himself. He felt like he needed to give this kid something more than a couple of lame compliments. Just as they reached the front door, Cooper put his hand on the teen's shoulder, like he was some sort of father figure. He knew he looked ridiculous and was probably scaring the shit out of Evan, but he didn't know how else to stall their exit.

"You told me your dream yesterday was to work with animals, and after seeing those, I believe you. I'm sure the fuckers here"—a phrase that made Cooper feel a sense of release, noticing for the first time that he had a new anger for all of AIP—"didn't give you much in terms of pay, and for sure no severance," he added, smirking. "I want to help you get wherever you want to go." He pulled out his wallet to see how much cash he had to give, realizing there wasn't nearly enough.

"Oh," Evan said, clearly uncomfortable. "You don't need to do that. You barely even know me."

"I don't need to know you any more than I already do. You're a good person. You deserve something better than another desk job somewhere, trying to make enough for some better future. Follow me to my car. I think I've got a checkbook in the dash." He noticed that he could have picked better wording since Evan looked like that was the last thing he wanted to do. Cooper persisted anyway. "I'm not going to take no for an answer." Probably an even worse choice of words.

Evan reluctantly followed him across the street as Cooper tried to delay being alone again, but also genuinely wanting to do something good and help the kid, hopefully making the world that was falling apart around him a tiny bit better. He dug around in the dash for his checkbook and a pen. Evan looked like he was about to make a run for it, but just before he did, Cooper popped back up, put the checkbook on the hood of the car, and began to write.

"How do you spell your last name?"

"H-A-R-T-L-E-Y, but really, you don't need to do this."

"Already done." Cooper ripped the check out and handed it to Evan.

Evan's jaw literally dropped, his mouth hanging open as he looked at the check for ten thousand dollars with his name on it. He was speechless. To think, just moments ago, Evan had probably been afraid this tired-looking man was going to kidnap him or something.

"Hopefully that lets you get out into the world for a while, so you don't have to sit at a desk and put on a smile for people who don't give a shit about you. Or maybe you can sit at a desk you want to be behind, learning about those animals in your sketchbook. Just promise me you'll follow your dreams, as stupid and cliché as that sounds," Cooper said, laughing at his poor attempt to end his motivational spiel.

Evan spoke, the words a jumble, before finally forcing out a "Thank you" as he instinctively hugged Cooper, a man he had only met yesterday.

Cooper didn't hug him back but didn't resist either, letting his arms hang limply at his sides as the kid showed his appreciation for an amount of money he probably couldn't even fathom at this point in his barely started life. After being released from Evan's grip, Cooper closed the passenger door.

He might not even have a way to deposit a check, Cooper thought, so he took a few hundred dollars out of his wallet and gave it to Evan too. He imagined Evan hopping on a plane to a better life that very day. The thought made Cooper feel less gloomy, no matter how unlikely it was.

Cooper nonchalantly made his way to the driver's side of the car and got in. He rolled down the window as Evan came around to his side, still looking as if he might try to give the check back.

Before he could utter any more words of resistance, Cooper said, "Go do whatever you want to do. Hopefully that's a good enough starting point to get rid of any excuses not to. Nobody's stopping you now, except for yourself. It was a pleasure to meet you, Evan. I'll be on the lookout for your work." He held out his hand for one last handshake, which Evan obliged.

"Thank you, Cooper. I promise I'll use it well and I'll never forget this." With that, he turned from the car and headed away from Cooper toward his own journey.

Cooper felt good about what he had done as he watched the kid walk further away, but after a few minutes, the pleasant feelings faded to jealousy.

He wished he had that open-ended and bright future ahead of him, not whatever ambiguous and most likely depressing future stood before him now. He tried to grasp at those warm feelings that came from helping someone, but resentment and jealousy had opened the floodgates enough for every other negative feeling to come crashing down on him.

There was no plane to take him to some picturesque place filled with magical animals. Instead, he sat there in the car, going over every detail of their exploration through the building and what it most likely meant. Trying to resist the torrential downpour of crazed theories pounding in his head, he remembered Evan's suggestion about the servers and computer rooms.

*Maybe AIP did just rent the floor to some crypto-mining company.*

He knew it wasn't true, but it was the only thing he could use to stay calm. He would have to hold on to that explanation in order to function well enough to get home. He was so thankful that Evan had been at the office in the first place.

Suddenly, he pictured those intricate and skillfully crafted sketches again, which brought a few good emotions back to stifle the others. Flipping through Evan's sketchbook after descending from that hell on the floors above was a moment he wished he could return to.

He looked at the big, empty brick building and turned to find that Evan had disappeared from sight. Cooper knew he would have the occasional thought about that kid for the rest of his life. He would wonder if he had ever made it to where he wanted. He would hope that Evan was out there somewhere, surrounded by nature and far from the technology ruining the world, observing and capturing whatever beautiful creature he was looking at with each stroke of his pencil.

# 18

*The duality of Elena's forgeries made Victor feel as though he was caught between parallel realities, each painting a mirror reflecting an unknowable past.*

Cooper pulled into the driveway and put the car in park. As he turned the keys, he realized the entire trip back had been a blur. Over an hour of hazy awareness, feeling like somebody else had gotten him from point A to point B. Many people paid little attention while driving, but this disconnection was so severe he felt lucky to even be alive, instead of in a ditch somewhere along the highway.

He collected himself and stepped out of the car, feeling a sense of déjà vu as he looked at the warm, yellow exterior lights of the house. Their glow illuminated the pale-blue siding that looked cool-gray in the night. He had just done this. Coming home with no new information and even more questions.

Yet his heart wasn't racing as much, he'd had no suicidal thoughts about being run over by a train, and he had reached a point where nothing could shock him anymore. More importantly, he knew he and Elena were in a good place and she was there for him, no matter what.

He made his way to the front door and headed inside, ready to confide in his one and only true companion.

"Elena, I'm back."

No response.

"Elena?"

The house seemed oddly darker than usual, with only

a few lights casting shadows in a way that was noticeably different. He stood silent, trying to listen for any sign of his dear wife.

"Elena?"

He called out to her again, this time much louder: "Elena!" but still received no response.

Maybe she had to do some edits and is in the booth again, he thought, hoping it was the truth. His pace quickened as he headed for her office. She wasn't there. The room oozed a cold, dark emptiness that sent goosebumps across Cooper's skin.

The house suddenly seemed obscenely large, and he felt like it would take an eternity to search. He still hadn't heard a single sound that told him someone else was there.

*Where is she?*

He searched every room as he moved through the house, but when he reached their bedroom, he was horrified. Clothes were scattered across the floor and half-folded piles lay abandoned on the bed. Her suitcase from their trip to the cabin, which had sat unpacked next to his, was missing. It didn't take a genius to realize what had happened. She had left, and in a hurry.

Elena was gone.

Cooper collapsed against the doorframe, his heart smashed to a pulp, feeling tears drip down his face.

"Why?" he cried, the word coming out all messed up and distorted, gargled like an old radio slightly off-channel. *After last night, why would she leave now?*

Deep down, he knew why, or at least assumed why. His spiral into insanity had driven her away—even though he now knew he wasn't crazy. She couldn't take it, couldn't watch what she had assumed was a one-way trip to the loony bin. She probably thought she would soon have to put him in a psychiatric ward herself. Whether any of this was true or not didn't matter, he believed it whole-heartedly.

As this realization sank in, he slid down to the floor, sobbing uncontrollably. He could already feel himself on the verge of passing out. It was just too much. Too much to come home to after everything that happened. That railroad crossing looked more appealing with every labored breath his body forced him to take.

Cooper sat there and cried harder than he had ever cried in his life, caught in an endless stretch of agony that made time disappear. He convulsed with pain and sorrow that tried to overtake him.

Eventually, he was able to right himself.

He looked at the room through his bloodshot eyes, trying to find anything, anything that could tell him it was just a giant misunderstanding. His head pounded and his vision was blurred, but he combed through the entire house, finding nothing. He could feel himself about to fully break, a single wrong thought away from his own implosion. But just before he crumpled in on himself, he began to think a little more rationally, his mind trying to save him from his own despair.

Cooper grabbed his phone, sat on the bed, and dialed her number, exactly what he should have done before jumping to conclusions and having the mental breakdown of a century. He expected it to go straight to voicemail, now so accustomed to every other person he knew ignoring his calls and emails. If it did, at least he would still get to hear her voice, even if it was just some silly prerecorded message. When her real, beautiful voice came across the line, he bolted up with so much surprise that he nearly fell off the edge of the bed.

"Hello . . ." Elena's voice, tinged with sadness, came faintly through the phone's tiny speaker.

He didn't know what to say at first and stalled by clearing the remnants of crying from his throat and nose.

"Where . . .are . . .you?" he asked, the words getting stuck in his mouth on their way out, whispered and hoarse, only fragments of their former selves.

"Nowhere yet."

"Where are you going?" His voice was still so quiet that he could barely hear his own question.

"I don't know yet. Just away for a while." A few breaths followed her response, giving the sorrowful words a chill that froze them in place.

"Why?"

"You know why."

"I'm sorry," Cooper wailed. The statement reignited the waterworks and gasping sobs. "I'm sorry! It's all true . . ." Cooper was about to argue that he wasn't crazy, then realized that was exactly what a crazy person would do. "None of it matters. I don't care, I'll forget about it all. Just come home." The begging made him feel pathetic even amid the immense pain he felt as the phone call confirmed his worst fear. Elena had left on purpose.

"Not now. Maybe later."

Cooper stifled his crying so he could respond and wiped the back of his arm across his face.

"When?" The question was as quiet and sharp as a needle dropping onto the floor.

"I don't know."

With a little bit of fire in his voice and a hint of anger, he asked, "What do you mean, you don't know?"

"I just don't."

The blunt coolness of the response quickly extinguished whatever rage had tried to build inside Cooper, leaving only a wisp of smoke that made him choke even more. *A cigarette.* Cooper scrambled around the room, tears streaming down his face, now re-wetting the tracks from the earlier ones. He made his way to the closet, unconscious of what he was doing, crying silently into the phone while looking for *a cigarette.*

"Are you still there?" Elena asked, her voice ghostly, sounding miles away.

"Yeah . . ." Cooper said as he pulled out a small box that contained the last pack of cigarettes he had bought over a decade ago. The one and only real *last pack.* It still had the cellophane wrapper on it, just as it had the day he brought it home and put it into the back of the closet for safekeeping, always there if he needed it. There when he quit cold turkey that day, and every day thereafter.

He crawled back over to the foot of the bed and leaned against it, holding the pack in his lap. Without hesitation, he opened the package and swore he could already smell the sweet taste of tobacco and its secret blend of chemicals and toxins. He pulled out a single cigarette from the crisp carton and rolled it in his fingers.

"I love you, Elena."

"I know you do." She paused, creating a silence that lasted an eternity. "I love you too."

Her statement of love was the only thing he wanted, but it split him down the middle, adding confusion to the *why* of it all. Cooper's heart broke and wanted to stop beating, begging him for the poison between his fingers. The poison that could kill him more slowly and more painfully than almost anything else in this world while making him feel so good at the same time.

"I know it's never been fair," he said.

"What hasn't?"

"Us . . ." Cooper realized he didn't know when he'd get to talk to his dear Elena again after this conversation and felt compelled to go down this path, fumbling along as he tried to say what he needed to say.

"What do you mean?"

"Us," he repeated. "Our relationship. You've been absolutely everything for me, because that's what I always needed."

Elena breathed, letting him know she was still there, but her silence felt like an acknowledgment of the truth Cooper was voicing—a truth that had always been there between them, one neither had dared to say aloud until now.

Cooper continued, his voice returning to its normal sound, his nose less stuffy and throat more open. "I always hoped I was that for you. In a way, maybe I was, but I don't think it was even close to the same level. The way I needed you was too much. Too much pressure to put on a single person. You became my whole world. All of it."

"You were mine too, though."

"That might be true, but I think you just felt like that was the way it had to be. Because of how I was." Elena went silent again. "Our relationship morphed into something so far from where it started. Over the years, we got closer while everything else in our lives drifted further away. The weight of something like that . . . becoming somebody's everything is crushing. Especially when the scales are tipped to one side."

"That's not true," Elena moaned into the phone in disagreement.

"You know it is, though." Elena went silent yet again and Cooper continued, no longer confident that his message was making any sense to anyone but himself. "You know it's never been fair. Especially not now. All the shit that's been going on. You don't deserve me pulling you into it, piling it all on.

Needing you even more than ever."

What he really wanted to say—but couldn't—rang in his head, desperate for an escape that wouldn't come. *I need you so badly. I don't know if I can do this without you.*

"I wanted to help you with it all," she replied, her words broken by sharp, restrained sobs. "I just couldn't. You're right. I couldn't watch you hurt. I couldn't watch you lose your mind like you were."

Her muffled cries sent spikes through Cooper's already aching heart. The urge to start blabbering about his day was so strong that he had to slap a hand over his mouth to stop all the craziness, *the truth*, from pouring out.

"I just need some time. I think time apart would be good for us."

His throat narrowed again, as if trying to stop the word from coming out. "Maybe." There was a long silence before he continued. "You didn't do anything wrong . . . I'm so sorry for everything."

"I'm sorry too." Her voice was frail now.

"I'll figure this out, and maybe then we can get back to how things were before," he said cautiously.

"Maybe," she whimpered. "The way things were going, I just didn't think we'd make it. I thought some space might help us get through."

"I know, I know, baby. You did the right thing." Cooper held his tongue, but his mind was screaming: *How could you do such a thing?*

"Figure this out, Cooper. I miss you already."

"I will, I promise." The determination rang through his words, the most solid his voice had been throughout the phone call. He could feel the conversation coming to its close and was trying to take in every fleeting second he had left with her, even if it was just through the phone. "I'm so sorry, this is all my fault." *MUSE's fault.* "I miss you too." *I miss you so fucking much.* "I'll give you some space . . . and I'll fix this. I love you, Elena."

"I love you too, Cooper. I'm sure your head's going to crazy places right now, but I promise I'm okay."

It hadn't until she said the words, but now the catastrophes and calamities came without hesitation.

"I haven't been taken hostage or anything like that. I really hope that we can work things out, but for now . . . I just can't be around you. It hurts too much. I have to go . . . don't call me again unless you know it's the right time. I'll love you forever, Cooper." Her despair and painful goodbye soared on the wings of her beautiful voice.

"I lo—" but the phone cut him off before he could finish, destroying him. It felt like somebody had pulled the plug on his life support. He continued speaking into the empty line for his own sanity: "love you, Elena." The words sent him into a hole he would have to work hard to climb out of, or maybe he'd be stuck in it forever.

Cooper let sorrow and its dark cloak envelop him, feeling more alone than he had felt in decades. He was angry, upset, and sad, feeling every ounce of these emotions and yet unable to differentiate between any of them.

*She still loves me.* At least there was that. This thought gave him a sliver of hope. It was the paper-thin tape that now held his pieces together. Elena used to be his superglue and only now did he grasp how fragile he truly was, how weak he was as an individual. No one to help him, no one to save him. For the first time in a long time, he had only himself.

He looked down at the cigarette still trembling between his fingers, brought it up to his nose and inhaled deeply, the aroma reigniting synapses in his brain that screamed with joy and excitement. Then he opened the carton lid and slid the cigarette back satisfyingly into the single open slot.

There was still hope. Not much, but he prayed it would be enough to make it through to the other side of this mess.

He grabbed one of Elena's shirts from the floor beside him and held it up to his face, just as he had done with the cigarette. He inhaled the sweet smell of his beloved wife, and wept.

# 19

*In the wake of Elena's departure, Victor wandered through the empty halls of their home, feeling the weight of solitude press down on him, the absence of her presence a haunting reminder of his newfound isolation.*

Cooper struggled to rise from bed the next morning, feeling as if all the life had been sucked out of him. He felt like a shell of the man he once was. He overcame the gravity keeping him down, which felt abnormally strong, and headed to the bathroom, once again hoping a shower would help him conquer the day. He let the warm water wash away the dried tears and other remnants of his wailing from his face, but didn't feel any relief or newfound energy. He needed to get through this.

He turned the water all the way to cold, gasping for air as its icy claws pierced his scalp first, the sensation making him pull away. He forced himself back under the showerhead, allowing the nearly freezing water to travel across every inch of his body, making him relearn how to breathe again. Cooper sat there well past the point of shivering, even through the burning sensation that came from near-zero temperatures. He only turned off the shower when he had fully collected his breath and was numb to the pain he was inflicting upon himself.

As he stood there dripping, the shivering returned to keep him alive, but he tried to resist. The cold had jolted him awake just enough to face the day, pushing away the urge to crawl back into bed, sulk, and hope things would somehow fix themselves. There was no going back now, only forward.

He stepped out of the shower and looked in the mirror. The mundane similarities between these tumultuous and terrifying days made him feel as if no time had passed, as though he was just sleepwalking through life. He looked worse than ever. His face was puffy and swollen, like he'd had a severe allergic reaction or been in a bar fight. The dark-purple circles under his eyes suggested the latter.

His hair hadn't been brushed or styled in who knew how long. Not a single strand could decide what it wanted to do anymore, yet it somehow looked flatter than usual. The stubble on his face had also officially crossed into beard territory.

A beard had never suited him, but now he couldn't care less about his appearance and decided to forgo the razor once more. Not wanting to take care of himself at all, he reached for the toothbrush with reluctance. He couldn't decide if choosing not to shave was for similar reasons, or if he still hoped the new scruff was actually helping him by turning him into someone he barely recognized, someone more capable of doing what he had to do.

Cooper took the toothbrush and a few other items from the bathroom and laid them on the bed. He walked over to his mostly unpacked suitcase and grabbed it off the floor, sadness welling up behind his face as he tried to ignore that Elena's was missing. Turning back to the bed as quickly as he could, he placed the suitcase on it and opened it. He stared at the clothes crammed inside, realizing none of them could be considered clean anymore.

"Fuck it," he said, throwing his toothbrush and other essentials on top. He zipped the suitcase back up.

After grabbing his wallet and passport, he tried to think of anything else he might need. He was just about to head out of the bedroom when he saw the pack of cigarettes sitting on the floor. Cooper picked them up and put them in his jacket pocket. *Just in case.*

He made his way to the front door, placing the suitcase next to it. For a moment, he considered leaving right then and there just to escape the silence, the house now feeling so unsafe and cold, but he still had no plan of action. The weight of what he knew he had to do pressed on him as he stood there, building up the courage to voluntarily venture back into a world he'd tried so hard to escape.

Cooper went to his office and powered on the computer, navigating straight to MUSE. This thing had already stolen fucking everything from him. What was the point in hiding and not using it to his advantage? It was invented to make life easier, wasn't it?

His current situation was evidence to the contrary; his life had become a living hell because of its existence. He tried to remind himself that he still had no proof of any of this and that there was no time to dwell on his new and impossibly ruined reality. He had to search for answers.

For the first time since discovering the program, he began typing in the prompt box without fear. The idea that he could use it to his advantage eased his nerves. He was also no longer worried about pushing Elena away. He had already fucking done that. Now he could ask MUSE whatever he wanted without judgment.

I need you to tell me everything about the company that made you, and anything important about your programming.

Echelon Enterprises is a leading innovator in artificial intelligence, committed to advancing technology to enhance human experiences, and founded by Dr. Nathaniel Blake, who has a background in both computer science and ethics. Dr. Blake has been at the forefront of AI development, ensuring that Echelon's innovations are both cutting-edge and responsibly managed. His vision for the company is to create technology that not only advances human capabilities but also respects and enhances the human experience.

My programming is the result of years of research and development, combining advanced machine-learning algorithms with vast datasets to understand and predict human behavior, past, present, and future. I am designed to collect, analyze, and interpret data from a multitude of sources, providing insights and making predictions that can help guide decisions across various fields.

One of the key aspects of my programming is the ability to learn continuously. As I interact with users and process new information, I evolve and improve my responses, ensuring that I remain relevant and accurate. My creators at Echelon Enterprises have also implemented rigorous security protocols to protect the data I handle, ensuring privacy and confidentiality for all users.

In summary, I am a sophisticated AI designed to assist and enhance human capabilities, born from a company dedicated to innovation, ethics, and the future of technology.

Cooper read it carefully, taking notes on a sheet of paper, but the only thing that really stood out to him was this Dr. Nathaniel Blake. He needed more information.

Where is the headquarters responsible for you located and where is the technology behind you housed?

The headquarters of Echelon Enterprises is located in the heart of Zurich, Switzerland. Overlooking the pristine waters of Lake Zurich, this state-of-the-art facility is a blend of modern architecture and Alpine charm.

The technology behind me, MUSE, is housed in Echelon's advanced data centers, which are equipped with the latest in security and infrastructure to ensure both the efficiency and safety of their operations. These data centers are distributed across several key locations globally, ensuring redundancy and resilience in the face of any potential disruptions.

Can you give me the actual address of the headquarters?

Echelon Enterprises Headquarters
Bergstrasse 12
8001 Zurich, Switzerland

Cooper copied the address onto his now-full piece of paper, circling it repeatedly while trying to figure out more questions that might be of use to him.

What are the addresses associated with the technology responsible for you?

The exact locations associated with the technology behind me are confidential to ensure the utmost security and privacy. I apologize for any inconvenience, but I can assure you that I am here to assist with any other questions you may have.

Cooper realized he had most likely reached a dead end on this topic. He looked at his notes, hoping it was enough. Knowing the headquarters for Echelon Enterprises was all the way in Switzerland solidified his decision to head to New York first. He was already using the program, so he may as well keep going, he thought.

I need to go to New York today. Can you make a travel plan using my current location and recommend accommodations near Aldrich International Publishing?

I would be happy to help you with your trip. I need you to grant me permission to use your device's location before I can help.

A pop-up box appeared over the chat with two buttons. Cooper hovered the mouse over the Confirm button, about to click. He assumed this program had already seen everything on his computer, but he hesitated just long enough to change his mind. The fact that this box had appeared gave him some slight optimism that maybe it hadn't stolen everything from him. He'd be crazy to give it access now.

He moved the mouse a few inches and clicked Cancel instead. Cooper typed into the prompt bar:

Never mind

He closed the program, feeling stupid that he had responded to the thing he despised and treated it like a real person, as if it deserved the respect of closure. He would figure out the trip on his own. He didn't need some computer program telling him what to do. This new sense of human superiority gave him the willpower to grab his suitcase and leave the house, only to panic about having no plan and no guidance halfway through the drive to the airport.

Without Elena there to help him through life, he realized that MUSE, even though it was his new mortal enemy, was capable of filling a void within him. While he had mostly succeeded in resisting it this time by heading out without the itinerary it offered, he could see the allure and envisioned millions of people using MUSE. The thought was so terrifying that Cooper pressed on alone, and aside from a few wrong turns, he eventually made it to the airport.

"What do you mean I can't buy a ticket here?" Cooper asked the young woman at the front desk.

"Exactly that, sir. We don't really do that anymore. Most people"—she shot Cooper a sideways glance—"just buy their tickets online and well in advance of their departure."

"Well, I don't have access to the internet," Cooper lied.

The woman gave him an incredulous look, which made him painfully self-conscious. He pulled out his wallet, ID, and passport, worried that his appearance might be partly to blame for her reluctance to help him. After an hour of careful persuasion and pleading, Cooper finally had his bag checked and a boarding pass for LaGuardia Airport.

He headed toward the security checkpoint, the woman likely relieved to be done dealing with him. The only flight he could get wouldn't depart for hours, but what else did he have to do? At least the chaos of the airport would be distracting enough to keep him from breaking down again.

Cooper passed through the scanners, feeling more aware of the airport's technology than ever before. Again, the way he looked may have had something to do with this, as the TSA agents seemed to select him for every additional screening method ever invented, including an extra body scan and a thorough pat-down from a timid, lanky man who took forever to finish his search. They also selected him for explosive trace detection, swabbing his wrists and a few other areas of exposed skin.

At one point, a passing sniffer dog even stopped to smell him. This last one probably wasn't intentional; the dog had likely just wanted a better whiff of Cooper, who was barely holding it together.

The dog's handler stared at Cooper but seemed to remember they were already past the security checkpoint. When the dog didn't sit or signal, his stern expression softened slightly. He looked Cooper over once more, but there was nothing to see: no suspicious luggage, not even a personal item—just a weary traveler with a broken heart. Finally, he averted his gaze and moved on.

This also made Cooper realize he didn't have any luggage—not even a personal item. Suddenly, he felt rather naked, the spontaneity of what he was doing making his anxiety rise.

He found his way to his gate and sat down, hoping to let the stillness settle his nerves. He pulled out his phone to look at the time and saw that his overly scrutinized journey here had only taken a few minutes.

Cooper watched the thousands of people around him. People-watching was one of Elena's favorite things to do and was an excellent distraction. He imagined their life stories, all of which seemed better than his—the type of stories Elena would have imagined.

A family of four rushed past, dragging suitcases behind them, looking frantic yet excited and happy all at once as they scrambled to find their gate—and the airplane that would take them on their first vacation in years. They disappeared around the corner, but Cooper still heard one of the children ask, "How much longer?" before the sound of their luggage wheels faded.

Near a window stood a college-aged kid with a man bun, a beard, and a well-worn red backpack. He was alone, gazing out with quiet confidence, about to embark on a solo adventure around the world—a much-needed break from his studies. Cooper couldn't see the boy's face but caught the emotion in his silhouette framed by the open blue sky outside. He imagined all the sights the young traveler was about to see, probably more than he ever had.

Cooper continued scanning the area and noticed a soldier in uniform a few seats away. Beneath his serious expression, there was a mix of hope and unease as he patiently waited to board his final connecting flight—ready to finally reunite with his family after a long deployment overseas.

Across from him, Cooper watched an elderly couple wander into a shop. They browsed the wide selection of neck pillows, trying to decide which one would ease their tired bones best as they prepared for the romantic tropical getaway they'd saved years to afford. Just as they were about to choose the perfect pillow, something else in the store caught Cooper's eye.

He ran over and grabbed a copy of *Fake Creativity* from the rotating book carousel. For the book to have made its way into the airport, it had to be everywhere, he thought. As he held it in his hands, he realized he had stupidly forgotten to pack a copy to bring with him as evidence. Buying one made him feel ridiculous and sick to his stomach, but what was one more on top of the hundreds still sitting in the back of his car?

Throwing it into the empty seat next to him and trying not to look at it, Cooper searched for new people to watch. There was just one problem. He wasn't like Elena and could only people-watch for so long before the imagined stories became more depressing—a family of four, traveling to mourn a recently deceased relative; a college kid heading home, dreading normal life after a year of freedom; a soldier departing, hiding his pain, already missing his family before he'd even boarded the plane.

He looked at the time again. It had barely changed. Cooper picked up the book, even though it was the last thing he wanted to do, and started reading it. Word for word, this time. He hoped that maybe there would be something, some minor discrepancy or change. It might not be enough to prove to anyone else that it had been stolen, but if he could confirm it didn't match his final draft, at least that would be something.

Eventually, a message over the intercom informed him it was time to board. The crackly voice interrupted Cooper mid-chapter, and he still hadn't found a single thing out of place. As he waited in line, exhaustion finally began to take hold of him. Hopefully, he would be able to get some sleep on the flight.

After the plane had taken off and they were cruising at a comfortable altitude, the child across the aisle began screaming with no sign of stopping. Clearly, the noise was grating enough to sour his expression, because the mother of the inconsolable baby mouthed a silent "I'm sorry" to Cooper. He was perplexed as to why she hadn't just said the words. It wasn't like the cabin was quiet, at least not anymore.

Since sleeping was clearly out of the question, Cooper continued reading from what was likely his hundred-and-first copy of *Fake Creativity*. He plugged his ears with his own fingers to quiet the noise, but eventually a stewardess noticed and brought out a pair of complimentary headphones for him. They helped only slightly, but at least they were better than nothing.

Now that the screams were muffled and his ears were no longer bleeding, Cooper looked up from the book and at the mother again. Her hair was a mess, filled with tangles and knots. He thought he might have even seen a clump of dried baby food among the faded blonde streaks in her otherwise brown hair. The stress was plastered on her face as if it were the only makeup she ever wore now—not hidden from anyone, but accentuated instead. He watched as she tried everything to frantically soothe the poor child.

*Thank God that's not me,* he thought.

But then the mother began stroking the little tuft of wispy hair on the baby's head and started to sing. Singing as if nobody else was on the plane but her and that baby. Just a while ago, she hadn't even been able to say "I'm sorry" out loud.

Cooper took off his headphones and listened. The mother didn't seem to notice and continued the vulnerable act, something he would never dream of doing in a million years.

After just a few short verses of some lullaby he didn't recognize, the baby had quit crying. Then, surprisingly, it smiled—a smile so tiny that if you weren't paying attention, you would miss it. Slowly, its eyes grew heavier until they closed, and with one adorable yawn, the baby fell asleep. The mother continued to stare down at it lovingly as she sang the remainder of the song. The plane went silent. She looked like all she wanted to do was close her own eyes, but instead she continued to gently caress her child, the affectionate sparkle in her eyes never wavering.

*Do I wish that was me?*

If he and Elena had a child, maybe things would've been different.

They didn't though, and they weren't. He didn't have a screaming baby to console or a child that had the ability to make everything else in the world disappear, even if just for a moment. He didn't even have his wife anymore. All he had now was his book.

By the time he landed in New York, he had been unable to find a single scene, event, or character difference. He doubted reading further would lead to anything, but either way, it would have to wait.

At first, he considered renting a car but opted for a taxi instead. Hopefully, he wouldn't be going anywhere other than AIP and then straight back home. Sitting in the back seat as the driver tried to talk to him made Cooper feel alone again. He missed his driving conversations with Elena. Trying to avoid the small talk, he called every hotel within walking distance of AIP, even though the first one had already informed him they had rooms available.

Cooper realized he'd made a mistake when he asked to be dropped off at the first hotel he'd called. The cab driver gave him a dirty look when he paid the fare, not caring about the generous tip. Clearly, "How's the weather" conversations were more important than money to the old man.

The taxi sped off, and Cooper found himself back in the city he thought he had escaped. The sound of honking cars filled the air. Even though it was nearing midnight, numerous people were still maneuvering around him as he stood rooted to the spot.

The hotel towered above, its glowing yellow rectangles

scattered randomly as high as he could see. It wasn't the nicest place in downtown Manhattan, but it would do. As he walked up to the front doors, Cooper felt a little sorry for not engaging with the driver.

After checking in and making his way up to his room, Cooper unzipped his bag, and the stale, off-putting scent of his clothes filled the air. Notes of the cabin in Colorado intermingled with his deodorant and body odor. The aroma made his nose wrinkle. He couldn't go to AIP tomorrow smelling like that.

The hotel laundry service would likely be too slow to have his clothes ready by morning. Yet again, sleep would have to be put on hold. *Oh, the joys of not planning.* Cooper lugged his entire bag all the way back downstairs and made his way to the nearest laundromat. He dumped all the clothes into the machine carelessly. They just needed to smell halfway decent.

While waiting inside the nearly empty building, he continued reading the book, holding out hope that something would be different. The closer he got to the end, the less he wanted to look at it, finding nothing but his own story in its pages.

The words eventually blurred as his tired eyes lost focus. He closed the book and sat back. He watched his clothes go around in the machine in front of him, the occasional splash of water hiding them from sight. Their colors blurred together into shades that didn't match a single item he owned. Hypnotized by the spiraling visuals, he stared as if he'd never seen a washing machine before.

Nearly two hours later, Cooper had made his way back to the hotel room with fresh laundry crammed, unfolded, back into his suitcase. He was more tired than ever and longed for a restful sleep he knew he wouldn't get. Before going to bed, though, he decided to pick out what he was going to wear, just in case it needed ironing.

He had only made it halfway through the pile of clothes before finding one of Elena's shirts. The rip in his heart opened wide once again, and it throbbed with pain. He held the shirt up to his face, only to discover that he had just washed her scent off of it. It was all he had of her in this dimly lit, depressing hotel room.

Cooper knew keeping his attention on this item would only hurt him, but he did it anyway. Deciding he hadn't let out enough of his pain yet, he clutched it even tighter, telling himself this was the last time he could afford to be weak. He would need to be stronger. Tomorrow, he would need to wake up as a man who wasn't empty, broken, insecure, and terrified. For one more night, he allowed himself to be all of those things, and fully feel the painful possibility that he had pushed Elena, his wife and the love of his life, away forever.

# 20

*The gallery's security guards, with their stern gazes and meticulous routines, became unwitting participants in Elena's art. Unbeknownst to them, their movements were choreographed around forged masterpieces, guarding illusions with the same fervor as they did authentic treasures.*

He had been sitting on this couch all morning and well into the afternoon. The receptionist gave him an awkward smile each time he made eye contact or went up to ask how much longer it would be before he could see Cassandra. After a wait like this, any normal person would've let a hint of their temper show, just enough to prove they meant business and get things moving, but Cooper had always struggled to display his emotions in public, especially in professional settings.

Apparently, Cassandra had been out all morning doing who knew what, and she'd been caught up in meetings for the last few hours. Cooper hadn't left the waiting room except to go to the bathroom, something that was obviously making the woman behind the desk very uncomfortable. Each successive smile of hers got progressively more forced and fake.

Cooper's frustration grew, but it was still a long way from revealing itself. He knew he wasn't the be-all and end-all of writers, but he thought he had reached a level where he would receive a bit more respect than this. He could try to find somebody else, maybe even Alexander, but if Cassandra was this hard to get ahold of, he doubted seeing anyone else would be possible. Not to mention that he trusted Cassandra more than anyone here. If anybody was going to take his story seriously and actually try to help him out, it would be her. Now if only she would meet with him.

The only thing Cooper had brought with him was a copy of *his* book. He'd tried explaining the emergency to the woman at the desk, even showing her the book as evidence, but it had probably only made the wait longer. As she'd listened to his story, she still had that courteous grin pinned between her cheeks—the customer-service look that's perfect for all occasions—and her blinding white teeth looked about as real as her concern.

So now all he could do was sit there on the couch, which, compared to the one in Elena's office, felt like it had been stuffed with sharp rocks and a few stray sticks. As he patiently waited, attempting to keep his rising anger in check and stay calm, he continued reading through *Fake Creativity*, still hoping to find a difference, no matter how tiny.

After some time, he flipped to the last page and read the final paragraph of the book:

> As the last brushstroke dried, Victor and Elena stood at the threshold of their past, gazing into the expanse of an uncharted future, a blank canvas awaiting their touch. Tested by deception and heartbreak, their love had not only survived but flourished, growing stronger and more resilient with each trial. Hand in hand, they faced the unknown, ready to transform the remnants of their journey into a new masterpiece, a testament to their enduring love and the infinite possibilities that lay ahead.

He closed the book, his own words filling him with dread. Now he had nothing left to distract himself from this quiet room where he was being ignored. Sitting in this purgatory felt like being in a fever dream. He questioned whether he even existed anymore.

He did exist though, and didn't deserve to be treated like this, especially here. His books had probably helped furnish this office. His stories maybe even contributed to the salary of the rude woman behind the desk, who pretended not to know he was a *somebody* around here. Cooper looked at the clock on the wall and saw that it was nearly four.

"Excuse me, am I ever going to get to see Cassandra?" he asked through gritted teeth, the possibility of an explosion teetering on the poor receptionist's response.

"Um, hang on just a second," she said in her high-pitched tone, typing and clicking away on her computer.

Eventually she picked up the phone and began talking to someone else on the line, the fake, cheery tone piercing his ears, stabbing deep into his brain until the sound waves met in the middle and rang. Cooper did not like how the conversation was going. His anger felt desperate for release and he was unsure of how to prepare for such an event.

"I'm so sorry. It looks like Cassandra isn't going to be available to meet today. Her schedule looks more open tomorr—"

"What the fuck do you mean?" Cooper asked, uncomfortable with the confrontation already but unable to change course.

The receptionist trembled slightly but didn't say anything, her pearly white smile faltering at the edges as the corners of her lips quivered. None of this made Cooper pause; all the anger and hurt within him began pouring out, his words their only means of transportation.

"I've been sitting here all fucking day and now you tell

me this. I don't even believe you right now. Let me talk to Cassandra. Here, I'll just give her a call right now," Cooper said, realizing maybe he could still get her to pick up on the number he had for her.

"Mr. Owens, you need to calm down. Otherwise, I'm going to have to get security to escort you from the premises," she said with genuine fear in her eyes, somehow managing to maintain that stereotypical "How may I help you?" receptionist voice.

He stood there, hoping with all his might that Cassandra would pick up and smooth everything over, proving some sort of point to the receptionist. As the anticipation got to him, Cooper added, "Why don't you just get Mr. Graves down here too? He'll want to hear what I have to say." The phone stopped ringing as he said this.

For a split second, there was no noise. No one was talking. His own thumping heart jumped in to break the tense silence, beating in his ears. Suddenly, he felt like he was in the middle of a hostage situation, or some other tense standoff like in the old western movies.

Over the line came a robotic voice: "We're sorry, this number has been disconnected and is no longer in service." The words deflated Cooper like a popped balloon.

"Mr. Owens, just give me a phone number to reach you at and we'll let you know when Cassandra can see you," the receptionist said, her voice filling Cooper back up with the rage that hadn't escaped through the cracks in the tiny office just yet.

"Did you not understand when I said I'm here because it's a fucking emergency? This isn't something that can wait another day. I'm talking to Cassandra right now." Cooper walked behind the desk and toward the door that he assumed hid the friend he was looking for.

He tried the handle, but it was locked. He started slamming his shoulder into the door, trying to get it open, emotion fully taking control of his actions. There was no resistance on his part to the billowing fire now burning inside of him, rage and hurt becoming shovelfuls of coal that fueled the flames, slamming him forward into the wooden door.

The entire experience was so surreal, Cooper felt as if he was watching it from outside his body. This was some version of him he didn't even know existed. Decades of anger were coming out all at once, from small things like people cutting him off in traffic all the way up to not being good enough for the parents who'd never truly loved or supported him. The pent-up energy from every injustice he'd ever suffered in silence, holding his tongue and keeping his emotions in check, was put into an act he had only ever seen in TV and movies.

The force of it all was enough to bring the fictional into reality. He heard a crack as the doorframe broke, sending him tumbling into the room behind it. He stood up and found himself in a dark, empty room—no desk, no Cassandra, no sign of it being used for anything at all. *This can't be real.* He had to still be asleep in the hotel bed.

The receptionist must have dialed security the moment Cooper had made his way past the desk because two guards grabbed his arms and held him in place. He didn't resist, too confused at whatever he was looking at, the firm grip on his arms enough to tell him this wasn't a dream. They pulled him away and out of the room.

Slowly, he realized he wouldn't have any proof he'd been put through this entire ordeal. They would likely fill the office with something or someone to show that it had never been empty, and he would be made to look like a fool. He tried to stay rooted to the ground, but the guards just dragged him further toward the exit. He reached for his phone, hoping to get a picture, any semblance of proof to show he wasn't crazy, but the guards ensured this too was pointless.

"At least let me have my book," he yelled, expecting them to decline, but they stopped moving.

One of the guards went over and grabbed his book off the sofa, only to resume holding Cooper with his available hand.

"You need to leave, Mr. Owens. You can either be escorted by us or we'll call the police, which I'm sure you don't want, given how you just damaged private property." The burly guard pointed to the door that now stood drunkenly in its frame.

Cooper couldn't help but notice the man's size as he held his hulking and extremely hairy arm up, pointing at the scene of the crime. He was surprised he'd resisted the two guards as much as he did, but was even more surprised that he had succeeded in bashing the door open. He was becoming increasingly present and aware of what had just happened as the adrenaline left his body and defeat sank in.

He contemplated the guard's statement. Would the police believe his story? Could he twist the truth in a way that made him look like the victim? As he concluded that the more likely outcome would be them thinking him insane, he moved toward the exit of his own free will, causing the guards to slacken their grip slightly. They still escorted him all the way outside to the front steps of the building, not saying a word the entire time, leaving Cooper once again alone and unsure of what to do next, holding a copy of *his* book in his hands.

It was almost 4:30 now, and a vast sea of busy people rushed to and fro. One or two bumped into him, but nearly every faceless person moved effortlessly around him as if he weren't even there at all. He was nothing.

But in a way, so was everyone else in the crowd—each individual smaller, and perhaps even less important, than a single subatomic particle in the terrifying, moving mass of flesh that was humanity, which flowed past Cooper with utter indifference.

He stood motionless, an indistinguishable speck in front of AIP. The company had made him who he was, only to turn around and throw him out on the street like some stray animal after all these years. Now, he was almost certain they'd had something to do with his book being released seemingly of its own accord. The trajectory ahead of Cooper was narrowing, but there were still countless paths he could choose.

How did they think they could get away with this? How could such a blatant crime go unpunished? How could they publish his work without consent, still using his name, and more importantly . . . before he had even written it?

# 21

*His trusted appraiser and authenticator had missed every single one of Elena's forgeries, yet Victor couldn't bring himself to harbor resentment. Over countless discussions and shared frustrations, they had developed a bond that transcended the professional realm, becoming confidants in a world of uncertainty.*

Cooper was sitting in his hotel room, still undecided about how to move forward. The bed was almost perfectly made, save for a small indent on the neatly pressed covers where he'd slept the night before. He didn't want to have to stay in that unfamiliar room any longer than he had to. Not that his own house would feel any better. Nothing felt *right* anymore.

He leaned over and let his head hang to ease the discomfort of his bleak surroundings. The sirens and the commotion of a city that he was no longer used to, no matter how faintly they came through the window, were enough to make it impossible to think straight.

Suddenly, another sound startled him, this one coming from within the room. Cooper grabbed his phone and saw that whoever was calling him had blocked their number. Maybe it was Elena, or maybe it was someone at AIP. Both possibilities made him extremely nervous. He answered.

"Hello? Who is this?" His voice was weak and hoarse from yelling at the receptionist.

He heard Cassandra's voice come through the phone.

"Cooper, are you there? I can't talk for long . . . but I

just don't feel right about all of this." She spoke quietly, as if somebody was trying to eavesdrop on their conversation.

"What do you mean? And where were you today? I tried to find you at AIP, and you won't believe it . . . they threw me out of the—"

"Yeah, I know," she interrupted, sounding hurt. "I promise I had nothing to do with that. I don't have much time and I'm risking a lot for you right now, but I just couldn't live with myself if I didn't give you some sort of heads-up. We've known each other for decades and you're my friend. It's going to be hard, but you just need to listen to me, okay?"

"Okay," Cooper said. He stuffed the millions of questions he wanted to blurt out back down and metaphorically zipped his lips closed.

"I'm sure you've already seen it. Why else would you be in New York? So I'll try to get to the point. A few weeks ago, they told me your book was being handed over to someone else at AIP and I wouldn't be working with you anymore. I tried to fight them on it, but they offered to just fire me if I preferred. Anyway, obviously I found this all super odd, but then I saw your book being sold in some shop. Having already read your proposal, I became even more confused. I knew you wouldn't be back and ready to submit the book for weeks. I still don't know how they did it, but after some snooping around, I have a hunch."

"MUSE," Cooper stammered, unable to resist stepping into the conversation.

"So, you already know about the program?" she asked, surprised that Cooper had reached this conclusion so soon.

"That thing has been the bane of my existence since before I even left for Colorado. I assume that's how it got access to my novel and then AIP somehow used it to cut out the middleman?"

"Maybe," she replied. "What you probably don't know is that Echelon Enterprises, the company behind MUSE, is also connected to AIP. I've seen emails between them. I even found records of financial transactions made from AIP to Echelon."

Cooper had suspected this was the case, but if what Cassandra was saying was true, this confirmed it.

"Do you have any proof?" he asked. "Like enough that I could get a lawyer or even go to the police to try and prove they published my book without me?"

"I barely got away with the information I could get. The files were locked when I tried to download or print them, but I took a few pictures. I'll send them over. I doubt they'll be enough to do anything, but maybe they'll help you out somehow."

"Hopefully," Cooper said, unable to hide his dismay.

"I'm sorry Cooper, I wish I could do more. I heard about Elena too. I can't believe she left you to face this mess on your own."

"With the toll this has taken on me, I wouldn't want to have been in her shoes either," Cooper said, trying to defend his wife, even though he somewhat agreed. He didn't know how Cassandra already knew about Elena leaving, but that didn't really matter right now. "I appreciate your help, Cassandra. You've been the best manager I could've asked for. I wish none of this was happening and we could've just kept going until we were both old and retired. Or at least until one of us died." He chuckled awkwardly, trying to ease the overwhelming seriousness of the conversation.

"Me too. Makes you realize how small and powerless we really are, how little control we actually have." Cassandra sounded like she was thinking of her own situation just as much as his now. "I wish I could give you more to go on, but I can't afford to lose my job right now with three hungry kids and a husband on disability."

"Don't worry about it," Cooper said, sensing the guilt in her words and trying his best to convey that he really understood. He didn't fault her for still working for the people who were currently screwing him over. That was just the way the world worked. "Hopefully we can work together again, once I get this all sorted out," he said optimistically, but he knew that was likely never going to happen.

He heard someone talking in the background of the phone, their voice getting louder with each second.

"I have to go, Cooper, I hope you can come out of this right side up," Cassandra said, sounding more like a friend than a coworker as she hastily hung up the phone.

He still hadn't moved from the bed. The conversation didn't confirm much, but it had made him more confident about his assumptions, narrowing the path ahead, almost enough to solidify his next step. Just as he started contemplating his plan of attack, his phone dinged again as a few pictures came through from the blocked number.

The first showed what looked like a basic donation from AIP to Echelon Enterprises, or maybe some sort of loan. There were a few more pictures of similar transactions, but looking through them, he realized Cassandra was right— these wouldn't be enough to help his case. AIP knew what it was doing. Whatever he was looking at was probably by the book and wouldn't help him with any sort of legal action.

As he neared the end of the photos, he saw one transaction that made his heart stop. It was a document showing money going the other way, money being transferred from

Echelon to AIP. The transaction was listed as a Short-term Facility Rental, but the address of the facility was really what made every muscle in his body seize. It was the AIP branch near his house. Having seen all the mostly removed tech on its second floor, there was no longer a doubt in his mind.

Aldrich International Publishing and Echelon Enterprises had colluded together to steal his work. Hell, one was probably a front for the other.

This still wouldn't be enough, however. To a judge, it would look like AIP was just trying to make money off of their extra office space. Maybe, if he could show that he had received no money from the book in addition to the transaction record, there would be enough to at least get someone with more authority to go looking for answers.

As if they had been listening to his thoughts, or more realistically, using MUSE to predict them, Cooper received another notification on his phone. This time it was a message alerting him to a deposit into his account. He opened it up, horrified at the description of the deposit: Royalties for *Fake Creativity*. The expression this brought to Cooper's face literally hurt as the possibility of pursuing legal action faded away.

*If they were going to publish it without me, why would they still be paying me?* he thought, more confused than he had been yet.

He scrolled up through the bank's app and noticed there had also been a deposit from AIP months ago that matched his typical advance for the novel, something he must have missed because of his internet hiatus. This was less odd, as he normally received it after submitting his proposal, but he'd assumed they were trying to make money from his book without paying him. What was the point of all this, otherwise?

Having tried so hard to separate himself from technology,

he suddenly remembered he had other apps and accounts that would tell him about his book's sales. He opened them and, surprisingly, still had access. As he went over each available record and scanned the numbers, none added up. The royalty deposits were much lower than they should have been, given the number of copies sold.

So maybe they were shorting him somehow. Whether it was legal or not, he couldn't be sure. Given how everyone signed their life away just to visit a website nowadays, the contract he had with AIP probably gave them an infinite number of loopholes to change his pay whenever they pleased. By now, he had lost all faith that they had any morality at all.

These deposits would make it impossible to argue his case. He could already picture a judge looking at him, unsure of whether to throw him in the loony bin or yell at him for wasting his time and taxpayer money: *So, you're telling me they published your book that you hadn't finished without your permission? Even though you have a working contract with them and they're still paying you for it? Not to mention it still has your name on it. I really don't see what the problem is here, Mr. Owens, other than your story being batshit crazy.* He doubted an upholder of the law would use that phrasing, but still.

This meant he really only had two options left. Give up, or continue trying to find concrete proof that he had been wronged. To do that, he would need evidence that MUSE was capable of stealing his work.

Alexander's email portrait floated through his mind. He could try to get in contact with him, but Cooper's sudden distrust in his old partner, colleague, and boss made him feel like that was probably the last thing he should do. Not to mention, he knew he would have trouble getting back into AIP to find him.

He still didn't want to believe it, but he felt like the last twenty or so years of knowing Alexander had been a lie. The celebration at his estate and Alexander's enthusiastic speech about Cooper's work, just one short year ago, had all been for show. A show put on to protect the lie. Cooper quickly nixed this option.

He sat there, trying to organize his thoughts into a more coherent order from the scattered mess they currently were. His brain felt similar to Elena's workspace, a box of books dumped onto a coffee table. A jumble of ideas, words, and meanings all piled on top of each other, separated by broad, ambiguous titles. After a few minutes, Cooper finally picked from the pile.

*AIP is definitely working with Echelon Enterprises.* Cassandra had practically confirmed it. He quickly realized that going to Echelon Enterprises in Switzerland was the next logical step toward the answers and potential proof he was looking for. Hopefully they wouldn't be expecting him there and security wouldn't throw him out the moment he stepped into the building.

He wasn't going to stay another lonely night in this hotel. Cassandra's call had given him strength enough to find some forward momentum. At least someone was on his side, as much as they could be. He didn't want to sit around twiddling his thumbs anymore. He needed to reach the end of this rollercoaster before he either puked or it went barreling off the tracks.

Cooper searched for flights leaving for Zurich that evening, crossing his fingers that there would be something. After navigating through a multitude of options, he saw a nonstop flight out of JFK that he could make if he hurried. Still opting to buy the tickets at the airport, he put the book on top of all his clothes and zipped up his suitcase. This act was starting to feel like tying his shoes or zipping up his jacket before going out into the cold.

He checked out of the hotel and got another cab to the airport, this time with a driver who didn't want to ask him about his family or life story. Cooper once again felt as if he was two steps behind, no matter what choice he made. He had just done this yesterday and here he was again, rushing off to catch a flight, hoping to make some headway.

How could every day feel so much like the last, always adding to the feeling that he wasn't getting anywhere? He didn't know how much more of this he could take. Before he could even begin to answer such a question, he found himself back at an airport.

Getting on a spontaneous flight to Switzerland proved to be much more difficult than heading to New York on a whim, but he lucked out and grabbed one of the few seats left on the plane. As he boarded the red-eye and found his seat, he had the sudden realization that he was going to a place he had never even dreamed of visiting before.

Everything was pushing him forward into a life that bore no resemblance to the one he'd known. He was losing his sense of identity, questioning which actions were his choice and which were forced because of his external circumstances.

*Who is Cooper Owens?*

The version he knew would never hop on a plane by himself to some foreign country where he didn't even know if they spoke English. Luckily, he didn't have to worry about this for long, since there was no screaming child on this flight, which allowed him to sleep, teleporting to a destination that would have made even Elena jealous.

# 22

*Amidst the serene, age-old landscapes and delicate portraits, the contemporary works stood out, their stark contrasts and abstract forms disrupting the harmony of tradition. While classics required mastery of subtlety, the chaotic and brash nature of modern art made them nearly impossible to replicate. Forging these pieces demanded not just skill but a daring understanding of chaos, making them a perplexing challenge for even the most experienced forger.*

Cooper awoke just as the plane pulled up to the gate, surprised that he had slept through the landing. He was shocked that a flight attendant hadn't woken him, which they normally did just before touching down.

He followed others who'd exited the plane before him through the airport, hoping they knew where they were going. As he saw the first security checkpoint for international travelers, he panicked, worried that his seemingly random and chaotic travel might raise a few red flags.

Luckily, he came up with some halfway-believable story that slightly resembled the truth. Cooper left out the part about AI stealing his and everyone else's livelihoods. He didn't want any more altercations with security. He'd had enough manhandling for that week, and maybe for a lifetime.

While waiting for his luggage to appear on the carousel, he noticed for the first time the sounds of unfamiliar words being spoken all around him. The feeling of being somewhere he wasn't supposed to be crept in quickly, causing him to question even the tiniest of his actions. Just as he felt the urge to turn around and find a plane back home, his suitcase slid out from the hidden world behind the wall.

He stared at it and almost let it pass. The fact that it would come back around on the carousel if he missed it was completely gone—or at best temporarily inaccessible—from his database of knowledge. At the last second, he reached over the person standing next to him to grab the suitcase.

"Sorry about that," he said.

Cooper felt even more out of place as the sharply dressed gentleman replied in a language he couldn't understand.

With his luggage in hand, Cooper still seriously considered trying to turn around. But changing his mind and going backwards in an airport wasn't possible. This was especially true in international terminals, where departing and arriving passengers were herded like cattle, passing through gates, being corralled into certain areas, and occasionally waiting in line to get stamped. Luckily, it was just with ink and not a scalding-hot iron—otherwise, no one in their right mind would take that vacation.

Since he also hadn't changed his mind about being tackled by security, he continued on, propelled forward again, knowing he didn't have much say in the matter.

Cooper still had to go through customs because of his checked bag, and his appearance once again sent him for further inspection. The story he had bumbled through earlier when talking to the passport officer also may have been to blame for the extra scrutiny. Either way, he was happy that his suitcase was filled with freshly washed clothes as he watched its contents being examined.

The security agent held up the book, the only other item

in the suitcase, probably feeling rather silly for having done an extensive search.

"This was an excellent read," the man remarked, his English clear enough for Cooper to understand.

He felt a pang of discomfort as he realized that even here, people had already read the book. The man put *Fake Creativity* back in the suitcase and motioned for Cooper to make his way to the exit.

Once outside the airport, he was thankful the weather wasn't that different from New York's. Even though his suitcase contained just his leftovers from Colorado—attire suited for winter—he was surprisingly prepared for a trip to a place an ocean away. Cooper pulled out his note with the address for Echelon Enterprises. Now, all he had to do was find a way to get there.

Apparently, Zurich was known for its excellent public transportation and there were numerous options for getting to the city center. He could go by tram or train, but opted for a taxi, hoping to feel some sense of familiarity. Cooper was also trying to stay as far away from trains as he possibly could.

Interestingly enough, he had only ridden a train one other time in his life, a spontaneous surprise trip orchestrated by Elena. *Elena.* That had been one of their best dates ever . . . they'd been so happy. As Cooper climbed into the back seat, his trip down memory lane was quickly interrupted by the taxi driver.

"Where you headed?" he asked, his accent practically nonexistent. His tone was aggressive and sharp, yet carried hints of friendliness beneath its low, gruff growl.

"Echelon Enterprises." Cooper could see the driver in the rearview mirror and noticed the recognition on his face after hearing the destination. He put the note away, clearly not needing the full address.

"I can take you there. You sure you don't wanna go somewhere else?" he added sarcastically, a rough chuckle rumbling from somewhere deep within his chest.

"Yeah, I'm sure," Cooper said, now feeling entirely not sure.

"I'm just messing with ya." Another low rumble of laughter along with a quick glance in the mirror to make sure his passenger got the joke. "That seems to be the only place I ever take people anymore. Back and forth, back and forth. Airport, Echelon, back and forth. Why do you want to go there?"

"Um . . ." After hearing the driver say he knew of Cooper's destination and apparently drove their employees around all the time, the need for secrecy became apparent to him. Cooper decided a white lie wouldn't hurt. "My firm in New York sent me over to discuss a potential partnership with Echelon. From what we've seen, they have some great new technology that could be helpful for some of our upcoming projects."

This response appeared to make the driver lose his charm and friendliness. Cooper worried he had gotten caught in a lie somehow, but eventually the driver responded, easing his nerves.

"I don't like that place. What they're doing seems dangerous. Not to mention the number of travelers like you coming all the time to visit that big ugly building. Something about it all just seems off." Suddenly, as if realizing he might have just offended his paying passenger, he added, "No offense to you. I'm sure the work you're doing is important."

The cab went quiet for a while after this, but eventually the man broached more simple topics, giving advice on places to visit, various attractions to see, and other interesting tidbits of information about Lake Zurich.

"This place is home to one of the earliest settlements," he said. "Pretty sure it was four thousand, no, five thousand years ago, people lived all along this lake on stilt houses. Course, they're all under water now, whatever's left of them. But still, makes ya feel something, living in the same place people lived five thousand years ago. That's prehistory!"

Cooper looked out across the over-twenty-two-thousand-acre lake and pictured all those people living a simple life so long ago, waking up and worrying only about how to make it to the next day, what they were going to eat, and whatever else people worried about five thousand years ago. Cooper continued along with the friendly small talk, finding it funny that it now felt like a godsend and a comfort in this unfamiliar place.

When they finally pulled up to the building and Cooper had gotten out of the taxi, he didn't understand why the driver had called the building ugly. It was a marvel of modern architecture. Its clean lines and walls were made almost entirely of glass. Each pane was a right-angled triangle, and together they formed a diamond lattice. Every piece of glass had to have been nearly ten feet in length. They weren't pieced together to form a flat surface. Instead, the center of each diamond jutted out slightly, sending the sun's reflections off in various directions, just like a real diamond might. This was a building that would be admired and considered beautiful anywhere, especially in the city he had just left.

After his initial awe had worn off, Cooper noticed the surrounding structures and saw how out of place this glass prism of a building was. For as far as he could see down the street on either side, every other building was old and constructed of more traditional building materials such as stone, brick, and plaster. Many were adorned with beautiful accents and likely original details, and some buildings were painted in muted pastel colors toned down so much they were hard to notice unless you were paying attention.

Echelon Enterprises stuck out like a sore thumb, trying to squeeze itself into the midst of history, bringing the future to the past. Cooper glanced over his shoulder at the serene, mountain-fed waters of the lake across the street, its natural beauty a stark contrast to the unnaturalness of the glaring building in front of him.

He now wholeheartedly agreed with the taxi driver. Anywhere else it would be beautiful, but here . . . here it was fucking ugly. A pretentious piece of crystal displayed inappropriately.

Cooper was thankful it was early enough in the day that he wouldn't need to find a hotel just yet. Maybe if he was really lucky, he wouldn't even need to find one at all. Maybe he would just walk in, find whoever was in charge, get this all figured out, and be back on a plane home that evening. His real home, where he could call Elena and tell her he had fixed everything. This thought made Cooper antsy, more impatient than nervous, and he found himself walking toward the building with a blank mind.

His anxiety had always been a weak point for him, but now his fear had taken on an entirely new behavior—jumping between zero and ten, without ever stopping in the middle. Maybe the change had happened during his outburst at AIP, or maybe sometime before that, but it didn't matter. At this moment it was at a zero as he searched for the glass door, which was nearly indistinguishable from the rest of the building. He opened it and the heat of the building hit him square in the face as he walked inside.

He made his way to the front desk through the oddly empty entryway and suddenly realized he had no idea what he was about to say. His anxiety blasted straight to a ten like a speeding bullet.

Should he lie and try to get a tour of the place? Should he pretend to be a reporter looking to write a story about the company? He probably wouldn't get very far with either of these, so he decided being polite and telling a partial truth might be the best option.

"Hello." The man at the front desk looked at him, expressionless. "I'm Cooper Owens from Aldrich International Publishing in New York. I guess, if possible, I wanted to speak with Dr. Blake about an issue your new MUSE program has caused for us over there."

"Okay . . ." the man said with a look of utter bewilderment. He took his hands away from the keyboard he had been typing on and gave Cooper his full attention. "What sort of problem?" he asked, looking Cooper over with curiosity.

"It's a long story, but your program is seriously affecting our business. It's an extremely urgent matter."

"Sorry, what did you say your name was again?" the man asked, leaning over the desk to look at the suitcase.

Yet another interaction that reminded Cooper how absurd he probably looked right now. He adjusted his tone, adopting a more professional and authoritative demeanor, hoping to convince the man to take him seriously. As Cooper repeated his name, he thought he saw a flicker of recognition on the man's face.

"Like I said earlier, I'm from AIP, Aldrich International Publishing," Cooper added.

"Okay, I got it this time. I'll see if Dr. Blake has time to see you. If you wouldn't mind, just wait right over there." The man pointed off to Cooper's right, where there was a small seating area with benches that matched the rest of the building's aesthetic.

Cooper did as he was told and took a seat on a large, dark-gray block of granite. He quickly wished he'd sat in one of the chairs across from him because he was unsure if he was sitting on a bench or just a part of the building.

The minutes passed and Cooper thought he really might be caught in a cycle where every day echoed the last. Not a single person would come and he would wait there alone, and in a few hours he would once again go into a fit of rage, taking out his anger on the poor clerk behind the desk, who might or might not be in on the joke.

But it was only half an hour later that a younger man walked over to where he was sitting.

"Hi, I'm Dr. Blake. I heard you wanted to speak with me?" The man held out his hand to greet Cooper.

Cooper struggled to answer, the words and ideas in his head a jumble. Not only had he not expected to meet Dr. Blake so easily, but the man was nothing like he had envisioned. He was young, mid- to late-twenties maybe, and looked like he was fresh out of college. This *kid* had a PhD? He didn't have the graying hair or astute look of intelligence that only came with age.

Instead, he had semi-shaggy brown hair that hung ever so slightly over the bold, black lines of his horn-rimmed glasses. His face was perfectly shaved with no sign of stubble. Cooper continued to scan Dr. Blake but didn't even know what he was looking for. His eyes went from the black, long-sleeved, untucked button-up shirt down to the crisp, perfectly fitted khaki slacks. Only then did his searching gaze reach the floor and find what appeared to be a pair of skateboard sneakers, which looked as if they had been used for their intended purpose.

This couldn't be the real Dr. Blake. This had to be some intern they'd grabbed from the back and sent to occupy Cooper. Some sort of trick to distract him or get him to leave the property peacefully. Realizing he had been sitting there dumbfounded for too long, Cooper shook his hand, even though he was probably being bamboozled. *May as well see where this goes*, he thought.

"It's good to meet you, Mr. Blake." This kid didn't deserve to be called a doctor. "I don't know if you were told, but we're having some serious problems because of your MUSE program that need to be fixed right away."

"I'm sorry to hear that. If you want to follow me back to my office, we can discuss whatever issues you're having and hopefully figure out what to do about them."

Cooper nodded in acknowledgement and followed Dr. Blake away from the seating area, rolling his suitcase along behind him. The sound of the wheels echoed through the empty entryway, their frantic clicking reverberating off the tall ceiling. Dr. Blake stopped at the front desk and turned around.

"You can leave your things here. Andrew will keep an eye on them for you. It's a bit of a distance to where we're going, plus a couple flights of stairs."

Cooper didn't really want to leave his suitcase with these people he had absolutely zero trust in, but what else could he do? Then he remembered it was only filled with clothes and a single copy of his book. He placed the suitcase behind the desk and followed the supposed founder of Echelon Enterprises, almost excited to see how long they were going to keep this charade going.

"I work at the very far end of the building, so we may as well take a tour of everything. I mean, that is, if you would like one?"

How could Cooper turn down such an offer? The more information he had, the better.

"I guess we may as well," he said, still trying to sound unhappy and hinting at the urgency of the problem he was there for.

Dr. Blake led him through a labyrinth of rooms. Many were framed by glass walls similar in appearance to those on the building's exterior. Their hazy and frosted triangular panes divided the space in such a way that each room felt like a puzzle you had to solve before you could see inside. Walking through Echelon made Cooper feel as if he had stumbled into an upscale carnival and its luxurious fun house.

"This is the research and development wing of the building, where we hope to use our software to push other current technology into the future. Take everything and make it even smarter. Over there is our robotics department, and then we have automation down that hall, and concept design that way."

Cooper appreciated the tour, but he wasn't getting as much from it as he'd hoped. Everything looked pretty standard. Whenever Dr. Blake opened a door or let him peek into a particular workspace, they just looked normal. Most were filled with people typing away on keyboards or fiddling with some sort of prototype or other contraption. Maybe it was *too* normal.

"Now we are kind of getting to the boring stuff, like the

break room, presentation area, and lounge. There's not really much to see here," Dr. Blake said as he led them further.

The building seemed impossibly long to Cooper as they continued deeper into Echelon Enterprises. He noticed a few employees eating and chatting over their lunch. Off in another area of the lounge, others were playing table tennis. This place was beginning to look like any other stereotypical tech startup, complete with a bunch of kids playing pretend instead of actually working. Kids who believed the *work* they did was going to make the world a better place and improve things, or some other bullshit like that.

From what Cooper had seen, companies that looked like this one made a fuck-ton of money almost entirely on just the promise of advancement and progress. Empty words and ideas got people to pull out their checkbooks. Then, after they'd sucked the well dry and made things worse, they disappeared, leaving everyone to wait around for the next company to come in with a promise to fix the mess. A never-ending cycle of false progress. Cooper thought he had read a word for something like this once. *What was it? Enshittification.* Normally this word was only used for digital services, but Cooper was beginning to think it applied to all of life. An utter decline in society masked by shiny slogans and fucking ping-pong tables at the office. He could sense his worldview growing darker by the second, but could anybody blame him?

"Most of our employees aren't from around here, but so far, we've had some great people come and work for us. It's not the most glamorous or exciting job, but we have fun pretending to be smart. Hopefully, we can make some tech that will make life easier for everyone someday," Dr. Blake said, smiling.

Cooper stared intently into that smile, wanting to hate

Dr. Blake so badly, whether he was real or not. He wanted to watch that smile turn into an evil grin, but all he could see was a bright-eyed, bushy-tailed young adult not yet beaten down by the world. A man not that different from Evan Hartley, slightly older but still filled to the brim with dreams, wishes, and optimistic ideas. He could tell Dr. Blake wasn't lying, that he really hoped to make things better for everyone. Cooper couldn't fault the man for such aspirations and decided to give up on his pursuit of hatred for this enigma of a person.

"We're not always hard at work, though. We actually have a contest here every year where the employees submit ideas for the most ridiculous AI inventions. If they're even possible, we try to make them. It's sort of a fun side project for everyone to chip in on when they have some spare time."

Dr. Blake stopped in front of a mishmash of metal hardware recessed into the lounge wall.

"This is the winner from two years ago, the Baristai 2400. An AI-powered beverage dispenser. It scans your face and tries to decide what you need. If you're tired, maybe it'll brew you a double shot of espresso. But if you look stressed out, it might make you a warm cup of decaf tea to calm you down. You want to give it a try?"

"No thanks, I'm fine," Cooper said. He didn't want this company to have a scan of his face on top of whatever else of his they already had.

"Suit yourself," Dr. Blake said as he positioned his face in front of the machine. After a few seconds, a disposable cup came out from a slot, and then ice went tumbling into it, followed by some clear, fizzing liquid. He grabbed the cup and drank from it. "Well, it's refreshing, but I think we need to work on its weather-recognition software, because I was really hoping for something to warm me up on this brisk day. You sure you don't want to try it?"

Despite being his potential nemesis, Dr. Blake's friendliness was almost enough to tempt him, but Cooper stood firm in his response.

They walked further, finally reaching what appeared to be the end of the building.

"Here we are. My department, MUSE," Dr. Blake said as if unveiling the *Mona Lisa*.

They entered a large room. Cooper found it very anticlimactic. There were a bunch of desks and computers, and it looked like almost every other room they had seen on their journey here. The people who were working at the computers looked oddly similar to Dr. Blake, but more tired. Even from this distance, he could see their eyes were bloodshot, likely from the hours they had been glued to the screens in front of them.

"This is it? This is MUSE?"

"Yes, sir. This is where it all started, just a couple of guys fresh out of college playing around with lines of code and whatever learning models were the new hot topic. At the time, we never thought it would turn into this," he said, clearly reminiscing. "Anyway, I'm sure this is all pretty boring to you. We can head back to my office to see what we can do about the problem you're having."

Cooper followed him into a fairly small office. The first thing he saw was a skateboard leaning against the desk. All his doubts about the true identity of this Dr. Blake came rushing back, but then he noticed a picture on the desk of what appeared to be Dr. Blake with his wife and two children. He also caught sight of a framed, official-looking PhD certificate hanging on the wall.

Suddenly, Dr. Blake looked much older. Cooper was starting to believe this might really be the founder of Echelon Enterprises, skateboarder or not. How could this down-to-earth, seemingly nice guy be responsible for all of his suffering?

Maybe it was just Dr. Blake's charming and gentle nature, but Cooper quickly found himself retelling his entire story as accurately as he could, relaying every little detail he could remember—other than Elena leaving him, of course. It took quite a while to make his way through the whole thing, but Dr. Blake didn't interrupt once. With each new development, Dr. Blake's placid expression had become more effortful. Cooper could almost see the cogs turning in his head.

"Well, that's quite a story, Mr. Owens, but unfortunately, I think you've come to the wrong person. I can assure you MUSE is not nearly as advanced as you're describing. We even like to refer to it as our Marginally Useful Somewhat-intelligent Entity." Dr Blake laughed, but Cooper's seriousness didn't waver. "Anyway, the ability to predict the future to the individual word, as you say it has . . . I don't even know if that would ever be possible."

"Well, it is, and your program has done it, so I'm pretty sure I am talking to the right person," Cooper said, feeling his anger building. "So, are you going to help make this right?"

"I'm being entirely honest with you. Our program can be quite correct factually, but in terms of predictions, it has had a success rate literally equivalent to flipping a coin, even on the easiest of questions. There's just no way it would have correctly flipped that coin for every single word in your novel."

"If that's true, then it must've stolen it somehow,"

Cooper said, even though he knew that was impossible given the book's release date. Still, he was running out of directions to take this conversation.

"Even if it somehow did get access to your files, accidentally or otherwise, it wouldn't have done anything with them. It wouldn't be able to send them to anyone or, if you're telling the truth, publish the book before you had even written it. That would have required real human interaction."

"Who's to say you're not that human? I have copies of records that prove your company has done business with Aldrich International Publishing, the people who are responsible for publishing my book. What do you have to say to that?"

"I can't attest to that, but I think you don't really understand who I am. I don't do much around here other than fiddle around with computers. Myself and a few others created MUSE, but we're not the ones responsible for all of Echelon Enterprises."

"What do you mean?" Cooper asked.

"Well, once people started to see promise in our technology, we did start expanding, but somebody came in and offered to handle the business side of things. We were happy to hand that over, because it meant we could just focus on the work that we wanted to do. If I was some big, important person higher up, do you think my office would be crammed all the way in the back of the building?"

Cooper had bounced back to not trusting Dr. Blake, but the man's calm responses and genuine reaction to his story gave him pause. Dr. Blake was making sense and seemed unfazed by the interrogation he was enduring. Cooper's only choice was to keep following the trail laid out in front of him.

"Who's in charge, then?" he asked.

"I don't know if he does everything alone, but Hans-Peter Müller is the one who came in and took over as acting CEO of Echelon Enterprises, but he left MUSE as a subsidiary of the company under my ownership."

"Well, if you can't help me, can I speak to this Hans-Peter Müller?" Cooper could hear the irritation in his own voice.

"He comes and goes a lot, but I'm pretty sure he is in the office today. We could probably find him somewhere around here," Dr. Blake said, getting up from the desk, as courteous as he had been from the moment Cooper had met him. "Just follow me and we'll see if we can't find old Hansi."

As they made their way back to the front of the building, Cooper still couldn't help but feel like he was on a giant wild-goose chase.

"If only I'd asked about your problem before taking you on a giant tour, I wouldn't have wasted so much of your time. Sorry about that," Dr. Blake said sincerely as he knocked on the big black door they had stopped at.

"Come in," an oddly familiar voice said from inside the room.

Cooper followed Dr. Blake through the door, and his stomach dropped at the sight of the person seated behind the ornate desk.

"This is Hans-Peter Müller. It was a pleasure to meet you, Mr. Owens, and I enjoyed giving you a tour of our facilities. Hopefully Hansi here can help you out. I'll leave you two to it," Dr. Blake said as he exited the spacious room. The click of the door closing was nauseating to Cooper.

The man behind the desk began talking with an accent that was pasted on and out of place.

"What a pleasant surprise, old friend. I'm impressed with

how quickly you made your way here. Let's sit and chat," he said, motioning toward the chair on the opposite side of the desk.

Cooper stood frozen in place, eyes fixed on the man he thought had cared for him—or at least respected him enough not to be behind all of this. At the bare minimum, he figured the man had enough reverence for the publishing industry. Yet here he was, face to face with Alexander Graves, CEO of Aldrich International Publishing.

# 23

*As they crafted their forgeries, they were like moths drawn to the flame of their own talent, oblivious to the shadows their work cast on the walls of integrity. Their creations were beautiful lies, whispered tales that seduced the world with their perfection while concealing the quiet destruction they heralded.*

"Welcome to Switzerland, Cooper." Alexander's smile spread from ear to ear, as if he didn't have a care in the world.

"How? How could you, of all people, do this?"

"No time for hellos, I guess." Alexander dropped the forced accent but didn't let go of that big grin. "So be it."

He situated himself more comfortably behind the desk, seemingly unaffected by Cooper's piercing gaze.

"I'm just looking toward the future. That's what I've always done, and AI is what's next for society and the world. I can tell you're quite angry with me at the moment, and that's completely understandable, but by the end of our discussion, I hope you'll understand that this was the best option." Alexander averted his gaze slightly. "Not to mention the best outcome for all of us."

"How is this good for anybody but you?"

"I'll explain everything, but you're going to need to try and listen. I know it will be difficult, I can practically see the anger radiating off you, but you need to at least give me a chance. Just hear me out before you go busting down another door like you did back in New York."

"You saw that?" Cooper suddenly felt embarrassed,

barely able to remind himself that it had been justified. *That room was empty!* They had lied to him.

"Of course I saw that. What room doesn't have a security camera nowadays? I was actually rather impressed. We've been friends forever and I didn't know you had that in you."

"Friends? We're not fucking friends anymore."

Alexander made an exaggerated face of pain, his mouth puckered into a tiny O. "Ouch, that hurt. Like I said, hopefully by the end of this, you'll change your mind and see that I was only trying to look out for all of us."

"Nothing you will say will change the fact that you have ruined my life. I'm going to do everything I can to try and return the favor. I've lost my book, I've lost my passion, a few friends, and most importantly, my wife. My fucking wife!"

Alexander was staring intently into Cooper's eyes, taking in his anger and letting that smile fade for the first time since they had started talking.

"You're going to pay for all of it," Cooper said through clenched teeth. "I've made it all the way here and found you. It's proof that I'm not crazy and you're the one responsible."

"I won't stop you. You have every right to try your best, but by the end of our conversation, I can almost guarantee your feelings will have at least partially changed. Let's make our way down that list of complaints of yours, shall we?" Alexander motioned for Cooper to sit.

Cooper remained standing.

"Have it your way. Let's see, you said you've lost your book. As far as I can tell, it's still your book, isn't it?"

Cooper didn't answer.

"Is it not the same book you were writing?"

Cooper still didn't utter a sound.

"I'll take that as a yes, then," Alexander said airily.

"Just because they look the fucking same doesn't mean they are," Cooper snapped back at last.

Alexander nodded more in acknowledgment than in agreement.

"Okay, passion," he continued. "Well, I'm pretty sure that's not something I can take away from you. It's up to you whether you keep a particular passion burning or let it slowly burn out, wouldn't you agree?"

Resuming his silent defiance, Cooper scowled furiously, his eyes burning holes into Alexander's smug, know-it-all face.

"Now, on to the heavier stuff. You said you lost friends. If you're referring to Cassandra, I can assure you she is most definitely still your friend. That's why I had to send her back to New York. It wasn't personal. I just knew she would struggle to separate her feelings enough to follow orders and do her job, and I was correct. I know she called you."

This last part caused Cooper's intense stare to waver.

"If anything, I respect her even more now. A person that loyal is hard to find these days. Risking her job like that, especially given her current family situation." A look of admiration twinkled on Alexander's face for a split second and then disappeared. "Even though I can't trust her, at least I know who she really is now. You can't blame her for any of this. She was just following orders."

Alexander sat back. His expression went sour and almost sad as he continued.

"As for Elena, I know about that too. I'm genuinely sorry that you're having to go through that right now."

Every feature of Alexander's face went soft, and Cooper saw he actually meant what he had said. It was a true and sincere apology. It didn't change anything, Cooper told himself, trying to hold on to his anger with all his might. He may need it after all this talking was over.

"You two have been together practically forever. I'm sure adjusting to your new reality is tough."

"She hasn't left me forever! She just needed some space while I dealt with the clusterfuck you put me in. I wasn't the best husband while I tried to unravel the mess you created with your fucking greed." The last word came out of Cooper's mouth like poison.

"Greed?" Alexander scoffed. "Cooper, you sadly still don't comprehend what's going on. I'm sorry for bringing up Elena. I shouldn't have done that so early in our conversation. I apologize. Once you've heard a little more of what I have to say, it'll all make sense." Alexander shook his head as his all-knowing smile returned. "Greed. Have you not looked at your accounts? You're still getting paid for your work."

"The numbers don't add up. It's not enough for how many copies have been sold."

"We'll get to the reason for that shortly, but I can promise that the missing money isn't going into my pocket. Now . . . are you finally ready to listen? If we keep going on like this, we're not going to make it anywhere."

Even though Cooper wanted to continue attacking Alexander both verbally and physically, he knew he wouldn't gain much other than a one-way ticket out of the building or into a jail cell, depending on how far he went. Vengeance would have to be put on pause, at least for the time being. His curiosity tempered his anger just enough for him to want to see where this was all leading.

"Fine, but you're an evil, despicable, and pathetic excuse for a human. Now . . . I'll listen," he said, feeling like he had at least got one last punch in before enduring whatever explanation Alexander was about to throw at him.

"I really do hope I can change your mind on a few of those traits, but your feelings are completely valid." Alexander stood up from the desk and turned around. "Now, if you'll kindly follow me, it'll be easier to explain in here."

He didn't walk around the desk to exit the room, which confused Cooper until Alexander unlocked some sort of mechanism and slid a large section of filing cabinets on the back wall aside, revealing a steel door. Cooper felt as if he had left reality and now existed instead in some science fiction horror film. Alexander opened the door and stepped inside. Cooper cautiously followed, now fully considering the possibility that his AI clone could be on the other side, ready to kill him and assume his existence.

Cooper walked into a room not entirely unlike the one Dr. Blake had just shown him on the tour, but the differences stood out right away. It was more modern, sparsely furnished, and everything looked expensive. The few employees typing away on keyboards weren't college graduates in casual clothes. They looked older, well groomed, and professionally dressed. They exuded importance, like what they were typing was a matter of life or death, destruction or salvation. Everything from the screens they stared at to the chairs they sat in looked at least twice as nice as anything in Dr. Blake's department. Even the decor, accents, and lighting looked luxurious and futuristic.

The room had no windows, just a single door at the back, which Cooper assumed was an exit so workers could leave undetected instead of coming and going through Alexander's secret door. For someone who believed he wasn't evil, Alexander was certainly going to great lengths to keep all of this hidden.

"Welcome to MUSE. The real MUSE," Alexander said, spreading his arms to show what was obviously his pride and joy, his baby.

Cooper looked around the room, unsure about how to respond to such a reveal. He wasn't being murdered by his robot clone, but the monologue he was likely about to endure might be just as bad. Alexander didn't start talking though, and was apparently willing to wait as long as it took to get some sort of praise or astonishment out of Cooper.

Trying not to stroke Alexander's ego, Cooper asked a single question: "What makes this any different from what Dr. Blake and his team are doing at the back of the building?"

"They are tinkering with a toy," Alexander hissed, sounding more pretentious with each word. "They have no idea what they have created. And maybe never will. I'm sure Dr. Blake already told you what they call it. I know I've heard it a thousand times. *Marginally Useful. Somewhat-intelligent. Pfft.* That may be the case for their program, but it is only the backbone of *my* MUSE. With a little help, we have added a brain on top of it. A mind that can rival any human's. We've ignited the next phase of evolution."

Cooper stood there, trying to seem unamused, knowing it would hurt someone like Alexander, who was clearly a narcissist, if not a full-blown psychopath—not thinking about anyone but himself. But as Cooper should've expected, his lack of enthusiasm didn't seem to bother Alexander in the slightest.

"I think it's safe to say MUSE has been upgraded and is deserving of the title Most Useful Superintelligent Entity. All thanks to you, Cooper." Alexander's lips curled into a smile.

Cooper knew Alexander had added this last part hoping it would sting, hoping it would make him feel like he had somehow contributed to the program's creation. It worked, but he kept his mouth shut, and Alexander's smile turned down a few notches.

"Anyway, Dr. Blake's version of the program is fun and can help you do simple math or write your résumé for you. Ours is so much more. Ours is the next phase of humanity."

*Or the end of it*, Cooper thought. But then he changed his mind and decided it wouldn't be the end, it would just steal humanity from them. Little by little, until there was nothing left but empty shells, husks of humans with no purpose, no meaning, no reason to live other than existence itself.

"You are our first success story, Cooper. You will now forever be a part of history. The fact that you are here proves that we have accomplished what we set out to do. We have perfectly predicted the future by replicating you. We have created a version of Dr. Blake's silly little AI that can think like you faster than even you can. It makes the same decisions you will make. It tells the same stories you will tell. If it had a body and freedom . . . it would live the same life you would, step for step. So, tell me, how close was it?"

"What do you mean?" Cooper asked, the surprise of Alexander's question making him break his vow of silence once again.

"You never sent a copy of your novel in, so we weren't sure about the accuracy. But the lengths you've gone to already . . . it must have been pretty damn good this time." His lips curled and a greedy grin appeared on Alexander's face. It was the smile of a man who knew he had everything he could ever wish for. "So, how close was it to your original story?" he asked again, almost breathless with anticipation.

"Exact," Cooper said, still trying to be as expressionless as he could.

"Exact . . ." Alexander repeated, practically teetering with excitement. "You hear that?" he yelled to everyone who was silently working away on the computers. "Word for word! We've done it! We've done it."

The typing stopped. Simultaneously, everyone turned, applauded, and went back to their screens as if they were all robots.

"That's better than we could have hoped for. Honestly, there might not be much left for us to do here anymore," Alexander said, mostly talking to Cooper again.

Cooper couldn't take much more of this showboating, so before Alexander could open his mouth again, he interjected, "None of that explains why. Why me? Why still pay me? Why do any of it?"

"AI, the real deal, was coming no matter what, and I wasn't going to get left behind. Everybody always argued that the last thing it would replace would be creatives. I didn't believe that. I actually thought it would be the first thing. I imagined it wouldn't be that hard for a machine to analyze the entire catalog of Bach or Beethoven and create something similar but new. Or to learn what really makes a Picasso a Picasso or a Van Gogh a Van Gogh, and then render pieces that are just as beautiful, true to their styles, and yet, unlike anything we've ever seen."

Alexander paused for a moment before continuing, looking off into the distance with a proud, almost prophetic look on his face.

"The ability to resurrect the great artists from the dead. I was pretty confident the world of art would be one of the first things to be affected, because one could argue you don't need a body to make great art, you just need a brain. I knew it didn't matter whether that brain was organic or electronic."

Cooper's mind flashed with images of mechanical renditions of artists from the past. A Mozart on stage made of metal and electronics performing twenty-four seven, playing new and old works—a grotesque monstrosity that should be considered an abomination by anyone in their right mind, or at least anyone who considered themself a genuine lover of art. Cooper felt as if his own brain was transitioning to cold, hard circuitry at that very moment, but he kept his jaw soldered shut.

"If anybody was going to do it, why not me? Sure, a lot of other companies were already messing around with similar tech, but they were going about it in the wrong way. They were missing the crucial piece of the puzzle. Creativity. How about you take a seat, this might take a while," Alexander said, motioning to a couch in the far corner of the room.

Cooper reluctantly obliged this request. He felt like he was going to pass out, unsure if it was from the overwhelming circumstances he found himself in, the heat of the room, the lack of sleep, or something else entirely. The comfiness of the sofa held him up just enough to untie the knots in his stomach.

Suddenly, he noticed this was the same couch as Elena's, just a different color. This realization flooded his awareness momentarily and he wished he was with her, sitting on one of her excellently selected pieces of furniture, listening to her work. Just as he tried to imagine that beautiful voice reading to him again, Alexander's grating tone came through the dream, causing Cooper to once again reside in the nightmare.

"So, where were we? Ah yes, creativity. For an AI to truly be smart, it actually needs to be creative, too. We didn't have a set goal in mind when beginning this project, so we started out just trying to expand AIP using Dr. Blake's software.

"At first, we tried to have it create stories from scratch, write poems, and other things like that, but the results were god-awful. Then we tried to create stories in the voices of authors like Mark Twain, Dickens, Shakespeare, and a few others. Those turned out better, but there was no way to tell how good or accurate they were. Either way, releasing some imitation-Shakespeare is risky and a good way to get an angry mob after you, especially if it's bad. Finally, we arrived at the idea of trying to replicate authors who were still alive and currently writing, like yourself. You weren't the first writer to be put into MUSE."

Cooper was unsure about how this made him feel. Was the fact that he wasn't alone intended to comfort him? All it did was make him hate the man he was looking at more. He wondered how the others before him could have let this continue. If nobody else had succeeded in stopping this, or even tried, why would he be special?

Cooper wanted to regain some control over the conversation, so he reached for one of the many questions spinning through his head—but ended up asking two instead.

"Why try and replicate somebody who already exists? Isn't AI supposed to be its own thing, its own entity?"

"Yes, but that's why the thousands of other companies trying to create it have failed so far. Jumping to the thing you're talking about is a bit of a stretch, given our current understanding of how it all works. In other words, it's much easier to copy a person than it is to create one from scratch.

"For example, if I told you to draw a dolphin, but they didn't exist, it would be almost impossible. The statistical likelihood of you getting it right is essentially zero. Successfully copying a living human was a more attainable goal, and the perfect stepping stone for what comes next. If we can precisely replicate a human digitally, somewhere in all those lines of code would be the essence of conscious life. Then, all we need to figure out is how to pick that one piece of information out and reverse-engineer it to create a new form of life. Real AI."

"Why me?" The words barely escaped Cooper's lips, but he just needed to know why he was so unlucky.

"Because people like you are the perfect test subjects. We can put all of your past work into MUSE's database and then ask it to predict what your next novel will be. Then, all we have to do is wait until the real version of that novel is submitted to AIP. We put the two side by side and see how similar they are in their story elements, tone, and most importantly, words. We did this over and over again in the last few years, tweaking the program every time, trying to get MUSE better and better.

"Like I said, you're the program's most recent test subject, but it wasn't until your last book, *Us and the End,* that MUSE was 99.2% accurate in predicting what you would write. The best we got with other writers before you was sixty percent! It was quite an improvement, but ninety-nine percent still wasn't good enough for me. With a smidgen more help from . . ." Alexander paused and caught some singular word before it left his mouth. "I mean, after we got a little more data, we finally felt confident in the program's ability to actually implement it. To use it for our benefit."

"You mean your benefit?" Cooper asked, with as much hatred as he could convey.

"You're still not grasping that this is good, not just for me, but for you too. And eventually, the entire world!"

"How the fuck is this good for me? Look at my life!"

"Clearly, I haven't gotten to the point yet. Just calm down. We're getting there."

Cooper relaxed slightly, still feeling the urge to reach across the couch and punch Alexander in his smug face. But he knew it wouldn't go well; not once in his life had he ever hit anyone. If anything, the attempt would probably make Alexander laugh.

"For your most recent novel, we strongly believed we would get pretty darn close to one hundred percent accuracy, or maybe just slightly below it. I felt confident releasing MUSE's prediction this time because I knew it would be your book, just as you intended it to be. And I was right. According to you, we've done just that."

Cooper stared furiously at Alexander but held his tongue. *Just fucking get on with it . . . or kill me now.*

"The fact that you run away to that cabin of yours—the one you've never invited me to—to go on your little writing retreats, a luxury even I'm jealous of, allowed AIP to release your book exactly how you would have wanted it released, without any interference on your part. I don't think you would have believed it unless we released the book before you were finished."

A single question came to the forefront of Cooper's mind, highlighted like a neon sign. The question that had plagued him from the moment he had suspected that MUSE had copied his novel.

"If it is predicting my life, how could it finish the book before I did?"

"That's an excellent question, my friend." Alexander leaned forward, conspiratorial. Cooper recoiled and Alexander also pulled back with an apologetic gesture. "The moment you sat down to write that story, the whole thing was already in your head. It just takes you a while to collect and craft each idea and thought into one cohesive story. What takes you months, maybe even years to finish, only takes MUSE a fraction of a second. Just because I said it would live the same life you would live doesn't mean it has to do it at the same speed."

"What if some crazy, monumental event outside of my control changed the way I think or altered my behavior?"

"Do you really believe in free will all that much?" Alexander's words sounded more like a statement than a question. "Everything that came before almost always pushes you forward in a certain direction, and we mostly just follow the tracks we've been put on."

"What if Elena died while I was writing? What if she got sick? What if she left me . . . mid-book?" Cooper's own question punched a hole straight through his chest. He couldn't believe he wasn't bleeding out right at that very moment on the couch. *Her couch.*

"Before this last test was run, maybe it would've mattered. But now, at most, things like that will just cause a temporary reduction in accuracy. Even if the change in your head perfectly aligned with a new idea for a book, the percentage difference would probably be negligible. The idea of those life-changing events are already in your head, built into your sense of the world.

"But more importantly, you're forgetting that this is a connected world and humans have become permanently inseparable from technology. If Elena died, MUSE would eventually know and adjust its predictive model. If you searched for information about a new religion, MUSE would know and adjust. If a security camera caught you shopping at a new store and it somehow resulted in a miraculously life-altering experience"—Alexander raised his eyebrows and gave him a look of disbelief—"MUSE would find out and adjust."

Cooper felt like a lab rat in a maze and was frantically

searching for an exit, a question that Alexander wouldn't have an answer to. A question that wouldn't block another route of escape, that would prove Alexander wrong instead. Prove that this was all one giant farce, a cosmic coincidence, and that his program hadn't actually worked. He could find none.

"Anyway, like I said, I released it while you were away on purpose so I could prove to you that it was real. After our disagreement and my mishandling of your cover art last year, I even went ahead with asking MUSE to try to predict the cover you wanted for this book, even though we hadn't done any testing on something like that."

Cooper's eyes filled with horror, and Alexander must have only seen the truth in them, because his face lit up and then a look of satisfaction washed over his expression.

"So that was right, too? Holy . . . it really is perfect. Do you understand yet?"

The shock that gripped Cooper was indescribable. The fact that his words had been perfectly copied had, at the time, seemed like the only thing that mattered. But the machine had also plucked an imagined image from his fucking brain and made it a reality on the cover of *his* book. Cooper's head felt as if it might burst as he envisioned the vast, infinite MUSE filling up his skull. Cramming itself into every nook and cranny, squeezing into every fold of pink, mushy, gray matter, waiting in anticipation of its next directive.

"It's the future," Alexander said. "But for now, the lucky few like me and you will benefit from it the most."

"How am I benefiting from it?"

"You're still getting paid, aren't you?"

Feeling more and more like a child being told how he was wrong by a parent, Cooper nodded reluctantly before saying, "But it's not the right amount."

"That's not because of me. I always planned to pay you just as much as usual. You could keep writing your stories and we'd keep publishing your books at a faster rate than you could ever dream of. Hell, you don't even have to write them all the way to the end if you don't want to. Get bored halfway through, it doesn't matter, it's already finished. We could even send you over the finished versions for your approval before release if you wanted. You could retire tomorrow, let MUSE pump out every book you'll ever dream of, and we'd keep putting your name on it and you'd keep collecting the checks."

This made Cooper wonder if any court or legal system would even consider his assertion that he had been wronged at all. As long as Alexander kept paying him, it would probably fall into some legal gray area, much like when doctors performed an incorrect procedure that somehow led to a positive outcome, and they avoided a malpractice lawsuit by sheer dumb luck. *Well, we accidentally amputated the wrong leg, but it was full of cancer anyway, so in truth, we saved the patient's life.* He could envision Alexander's team of top lawyers arguing a similar case: *Well, we did kind of create a clone without consent, but Cooper never has to work another day in his life and he still gets to keep getting paid millions of dollars.*

"So if it wasn't your idea to cut my pay in half, whose was it?" Cooper asked, hoping he wouldn't have to hunt down another person who might be to blame for everything he had suffered.

"You are still a step behind, Cooper, and missing the important points. Not to mention I thought you would have already known this by now. Using authors as the starting point for an AI was ingenious, but it still wasn't enough. People convey a lot about themselves in their writing, but we needed more. That's where Elena came in."

# 24

*Victor's heart ached as he stood at the crossroads of affection and disillusionment, knowing that every secret unveiled about Elena would reshape the landscape of their love forever.*

*Elena.* Her name made the hole in Cooper's chest grow into a meteor-sized crater. He felt as if he would be extinct before this horrible day was over. He clambered out of the scorched earth and rubble of his mind, barely able to find his footing in the present. His ears were ringing so loudly he could hardly hear the words coming out of his own mouth.

"What the fuck do you mean by that? Elena. What does she have to do with this?"

Alexander looked at Cooper with eyes that glowed with power, the sort of power that destroys men.

"She had everything to do with this, Cooper. Without her help, we wouldn't have been able to make that jump from sixty to one hundred percent accuracy."

"What . . .what . . . are you saying?" Cooper felt as if all the energy had been sapped out of his being. No electricity ran through his nerves, no blood reached his vitals. Was his heart still beating? Was any of this even real?

"Well, we can't very well ask you to help train an AI that's trying to be you." Alexander said this as if it was common knowledge. "If you had learned about MUSE too soon, before we had perfected it, it could've ruined everything. The problem was, we still needed more details about your life and the way you think. Elena was reluctant at first, but she came around after she realized what life would look like if it worked, and more importantly, what it would look like if she didn't take advantage of the opportunity."

"You're lying! She wouldn't do that." Cooper could feel his eyes welling with tears, but the thought of crying in front of Alexander quickly made them recede.

"She did."

"You're a fucking liar!"

Alexander let out a long and low sigh and began speaking in a manner so calm, it was eerie.

"I swear to you, it's the truth. She had two options. Either help you become the first writer who doesn't even have to write in the traditional sense to make a living, or, wait around until either I succeeded with another of AIP's authors or somebody else beat us to the finish line, leaving us all in the dust to fight over whatever scraps were left."

"I would rather that."

"Think about it, Cooper. You're the lucky one. If somebody other than your good friend Alexander here had figured this out, they might have just stolen your stories entirely, or worse yet, released mediocre versions of them under a different name." Alexander paused. "And you call me greedy. Elena finally saw what I was saying and did what she had to do in order to protect you."

"You make it sound like everything she did was for me. So explain to me why she's gone. Why would she run off with half the money?"

"Yes, that's where the story took a turn. I truly believed she was doing it all with good intentions until a few weeks ago. She called me and told me she planned to leave you, and in return for her help with MUSE, wanted half of the proceeds from your future books to go directly into her account."

"Why? Why would she do that?" Cooper stammered.

"I asked her that same question. All she said was that she couldn't do it anymore and she needed her own life now."

"Liar! All of it. Tell me the fucking truth, Alexander!"

"It's true and I'm sorry. I really am." He grabbed Cooper by the shoulder as if they were still friends, before getting up from the couch and walking over to a nearby filing cabinet. "It's all right here. You can come take a look for yourself."

Cooper felt like gravity had increased tenfold. No amount of force would get him up from the couch. The look in Alexander's eyes said he was telling the truth as he waited patiently by the open drawer.

He needed to see.

He had to see the proof.

It took almost all the energy he had left to stand upright. Each step toward the filing cabinet was the hardest thing he had ever done. When he finally got there, Alexander backed away so Cooper could flip through the manila folders himself.

The drawer was filled from front to back with records upon records of Cooper's life. He pulled out a random folder with his trembling hands and struggled to open it.

This particular document detailed what he had eaten for breakfast on the morning of May 14th, and included a short summary of the nightmare he had the previous night. He suddenly remembered telling Elena about this dream over breakfast, telling her how he had been re-enrolled in school the day of final exams and was still expected to take them all. Hours of knowing nothing, hours of feeling stupid, hours of not being good enough.

Cooper's mind swam, the vast swaths of information in front of him sucking him under. The first page he looked at had confirmed it was true. It was undeniable proof that

Elena had been spying on him. Sharing his life with AIP, with Alexander, with MUSE. He needed to see more, to find something that somehow invalidated all of it.

He flipped to another page. This one had details about a terrible movie they had gone to see in early September, and how Cooper had said, "If I ever write anything that bad, promise to shoot me?" He remembered saying those exact words.

The next page was filled with transcripts of texts between him and Elena. Another page. A photo of him goofing around with a few of their friends at a bar. Another page. A list of questions and answers he had given throughout their daily conversations. Cooper threw the folder behind him, its papers floating down like identical rectangular snowflakes, and grabbed another.

He skimmed the information faster now, his eyes barely able to register anything he was looking at as his vision narrowed and the world around him became a blur. It was like he was looking through an old camera lens and the only thing in focus was this filing cabinet filled with . . . him. Suddenly, he stopped on one particular note. It read like a personal journal entry, intermingled with seemingly unimportant observations.

Cooper took me out to dinner tonight, and it was magical. I wore that dark blue dress he likes so much with the elegantly patterned thigh-high stockings that drive him crazy. He wore his favorite pair of pants and a striped button-up. He looked so handsome, I just couldn't stop staring at him.

He ordered the weirdest thing he could find on the menu just like he always does, Charred Octopus with Black Garlic Aioli. I love that about him, the way he just tries to be different. The way he does these little things to try and make life more exciting, more interesting. Of course, just like always, he still ended up taking a few bites from my plate of Chicken Parmesan.

After dinner, we came home and before the front door had even closed, he pushed me against it and kissed me with so much passion. Then he took me to bed. He slid my dress up and used his mouth on me until I came, but before I could even catch my breath and pull him up into an embrace, he did it again. Only then did he undo his belt and take his own pants off and make love to me until we both orgasmed at the same time. We crawled into bed and held each other so tightly, nothing separating our bodies, and fell asleep just like that. It was one of the best nights we've had together in a while.

*This can't be real. There's no way Elena would share that type of information.*

But she had. Like everything else he'd read so far, this night had happened too—just as the entry described. The way Elena had described.

Cooper frantically searched through more folders and then opened up another drawer of the filing cabinet. This too was filled to the brim with more folders of details, unimportant and important, about his life. He opened another drawer and found the same thing. That aperture he was viewing the world through was shrinking, like at the end of old cartoons, until all Cooper saw was black. He had one last thought before he disappeared, too.

*Please let me not wake up.*

Nobody really gets what they want in this life.

* * *

He felt an odd sensation as he tried to open his eyes. With each attempt, the bright overhead lights crept through the cracks in his eyelids and sent bolts of pain through his head. Through repetition, the sensation finally dulled enough for Cooper to look around, only to discover that he was still in the hell that he so desperately wanted to escape.

It hadn't been a dream. There was no denying it; Elena had played a part in all of this. Maybe she had thought she was doing the right thing, but now? Now that she had left him, what was he supposed to think?

Becoming more aware by the second, he saw Alexander looming over him, then quickly realized his friend was pressing something cold to his head. Panic set in as Cooper imagined his brain blowing out the back of his skull, Alexander pulling the trigger. Maybe Alexander had decided to just kill him, since he clearly wouldn't let this go quietly. Then again, maybe at this point Cooper wanted to die.

As his rational brain took over and connected the dots between Alexander's concerned expression and the cold thing he was holding to Cooper's forehead, he realized it was merely a bag of ice.

"You had quite a nasty fall. We thought we were going to have to take you to the hospital.

Cooper sat up quickly and felt the throbbing in his head again as the blood drained from it. He had a powerful urge to lie back down. Alexander must have seen the expression of pain on his friend's face, because he gently put the ice back where it was needed. This genuine gesture of care made Cooper feel uncomfortable and even more conflicted about his feelings.

Was Elena to blame for everything? Without her help, none of this would have happened. Did she even love him? When did her feelings change? Was Alexander actually not evil, but just oblivious to the error of his ways? Did he really believe all their lives would be better if MUSE worked? So many questions and he had zero inkling of how he felt about any of them.

Alexander pulled the ice away, still looking concerned. Cooper reached up to touch his now-freezing forehead, only to find pain with the slightest amount of pressure. When he looked at his fingers, he saw there was no blood.

"Are you feeling okay?" Alexander asked.

"Yeah, I'll be alright." His anger and rage were completely gone. Both had leaked out all over the floor when he cracked his head on it.

"I know it's a lot to take in. That curveball our dear Elena threw us didn't make it easier, though." Alexander put his hand on Cooper's shoulder and looked directly into his eyes. "It's a bloody shame that she just left you like that. I'm sincerely sorry she's gone, Cooper."

Cooper quickly averted his gaze, no longer sure of anything. He went to rub his head, trying to ease the pain and hopefully put some distance between him and his *friend*. It worked, and Alexander got up and returned with a glass of water and a few painkillers. No longer thinking that he was on the verge of being murdered, Cooper happily took them.

"Now what?" he asked.

"That's up to you. You can keep writing just as you always have, or you can stop. We can't force you to do anything. But MUSE is what it is, and will keep doing what it was designed to do. We'll handle all the hard stuff and your paychecks will keep coming. Just expect them to be half the usual amount."

Alexander gave him a sympathetic glance. "It really is a pretty awful thing, what she did to you, but again, I promise I had no idea that was her plan."

Cooper nodded. The urge to talk was gone.

"Hey, look on the bright side, now you can retire to that winter getaway of yours permanently and live out the rest of your life doing whatever you want. Enjoy the summer there even, I hear the hiking is excellent."

Cooper's head was still pounding, but for the first time since he had walked into Alexander's—Hans-Peter Müller's—office, he was seeing things as they were. He now believed Alexander wasn't evil, but dramatically unaware that anybody aside from him was human and alive. He had dropped a bomb on Cooper that would impress even Oppenheimer, and all he could say to try and ease the aftermath was that Cooper should take a hike. There was no point in arguing or being angry with someone who was this delusional. Cooper's life was in tatters and Alexander had just put the final nail in the coffin, a nail Elena had supplied to him. He couldn't see a way forward. Even if he wanted to stop this, to seek some sort of retribution, who would he go after? Alexander or Elena?

He wanted to hate her more than anything in the whole world, but . . . he still loved her. *How can I still love her?*

# 25

*Victor felt the crushing weight of futility, every decision seeming like a drop in an ocean of despair. The sense of hopelessness left him paralyzed, feeling as if no choice could change the inevitable tide of darkness.*

The phone continued to ring. Cooper had been trying all morning to get ahold of Elena. He needed her to tell him it was all true, that she had betrayed him. He couldn't believe any of it. Still no answer.

By this point, he had left nearly a hundred messages, some pleading for forgiveness, others insulting her character, some filled only with silence when he couldn't find the right words. Cooper flooded Elena's inbox with anger, sadness, and every emotion in between. He listened as the voicemail picked up again, but ended the call before leaving another message.

He dialed the number again and told himself this would be the last attempt. This time, he called just to listen to her voice, even if it was only the short, prerecorded message that said, "Hey. You've reached Elena. I'm probably off in some fairytale right now, but I'll get back to you as soon as I can." He didn't expect her to answer—this time he would just be fully present in the beauty of that voice.

The first ring came through the speaker, but then he heard a blaring beeping and then silence. A robotic voice came on the line, a voice that was nothing like Elena's: "We're sorry. The number you have dialed is no longer in service."

It really was over. Elena had abandoned him. She had betrayed him and left him to the wolves. Cooper didn't know who he was without her. For the longest time, they had been two halves. Now he was no longer whole, and he knew he might never be again. Was there even any point to a life spent separated from the one you loved?

His brain welcomed these dark thoughts, quickly taking him to a place he had spent his whole life running from. He was afraid to go home, *their home*, where these sorts of thoughts would only grow in the lonely confines of rooms that still smelled like her.

But he didn't have much choice; Alexander had booked him a flight home that day after *generously* getting him his current accommodations, as if these two menial acts made up for everything. When Cooper had given him a sarcastic "Thanks," he had even offered to increase his royalty percentages for all future book sales, which only refreshed Cooper's newfound distaste for his old friend. As if money would fix anything or prove that Alexander was the good guy in all of this.

The only thing Cooper really wanted from Alexander was a way to find Elena. If he could just talk to her in person, maybe he could still get his wife back. He had literally gotten on his knees to beg for her location or any sort of way to track her down. Just to spite Alexander's previous generosity, and to prove his own point, he even offered all of his royalties in exchange for such information.

Alexander declined, claiming he was "contractually obligated" not to share any information about Elena. But he'd also said he didn't know where she was, as if to imply he would've told Cooper if he did.

His behavior only solidified Cooper's impression that Alexander felt he had done no wrong. That his MUSE was the future and that it was a win-win for all parties involved.

He used to be a writer himself. How could he be so blind? How could he knowingly steal all his work and just hand it over to that thing?

The answer came quickly enough—now Alexander could think of himself as the true creator. He'd made something that could *be* every writer to ever exist. Maybe even more than that, as the years went on and they expanded MUSE's capabilities. He could feel like he'd played a part in all of it, like he was some sort of God over every new book, every new story told. The master behind it all.

That was all fine and dandy for Alexander, but every other soul trying to find some sort of meaning or purpose on this giant rock was absolutely and undeniably fucked now. If the ability to create is taken away, so too is our humanity.

If the program continued to write Cooper's books for him, he didn't know how long he would make it. If he had Elena, he could survive and maybe even be happy without writing, but now he'd be lucky to last through the year.

*Alexander.* Everything always had to be about him. Cooper couldn't believe it had taken him this long to see it. How had he been so stupid? Alexander had just stabbed him in the front, and now it was easy to see every other knife he had jabbed in his back. For God's sake, the man had thrown him a gigantic party last year and had given a heartfelt speech that made Cooper actually feel proud of himself for once. Only now did he see what that party had really been celebrating.

Cooper felt ashamed for being so oblivious. He wanted to focus all his efforts on seeking revenge on his egotistical and misguided boss, but what would be the point? What could he do, especially alone?

Alexander had won while honestly believing he was a hero. Not only would Cooper not be able to break through this delusion and get satisfaction by making him suffer for his wrongdoing, but Alexander also had a powerful and all-knowing tool under his control. His unimaginable wealth and connections would make any attempt at justice not only improbable, but impossible.

Cooper grabbed his suitcase from the bed and got ready to get on another plane, this time feeling even worse about it than he had before. The other times, he had been filled with adrenaline, overwhelmed by the unknown. There was none of that energy left, no chemicals being expelled by his adrenal glands, no obvious emotions to give him guidance. He had put so much effort into getting here only to hit a wall that stood so high he would never be able to climb it. All he could do now was go back home and try to live his life somehow while knowing full well it wasn't his life anymore. He had lost everything.

Maybe . . . maybe one day Elena might come back though. Maybe she would realize she still loved him. How could she not, after spending all those years with him?

Cooper sat on the plane trying to find the answers, thinking of ways to kill MUSE, and most importantly, how to get Elena back. After a long flight with no revelations or breakthroughs, he found himself crossing the train tracks again, able to see their house in the distance.

*Maybe Elena is at home right now.*

There was a glimmer of hope in his mind that she would be sitting inside, having changed her mind, or better yet, to tell him it had all been one giant practical joke. He stood outside the house, trying to build up the courage to go in as the cool night air and his own thoughts made him tremble.

He let the door swing open, and all that was behind it was darkness, an eternal loneliness he had to enter. He stepped inside with no idea of what to do, no path to follow anymore. Cooper wandered around the empty house like a ghost, looking at their pictures on the walls, not uttering a sound. He reminisced about all the memories they'd built in this small home by the railroad. The faint sound of a train in the background called out for him as he dove further into despair with every room he entered.

Eventually he made his way to Elena's office, having checked everywhere else for his dear wife. No sign of her. He fell onto the couch, its comfort now suffocating as it enveloped him. He lay there, wondering where she was. What was she doing? Was she even thinking about him?

Cooper didn't know how long he was lying there staring up at the ceiling, running through endless loops of questions and possibilities. It could have been hours, maybe even days. The line between death and his current existence was paper thin. Eventually, another train whistle pulled him out of the trance.

He couldn't stay here. This house would trap him until it swallowed him whole. It was too painful. It was their home.

If he went to the cabin, he might at least have a chance of escape. After all, that's exactly what it was designed for, a place to run away to. Maybe it would allow him to think of a way out, a way to win against the machine, a way to live. *At least it will take me away from these fucking trains.* The whistle grew louder as it warned nearby drivers not to tempt fate, the darkest parts of Cooper's mind telling him to do that very thing.

Cooper hastily packed another bag of clothes, realizing he didn't have the cabin stocked with anything for the warmer months. He grabbed the hard drive from his office and decided to also grab Elena's. Maybe there would be something on it that would hint at where she'd gone and why she had really done it all. He threw everything in the car, trying to get out of there as fast as he could, but before he could even turn the key in the ignition, his phone rang. The train's deafening whistle intermingled with the peaceful, serene ringtone. He looked at the glowing screen. It read, Private Number. He answered.

"Hello?" The train's cacophony faded into oblivion and Cooper could no longer feel the chill of the night air as he waited for a response. The silence seemed to last forever.

"Cooper." Her voice was quiet and eerie, but just as beautiful as always.

"Elena?"

"Yes."

Cooper's heart screamed, its piercing cries spreading into every part of him. He couldn't figure out right from left and had no idea what to say, how to feel, or if this was even real. There was only one thing he could possibly say.

"Why?" he asked, feeling the sadness ready to explode out of him, but her answer was too important, and it held him still and silent.

"I'm sorry, Cooper. I made a terrible mistake, and there's no going back."

He could hear the tears behind her words. He wanted to reach through the phone and hold her, tell her everything was all right. At the same time, he wanted to scream at the top of his lungs and let her know how much she had hurt him. He couldn't do either.

"None of that matters, baby. Just come home . . . come back," he wailed softly.

"I can't. I can't ever come back."

"What do you mean?"

"I fucked everything up." Elena was crying now, her beautiful voice intermingled with sad sobs and sniffles.

"No . . . no. You didn't do anything wrong. You did what you had to do," he said, yet Cooper couldn't help but wonder, *Did she?*

"How can you say that?" Elena asked. "You know it's the furthest thing from the truth."

It was, but Cooper would say anything right now to get his dear Elena back. He knew for certain that all of her lying and betrayal didn't matter, he still loved her with all of his heart. She could stick a blade into his chest while looking him dead in the eyes and he would still use his dying breath to tell her that he loved her.

"It isn't. I love you, Elena. Please, just come home."

"I can't. Don't you get it?" Cooper sat silent, not understanding. "I killed you! I helped create something that will destroy you piece by piece until there's nothing left."

Cooper already knew this to be true, but when the words came out of Elena's mouth, they were gospel. He finally understood what she was saying. Understood why she wouldn't come back.

"You will always love me," she said. "But you will resent me for the rest of your life. A part of you would hate me until we died, as long as that fucking thing continues to steal your other love. That would destroy me the same way I destroyed you." She paused for a moment. "I can't do it."

"Baby," Cooper begged, for the first time realizing the purpose of this conversation.

"I can't. I won't. I've undone us and if I come back, I'll have solidified the death of us. There's no going back. It will never be the same. It's the way it has to be."

"No." Now he was crying. The faucet handle of his tears was turned wide open.

"Yes. You know I'm right."

*She is*, he thought.

"I love you more than anything in this world, Cooper Owens, and always will until the day I die. I am so, so sorry."

"I love you." Enough pain and sorrow rang through his words that he could hear it echo back through the phone.

"Please understand. I can't come back just to watch our relationship slowly die until there's nothing left except your hatred and my own guilt. Please, Cooper." She was sobbing uncontrollably into the phone now.

"Okay . . ." His voice was shaky but oddly calm as he realized there was no escape. "Okay . . ." The single word numbed his sadness like a huge shot of novocain.

"I'm sorry," she repeated, her sobs beginning to subside, and Cooper felt as if they had come to some sort of awful agreement.

"I know that now. You won't believe me, but it's okay. I really do forgive you. I love you so much, Elena."

"I love you so much, Cooper."

"So, this is it? This is goodbye?"

"Yes."

"Does it really have to be?" He already knew the answer, but prayed it would somehow be different.

"Yes."

This time the silence that followed was unbearable. He wanted to say something, anything, to stop what was about to happen. But he couldn't utter a single syllable.

"Goodbye, Cooper. I love you so much. Please try to hold on to the memory of me from before all of this."

"I will. I still love you, Elena, I really do. Please don't forget that."

"I won't."

Cooper heard the phone click, and then nothing. He continued to hold it up to his ear, hoping that it would somehow magically reconnect to his lovely wife, a sign that they were making a terrible mistake.

No such miracle came.

Eventually he took the phone away from his face and sat quietly, staring through the windshield at their home, now more lost than ever. He felt everything and nothing. Then the sound of the train whistle filled his ears once again.

He slammed the car into drive and sped up to the tracks. The crossing arms weren't down and the lights weren't flashing, but he could still hear that screeching whistle somewhere off in the distance. He pulled onto the tracks and threw the car into park. He would wait. The last time he had paused in this very same spot, he had driven to safety because he still had Elena.

Now she was gone.

The car idled there in the dark, waiting for the cataclysmic event. Cooper reached into his pocket, grabbed the pack of cigarettes, and without hesitation, without thought, put one between his lips and lit it as he rolled down the window. The first inhale hit so good—the sting of the smoke in his lungs felt right. It was the best thing he had tasted in years. He coughed, struggled, and enjoyed every single drag from the small stick of death while listening to the approaching train whistle. As the cigarette evaporated into nothingness, Cooper flicked the butt out the window and onto the tracks. He looked curiously to his left and then to his right, but still saw no sign of his oncoming demise. No scarlet glow. No crossing arm locking him into his decision.

*I'll wait.*

He grabbed another cigarette and repeated the process, savoring this one even more than the last. Every smooth inhale and slow exhale changed him, making him feel less than he was, but better somehow. The train was so loud now it had to be right around the bend. If it didn't come soon, he was going to need to reach into his last pack of cigarettes for a third time. The one currently between his lips was already half gone when a loud *Beep!* cut through the train whistle, making him jump in his seat.

He looked into the rearview mirror and was blinded by the headlights of the car behind him, urging him to get a move on. He tried to motion the driver past him by waving his hand out the window but was only met with another furious round of honking.

"Motherfucker, just let me die in peace."

More honking. No train whistle. Cooper furiously put the car in drive and slowly drove off the tracks, pulling to the shoulder. The other car passed, its passenger angrily giving him the finger as they drove by. After he watched the red taillights disappear into the distance, he looked back in his mirror and saw no sign of a train. As he listened, he heard nothing, either. The night was dead still, and not a sound filled the air. There was no train.

*Fine.* Frustrated, he took one last drag, flicked the second cigarette out the window, and drove on. The angry driver had pushed him a few more feet off the tracks and toward the cabin—saving Cooper's life from an imagined train that eventually wouldn't have been so imaginary.

# 26

*Victor's reflection was a silent witness to his internal struggle, the battle between the wreckage left by Elena's actions and his desire to rebuild. He vowed to piece together the fragments of his shattered life and to rise above the chaos she had caused. He was determined to find a way forward from the ruins of their past, even if it meant confronting the darkest corners of his own conscience.*

It was still beautiful, but now it was more of a sad type of beauty, missing all of its bright and happy undertones. Spring had penetrated into the mountains and begun to kill winter. There was still snow precariously perched on the peaks in the distance, but his winter retreat was no longer blanketed in crisp, clean white. The surrounding property was instead covered in a slushy mess and some areas were even bare. Cooper wondered if coming back here was a bad idea.

As he approached the black hole of a cabin, nestled against the rough and rugged backdrop, he knew at least he could count on having a better view here. When he walked inside, the size of their second home overwhelmed him. It hadn't grown since they'd left, but now, without Elena, it felt impossibly massive.

Before doing anything else, he went and closed the door to Elena's office. He needed to pretend it didn't exist, to believe nothing was missing. Maybe he'd even try to pretend *she* didn't exist . . . at least for the time being. He needed to survive.

The drive back to Timber Creek, Colorado, had been

long, giving him plenty of time to think about how he'd sat on those train tracks. He didn't want to die, but the pain of Elena leaving made living feel almost unbearable. A few hours into his lonely trip, he was struck by the sudden realization that maybe there was a way to fix everything.

Elena was afraid he would grow to hate her, resent her more with each passing day, and that their love would die a slow, painful death. Cooper would never stop loving her, but he knew she was right. There was a tiny black drop of hatred somewhere deep in his heart. He could feel it spreading over his love for Elena, and it could coat everything in its darkness if MUSE continued to steal his life.

If . . . if he could actually figure out a way to stop MUSE, maybe things could go back to normal. If he could just beat the thing, find a loophole, the reason Elena had left him wouldn't be valid anymore.

He didn't fault her for making the decision she had. She was trapped between two options and picked the one she thought was the lesser of two evils. If he could just get his future back from that damned program, he might get rid of the dark thing that was growing inside of him. He might be able to convince Elena that it was gone and she wouldn't have to watch their relationship wither.

To do that, though, he would need to not desperately long for her like a starved man longs for food. Not crave her return like an orphaned child craves the return of their dead parents. She hadn't suddenly ceased to exist, and he realized there would always be a chance, a possibility that she might come back. But for him to regain his footing in this world alone and stand up on his own two feet, he would need to not think about her. He needed to focus and learn to live on his own, be strong on his own, so he could fix this.

In truth, he felt weaker than ever, but he prayed that he could overcome it.

And so, Cooper wiped the memory of Elena from his mind . . . to survive.


Now he was truly alone, living in his cherished cabin that could comfortably sleep ten. The expanse of the space begged for more than just him. The vaulted ceiling dimmed any noise while adding its own ominous chatter, every sound he made echoing. Without the presence of another, Cooper made sure there was always a TV on, a speaker playing music, or headphones adding noise to drown out his own thoughts. The only time he sat in silence was when he went out on the back porch to smoke, but even this wasn't totally quiet. The loudness of the chemicals hitting his brain, swirling in with the serene sounds of the man-made stream that trickled along the property, was enough to ensure his mind didn't wander too far.

His habit had returned as if it had never left, and before he had even made it to the cabin, that last pack of cigarettes was empty. It wasn't long until Cooper had found himself at a gas station on the outskirts of town, feeling twenty years younger as he bought a few cartons in order to satisfy his returning addiction.

He tried to act as if everything was perfectly normal, attempting to get back into some sort of routine. He pretended to work toward a new novel as if nothing had changed, knowing full well he wasn't going to write whatever he was scribbling in his notes, notes that MUSE was probably replicating at that very moment. Cooper read books, researched, and tried to learn everything he could about AI technology, hoping to find something of value, but he could only pay attention to the fact that MUSE was most likely watching him plot against it.

He even tried to get back into the swing of working out, the thing that used to be his coping mechanism, his crutch to get through the shit life threw at him. At this point though, he couldn't help but feel as if life was throwing more than just shit his way.

Even so, exercise helped a lot at first. But eventually, his old addiction combined with the exercise made him feel twenty years older when he tried to lift the same weights he had before. Each rep burned so sharply in his lungs that his rests between sets became more like breaks dedicated solely to coughing and expelling the ever-growing mucus in his lungs. The workouts were almost making him feel physically worse, but the old mental tricks were still there. The effort tired him out, cleared his head, and kept him grounded in his body instead of his brain.

More importantly, it was one part of his old routine that didn't make him feel like he was being watched. Even though MUSE still factored this aspect of his life into its predictive model, it didn't feel that way to Cooper, and that's what mattered. It was a small sliver of privacy in his day, away from imagined prying eyes of ones and zeros.

After a while, Cooper caught on to this feeling and decided it was the key to staying sane. He went all in on exercise but didn't quit the cigarettes, a part of his brain still holding out that they would kill him, saving him from having to do it himself. So there he was, a pack a day smoker who lifted weights every day.

One morning, while having his smoke and coffee on the back porch, he noticed a trail winding through the mountainside. The fact that it wasn't hidden by snow suddenly made him realize just how warm it was outside, and that the spring weather and changing landscape offered even more ways to get out of his head. By now, he craved that sense of privacy almost as much as the cigarette currently hanging from his stained lips.

He dropped all his reading, research, and book planning and replaced them with even more physical activity: hiking, climbing, and at one point even mountain biking. But after falling once, he quickly decided his aging body couldn't handle the sport. All of this was a way to tire himself out so he could actually get to sleep at night. A way to avoid being alone with his own thoughts, hoping one day to feel strong enough to face all the dark ideas running through his head.

Some nights, his demons would reveal themselves, peeking out from the shadowy recesses of his consciousness, waiting for an opportunity to overtake him and send him hurtling down their tracks toward a dead end. There were nights when he remembered that Elena did exist, and he would call her disconnected number or write her countless emails, telling her how much he loved her, how much he wanted her back, and that he would do anything to make it happen. Afterwards, Cooper would lie awake for hours, the sound of the train that wasn't there still haunting him when the TV got quiet or the music paused for too long between tracks.

The next day, he was always unsure if he had slept at all. He would push himself even harder by adding a few extra pounds to the barbell or a couple more miles to the hike, trying to make up for his moment of weakness.

Life stayed this way for weeks and Cooper could feel himself becoming more like a machine as time passed. More cold and numb, less human. He felt pathetic and questioned whether he even deserved to exist. Cooper felt nowhere near ready yet, but he knew he would have to start to live again soon. It terrified him. He couldn't just work himself to exhaustion day in and day out for the rest of his life.

So he started slowly, just a little at a time. A minute here, a couple minutes of silence there, testing the waters by dipping a single fingertip into his own thoughts to gauge the temperature. His mind was still screaming and writhing with pain under the surface, even though on the outside he looked rather calm and collected. It would take a lot of hard work to get the courage to jump into that freezing, raging ocean in his head. And once he managed to do so, it would take pure grit and a lot of luck not to get sucked into its undertow and be lost at sea, never to be found again.

With each passing day, he spent more and more time inside his head, and the fear of doing so gradually faded. After a while, he even cut back on his excessive and unhealthy amount of exercise, reading again instead.

In time, he began to accept that he might never feel truly okay again, but at least he was learning to function in this new reality. He could see the fragments of his identity being put back together and tried to ignore the missing pieces and the holes that might never be filled.

After a while, he had relearned how to live alone. Without Elena. He was still a sorry excuse for the man he had once been. At last, though, he had reached some solid ground to stand on. Rogue waves continued to lap at his feet, but he felt like he could finally try to change his fate.

One day, Cooper went to his office computer and searched to see if any new books had come out under his name. He found nothing; the last release was still *Fake Creativity*. This wasn't good news, but he was thankful that MUSE hadn't been polluting his name with books of its own devising. He knew MUSE had stolen his book and there was no doubt that it would do it again.

Cooper leaned back, looking at the list of his books on the computer screen, and finally opened his mind, trying to brainstorm his first plan of attack.

Maybe it hadn't written a new book yet because he hadn't. That was an option, never write again and hope that stopped MUSE. Alexander did say it perfectly replicated him, so he was pretty sure it would work.

It might also slowly destroy him, just like losing Elena had. He could already feel the urge to create growing within him. Over the last few months, he had worked so hard to become himself again . . . and he was a writer. He wouldn't be able to resist indefinitely and do nothing. He needed to find another way.

For days, he thought of every avenue of attack and his list of ideas grew. The problem was, implementing each idea would take time, and many required him to write full novels. He was only human and couldn't just shit out a story in a fraction of a second like MUSE could.

If he was going to beat the smartest computer to ever exist, he would need to take every precaution and use any advantage he could find. That meant trying to hide from its prying eyes once again.

After researching which models were the most reliable and easiest to use, he ordered a refurbished typewriter, along with everything needed to maintain it. Ideally, he would have preferred to find one locally to keep the purchase a secret, but trying to find a working model in the small town would be nearly impossible. A few days later, the typewriter arrived at the front gate. When he picked up the box, it was heavier than he could have imagined. He felt a pang of shame as his lungs rattled and his breath wheezed from the effort of carrying the behemoth and heaving it onto his desk.

The typewriter wasn't spectacular to look at, but hopefully it would serve its purpose. After printing off anything he might need from the computer, including a beginner's guide to typewriters—just in case—he unplugged his computer and everything else on the desk. He was more than happy to hide the entire setup from sight. Now, the ostensibly useful technology only reminded him of his own dwindling significance.

Now the desk lay empty except for paper, a few pens, and the giant, baby-blue hunk of metal, which was without a doubt older than him. There wasn't a cord to be seen, no highway to another world, no leak in the system. The primitive and simplistic nature of it all calmed Cooper's nerves in a way he hadn't predicted.

The only other thing that still sat where it always had was the beautiful black hourglass Elena had gotten him. He looked at it and got stuck on the memory of her, the memory he was trying so hard to avoid. He felt his cheeks get warm and his stomach churn as a tidal wave of sadness prepared to pull him under.

Quickly, but with the utmost care, he picked up the hourglass and placed it in the bottom drawer of his desk. Tears rolled down his face but he ignored the damp trails they left. He couldn't get lost again. He needed to focus and crawl his way out of this mess. Only then could he think about Elena. Then he could get her back. There was no need to measure time. He would chip away at the problem until it had been solved.

He sat down in his chair, pretending he was going to

write, and put his fingers on the cold keys. He typed, no paper inserted, only playing with the letters. Each action resulted in a satisfying and resounding *klack*. He couldn't believe he had thought less of all those hipster writers, had sneered at them for thinking they were cool and different for using their vintage typewriters. Here he was, his beard grown out, shaggy brown hair pushed back and almost down to his shoulders, drooling over his new, baby-blue toy.

He almost felt happy.

He also felt like a hypocrite, but he didn't care. The type-writer felt good under his hands, better than he thought it would, given what he was about to attempt.

Now that everything was ready, Cooper turned off the internet again. This time, it felt justified. He was about to turn his phone off too, but then realized he couldn't.

*What if she called?*

So instead, he put it into the drawer of his nightstand and promised himself he wouldn't use it. He prayed all this would help, even though none of it had when he'd sat down to write *Fake Creativity*. He still had to try, still had to hope he could outmaneuver the AI and find some weakness in its programming.

Cooper went back to his dark office to lose himself in whatever obscure story he could find deep within his mind. It needed to be something different, something he would never write in his wildest dreams. He needed to write as if he wasn't Cooper Owens, to pretend he wasn't alone, and to forget that his wife Elena was gone. But even more crucial to this particular plan was that he needed to write it fast.

# 27

*The act of creation felt like a delicate dance on the edge of a cliff; no matter how carefully you moved, the masterpiece you crafted could be toppled by the whims of those who envied its perfection. In art, every triumph was a prelude to potential ruin.*

Cooper had finished the nearly three-hundred-page novel. His hands sat motionless, but the sound of the typewriter still hung in the dimly lit office, a noise he had heard almost constantly over the last few weeks. He had worked day and night, hoping he would be too fast and too unpredictable for MUSE. It was the quickest he had ever written a book of this length, and while it wasn't his best, it was still pretty good. This surprised him, given that he had tried to write far outside his comfort zone and area of expertise.

Instead of a romance, he'd written an alternate history novel. He had filled the pages with a tale about how prohibition had resulted in a full-blown revolution. It was so far from his usual material it seemed impossible that he'd written it, yet there it was, sitting on the desk in front of him. There was still a minor plot thread about a couple trying to find love amid the chaos. He couldn't resist. Cooper was beginning to feel a little optimistic. There was no way that program could predict he would write something as absurd as *America's Last Round*.

He sat there, bleary-eyed, looking at the stack of papers, realizing that even though he had put himself through the wringer to write it, he had enjoyed crafting every line.

There was only one way to find out if it had worked. Cooper didn't even take the time to put the computer and its appendages back on the desk. He plugged them in on the floor where he had placed them a few weeks ago. He ran to turn the internet on and hoped that his mad dash to the finish line had been enough, but his doubts were doubling with every step.

Reconnecting that single ethernet cord would allow him to see . . . and be seen. By the time he had gotten back to his office, the computer screen was glowing, but it didn't sound happy about being awoken from its long slumber. Or maybe it wasn't happy about having been replaced by something so old.

The computer hummed and almost breathed as it tried to warm up its stiff, cold circuitry. After what felt like an eternity, Cooper got online and found what he was looking for. He wanted to throw himself off the mountain right then and there.

At the top of the list, front and center, was his new novel. Already available in hardcover, paperback, and digital, of course. His hopes faded so quickly it was as if they had never existed. He had written it so fast, in mere weeks, and somehow it was already there.

He bought the e-book and quickly grabbed the stack of papers that made up his first draft from the desk. He compared them page by page, and for a moment it looked like maybe MUSE hadn't been as accurate this time. But after a few chapters, he realized most of the changes were just minor corrections—ones he would've made during editing.

Cooper didn't want to turn another page, the crushing defeat already pulling him back into someone he didn't want to be. He flipped to the end, assuming that if it was right, it had almost certainly gotten everything else right. It was identical. He hadn't been fast enough or even remotely unpredictable.

It knew him inside and out, and Cooper could feel it there again. Could feel its presence, as if he wasn't the sole owner of his own body anymore. He was slowly becoming skin that MUSE could wear.

*Of course it wouldn't work. It was a dumb idea.*

Cooper tried to analyze what had happened, searching for something useful to take from this utter failure of a first attempt. Disconnecting from the internet didn't help. Trying to write absurdly different hadn't worked. AIP had somehow released the book on extremely short notice. These were things he had already assumed would happen, but at least now they were confirmed.

At the moment, these facts weren't of much use to him, and all he could do was move on to his next plan—write even faster. It sounded more idiotic now that he had arrived at it. Cooper felt the urge to give up, but he'd promised he wouldn't.

Rather than trying to write a full-fledged novel, he would write an entire short story in one day. It would be tough, but doable. He would need to plan the outline well and not stop writing once he sat down to start. Most importantly, it still needed to be good. What was the point in writing if the work he created was terrible?

So, without a single day's rest, Cooper began drafting the outline for a new short story in his overtired daze. He mostly ran through it in his own head while smoking on the back porch.

Out there was just nature, the sound of trickling water, and the warming weather. Inside, there was electricity running through the walls, cords that could be traced across the continent, and every other sign of modernization—things that reminded him of *it*, of the passenger taking a ride through his own life. A passenger getting all comfortable in the soft and squishy interior cushioning of his brain, where it might end up living forever.

The sun began to set, and Cooper felt as if it had only risen a mere hour ago. It had taken all day to flesh out the premise and plot of the story, and the work, as it so often does, devoured time like a starved, insatiable beast.

As night fell, he solidified the ending of the story in his head while smoking the last cigarette from the pack. A fine trail of smoke rose gently into the sky, and Cooper followed it, gazing up at the few twinkling stars above.

The temperature was perfect. The world was quiet. Peaceful. Beautiful.

Satisfactory.

Then he inhaled the final puff of his cigarette and crushed the butt into his disgustingly dirty and overflowing ashtray. He'd need to head to the gas station to buy a few more cartons before bed.

By this point, he was so used to running into town that he barely noticed the chore, a mindless act of his born-again addiction that had returned without any resistance. But this time, before he walked out the front door, he suddenly felt very naked, like he was forgetting something. He slapped his hands to his pockets out of habit to jog his memory.

It was his phone. That thing people couldn't survive without anymore, unable to take a few steps outside the comfort of their homes without them. The tiny devices that had become like second brains, that could under no circumstances be left behind. God forbid they got lost or forgotten.

Panic would almost certainly ensue, the separation anxiety severe enough to be classified as clinical.

Cooper hadn't even remembered he had a phone until that very moment, but he was far from the average person. His growing hatred of technology and his intense focus on the book he'd just written had made him forget about it. The second he opened the front door though, he was just like everyone else, needing that thing that he despised, unable to leave the house without it, not even for a short smoke run.

So he went back to the bedroom, opened the drawer, and grabbed the phone, only to realize it was dead. He put it into his pocket anyway and went to get more cigarettes, no longer feeling like a part of him was missing. No longer feeling naked and vulnerable.

When he got home from his toxic supply run, Cooper went straight to bed, hoping to get an early start tomorrow. He plugged in his phone. There was no putting it back in its previous hiding spot now. *What if Elena had called?* Before it had enough charge to answer his question, he drifted into that space in between—another night of tiptoeing the line of sleep and wakefulness, never fully crossing into either.

When morning finally brought him to something that resembled awareness, he scrambled for his phone, his eyes bulging and bloodshot. Just like the computer, his phone was also slow to wake up. Nobody could blame the poor thing, though, not even Cooper.

It had just gotten the best and longest sleep of its life, completely dead to the world, only to open its eyes and be instantly bombarded with countless notifications of unanswered calls and messages. Cooper scrolled through them all. Distant relatives were asking where he'd been, other distant relatives were asking for money, ad after ad, unpaid bill notice, ad, ad, ad, another bill, bill, ad, old high school buddies trying to reconnect, spam, more spam, a metric ton of spam, and another fucking bill for that subscription he kept forgetting to cancel.

He and his phone felt pretty similar at the moment, all of that hanging over them in the big comfy bed as they started the day. Both were supposed to be recharged and refreshed, and even might have been for a few milliseconds, but all their energy was sucked right the fuck out as the outside world came pouring back in. At least Cooper could turn off the phone if he really wanted to, but he didn't, and the phone didn't have much of a choice in the matter.

He needed to be certain Elena hadn't tried to contact him. He scanned the overwhelming mess on the tiny glowing rectangle in his hands, a portal to the life he had tried to run away from, tried to forget. Cooper saw all those reminders of normal life . . . but nothing from her. Not a single message that mattered, not a single thing that had any real importance to him.

Exhausted, he got out of bed and slipped the phone back into his pocket, as if it were a missing piece of the puzzle that was him. *She might still call.* He still had a flicker of hope, but to keep it alive he couldn't think about it, otherwise his own pain would extinguish it.

He needed to only think about work now.

Cooper wasn't a short-story writer and never had been. When an idea came to him, it was vast. Worlds upon worlds of information, details, and minutiae that might or might not become part of a book. The thought of trying to condense one of his ideas into so few words was already making him feel claustrophobic.

It made him crave his coffee and smoke break on the back

porch more than ever, but to his dismay, rain was pouring down outside and the wind was whipping each droplet into tiny wet bullets. He felt even more confined as he resorted to cracking the window in his office and inhaling his morning cigarette with record speed as he tried to shift his mindset and put himself into the world he was about to create.

He sat down at the hefty typewriter that he now rather enjoyed using, and the frantic nature of his morning persisted as he began writing. It was nearly eight p.m. when he finished. The typewriter made a satisfying *klunk* as the carriage returned to its resting position, and he pulled the last page out and laid it face down on top of the small stack of papers to his right. He had done it, written the smallest snapshot of one of his ideas. In truth, Cooper was quite proud of it.

He spun around in his chair and got down on the floor in front of the computer that was probably still upset about its new home. He sat there cross-legged like a child sitting in front of the television, wide-eyed and entranced by Sunday morning cartoons, only Cooper adopted a much more serious gaze. He was already telling himself it hadn't worked, but could feel himself getting antsy anyway. Luckily, the computer hadn't been asleep for as long this time.

There it was again, at the top of the list under his name. He had started and finished it in less than twenty-four hours, but it didn't matter.

As he struggled to look at the evidence of yet another defeat, he saw that this time it was only available digitally. Every other format had to be preordered. He may not have been faster than MUSE, but at least he'd been fast enough that AIP hadn't been able to fully release his book. A small win, so tiny that to anybody else it would be like comparing a single grain of sand to Mount Everest. Cooper clung to it. It was at least something.

He bought a copy of the short story and checked it side by side with his draft once again. There were many more revisions this time, but Cooper was convinced he had made more mistakes due to the speed with which he had written the short story. It was only his second attempt, but he was already beginning to doubt he would ever beat MUSE. That doubt was growing into a belief, and the option of just not writing was looking more enticing.

As he stared blankly at the product listing for his short story, he suddenly realized there were already a few reviews. The words Alexander had said came rushing back to him, words that were previously jumbled into one horrid memory that he had tried to forget: *What takes you months, maybe even years to finish, only takes MUSE a fraction of a second.*

It didn't matter how fast he wrote a story or how different it was; the second he sat down to write it, they would already have it. The book had been released at noon that day. Humans have never been able to outrun their own creations. Why had he thought this would be any different?

His eyes went out of focus and the screen became a glowing white square while he tried to accept his terrible mistakes and come to terms with how much time, energy, and effort he had wasted pursuing pointless plans.

"Write faster . . . just write faster. How fucking stupid can I be?"

Cooper buried his head in his hands. If only he had remembered what Alexander had said, but even now, as he tried to step back into his recollection of that day, there were no details, just a memory that was shrouded in thick fog that would only burn off little by little.

He gave up his search for past answers and forced himself to look at the computer again. He clicked on the reviews. Maybe they could be useful somehow.

Most readers had loved the short story, which made him feel almost good, but the pleasure felt tarnished and stained from the fact that it had been simultaneously written by an AI. He should be original enough—creative enough—to not be so easily replicated.

His work was still making it out into the world almost word for word, but it felt ruined. Hardly anybody else would understand, but Cooper felt violated and sick. He scrolled through the reviews, trying to suck as much positive energy from them as he could, anything that hadn't already been siphoned off to MUSE. After a while, he realized that some of his readers weren't entirely on board with his two most recent releases.

> I've been a fan of Cooper Owens for years. I never thought he would be switching up genres or writing short stories. They're still good, but it's pretty weird.

> Have been reading Owens' books for as long as I can remember and while his two newest aren't my cup of tea, they're still well written. I can only wonder why the sudden change. Also, how is he releasing them so quickly? Has he run out of ideas and is just pumping out old half-finished books he had lying around?

Cooper hadn't even thought about the impact his plans would have on his readers. He had been so focused on beating MUSE that he'd totally forgotten that he wrote books not just for himself, but so other people could read them. How had this crucial aspect of being an author escaped him?

Now that it was back in his framework, he questioned if he even wanted to move forward with his next plan—write a terrible book.

It might work, not because MUSE wouldn't write it, but because AIP and Alexander might not want it published. Even if it gave him another one of those single-grain-of-sand wins, it would be a lose-lose situation for him.

He would be creating something that might ruin his reputation forever, a stain on his otherwise sparkling record. A source of shame for the rest of his life. Now remembering that he had fans, the thought of making them suffer through something as horrendous as he had envisioned, something that would likely make over half of his reader base never touch one of his books again, made him physically ill.

The temptation to try anything to win almost made Cooper want to do it anyway, but he knew he would regret it. That meant he had only one last idea to try, barring the drastic option of attempting to give up writing for good. He was going to write a novel live on social media.

Once again, he felt like a toddler could come up with something better. If only he could find that toddler. Cooper had always hated the virtual cesspools of polarized opinions and fakeness, but now he would have to suck it up and become an active member of online society.

Even though this plan sounded more ridiculous than all of his previous ones combined, he really believed it would work, in a way. He was confident MUSE would know the story before he did, probably even more so since it would be uploaded piece by piece, but there was no way AIP would show its hand. They wouldn't risk releasing it before he had finished, or at least he hoped that was the case.

The next day the rain had subsided and Cooper basked

in the warmth of the morning sun as he had his coffee and cigarettes and planned his next novel. He had a few concerns about this final plan he was about to embark on, but he tried not to let them drag him down. After he'd made it through another pack of cigarettes and his skin had turned a few shades darker, Cooper went to put himself online, even though it was the last place he wanted to be.

He started by putting his new, cherished, favored type-writer on the floor and replaced it with its modern equivalent. Cooper was so used to the primitive baby-blue tool now that he struggled immensely to set up his old computer. He could have sworn its tangle of cords was attempting to strangle him.

Eventually, everything looked like it used to, like it had before MUSE. Only one thing was missing. Cooper was about to open the drawer that contained the hourglass from Elena, but stopped himself. He still wasn't ready for such reminders of her.

Cooper sat down at his desk, extremely nervous about what he was going to attempt. He wasn't one for being seen or heard. He had set up his writing career in such a way that he could have as little interaction with the public as possible. Here he was, though, about to create his first social media accounts and livestream his writing . . . for everyone to see.

It took him the rest of the day to make his online profiles and learn how to use them. He used every popular site, hoping that it would be enough to gather an audience. For this to work, he would need people to watch.

When he woke up the next morning and logged back into the computer, he couldn't believe how quickly people had found him online. In less than twelve hours, he had amassed nearly three million followers across all platforms.

"Do these people ever turn their phones off? How do

they even have time to read my books? Maybe they don't read them . . ." *Maybe they listen to Elena read them.* The last thought ricocheted painfully around in his skull like a bullet until it exploded out the back and let even more memories of *Elena* leak out. She was gone and he couldn't think about her . . . she couldn't exist right now.

Cooper put his hands on the keyboard, re-familiarizing himself with it. It felt cheap. If only he could go back and be a writer in a time before all of this, he thought. Go back to a time when that typewriter, now sitting on the floor, was brand new.

He reluctantly logged in to every single one of his newly created accounts and fumbled his way through setting up the livestream and sharing a link to it. There was no going back. Cooper watched in horror as, within seconds, the number of viewers shot up and thousands of people poured in to witness whatever he was about to do.

*What the fuck am I about to do?*

He could feel his heart pounding, his throat closing, and as he looked at the version of himself on the screen, could see the sweat glistening on his own forehead. He was suddenly very aware of his rough appearance and just how tired he looked. *I should've at least brushed my hair or shaved.* Cooper wanted to call it off right then and there.

"Um . . ." Even this pathetic sound couldn't come out right. Cooper tried to clear his throat, hoping that he could expel whatever monster was terrorizing his insides. "Hi. This is all new to me, so bear with me here."

He made sure he was in frame and that the blank white page, cursor blinking in anticipation, was also being displayed to those who had already tuned in. He stared at himself in the camera once again, feeling stage fright ten times greater than the time when he had read his own poetry aloud in the middle school talent show. Cooper could hear the thousands of viewers laughing at him already, just as his classmates had all those years ago. He pushed on anyway.

"So, I'm going to try something new this time and write an entire novel live. I don't know how well this is going to work, but hey, maybe some of you will enjoy it. And who knows, maybe it will turn out to be a decent story. I guess we'll all find out together." The words sounded so stupid coming out and the imagined laughter grew to a despicable roar. He trudged on. "Welcome to the show. Thanks for coming. I guess I'm going to get to work now."

Cooper began to write, trying hard to get into the flow state where the pressure of being recorded would fade away. He was so close, a few sentences from everything else disappearing, only the story left in the dark office.

*Ding!* A comment popped up on his screen, right over his writing:

This is weird. Why are you even doing this?

He had already been interrupted, so there was no point in not responding.

"Uh, yeah, I know this is pretty weird. I guess you could just say I wanted to change things up. Try something new. Thanks for your question, HeartThrobber32."

He went back to typing, just picking up steam when the computer dinged again.

So far so good, but you should make it take place in Australia instead of New Zealand. It would work better.

"Thanks for your input, but I didn't actually intend for this to be an interactive event."

Cooper struggled to find a way to turn the chat off, but before he could, he realized the action might also upset his viewers, most of whom were probably some of his biggest fans. He tried to get back to writing and was making decent progress when another *Ding!* rang from the computer. Before he could even read the comment, another *Ding!* and then another and another as messages filled his screen.

*Ding!* Have you lost it, old man?
*Ding!* Can you make the main character's name Harley instead? That's the name of my dog!
*Ding!* This story already sucks ASS!!!!
*Ding!* You should just retire already. You don't even know how to work a computer!
*Ding!* This is the most pretentious bullshit I've ever seen! Like, what is he even trying to do here? Live Streaming while writing a novel. For once, the phrase I'd rather watch paint dry might literally be applicable.

Cooper had plunged himself into a world he wasn't fully prepared for. He frantically searched for a way to at least turn off the comments on his own screen. After a few minutes of constant dinging, he found the button that hid all the comments and a sad silence settled over the office.

"Okay, I want to thank everybody for all their input, but unfortunately, if I had to respond to all of your comments, I think this book would never get done. Feel free to still discuss with each other and hopefully I'll have time to read all your messages after the book is done."

He would never voluntarily look at those messages ever, not in a million years. Before he had even finished talking, the number of viewers dropped to almost half, but that didn't really bother him. If anything, it actually made him feel better.

He was almost certain that just one would be enough to stop AIP from using MUSE.

The onslaught of opinions, requests, and vulgarity made it extremely difficult for Cooper to get back into a headspace where he could write. He knew comment sections were a brutal place, some of the worst places on the vast internet, but he had assumed his viewers would be different. How wrong he had been.

After a few rough pages, he got back into a groove. He already felt burnt out, but he had to keep going. If he stopped, he might give up for good. So, he wrote.

Every night he would end the livestream and check to see if the unfinished book had been pushed to the stores, but it never was. For weeks he continued to log in and turn on the webcam, writing his story live for everyone to see. Sometimes thousands tuned in, other times just a few hundred, but there was always someone watching him struggle to write in front of an audience he knew was there, even if he couldn't see them.

Occasionally he found himself wondering about the comments, questioning whether his imagination was worse than reality. He succumbed to temptation once and opened them again, despite swearing he never would, and observed some of the most vulgar conversations he had ever witnessed. Worst of all, they were about him. In this case, curiosity really almost did kill the cat.

The small glimpse of what he had seen people saying about him nearly made him quit entirely. He held on though because so far, his plan was working. He was the one delivering the story to the world, giving it to his readers.

The only problem was he could feel it deteriorating. The stress of being watched and critiqued was throwing off his writing. The plot was good, but he could already see it was falling apart at the seams as he neared the end. He wasn't entirely happy with it, but prayed that once it was done, it would be good enough.

It was a beautiful day outside when Cooper finally finished his newest novel, an act that normally lifted a weight from him, but this time seemed to only add more onto his shoulders. He didn't know how to feel. His emotions were so tangled that he couldn't differentiate one from the other.

The office was unusually bright as the hot midday sun streamed in, making Cooper's face glow on the screen as he stared first at the blinking cursor, then at his own expression-less face. He realized he needed to say something to the few viewers left, so he pushed the hair out of his eyes and looked directly into the camera.

"I appreciate everyone who's watched me write this book. I hope you enjoyed it and maybe even learned a bit about the writing process. If you want to show your support for the project, the final version of the book should be available soon. Thanks again for following along with this little experiment."

Cooper ended the livestream, still unsure of where his feelings were going to land. He had written three books faster than he'd thought possible, and doing this one live had seemingly stopped AIP from pushing his work out into the world. But at what cost?

He looked to see if the book was available for purchase, and there it was, open for preorders just minutes after he had finished it. Could he even count this as a win? What had he accomplished? He was completely wiped. His brain literally ached, either from the screen or from pulling stories out of it at such a rapid pace. He needed to rest.

For days, he tried to unravel his thoughts on what had

happened and searched for new plans to reclaim his life. Writing the book live had made it feel more like his, but being watched made his work suffer and he'd hated almost every minute of it.

The conversations that he knew were happening in the comment section had ruined his work in a way that was almost worse than MUSE ever could. Those were real people saying all those horrible things.

After building up some courage, he looked at what some of his other readers had said in their reviews of his latest novel. They didn't do a great job of lifting Cooper's spirits. Many claimed it had been his weakest story so far, while others said he had lost his mind, attributing his insanity to Elena separating from him.

> Haven't you guys noticed? None of these new books have Elena as a character. I heard rumors that she left him. It's clear he's having a mental breakdown. He needs help!

This review stuck like a knife in his side, the blade twisting every time he thought about it. He hadn't even realized he had left her out of these stories. The goal had been to not think about her, but his brain had apparently opted for total, voluntary amnesia. This painful review gave him a moment of clarity and sent him into a bout of despair, leaving him bedridden for days until he was able to forget his dear wife once more.

The reviews had been bad enough, but when he checked the book's sales, he really questioned what exactly he was trying to accomplish. The numbers were abysmal. Clearly people didn't want to pay for something they could read online, or maybe the whole livestream idea was just too strange.

Further research showed that many of his readers really thought he was going crazy. This made Cooper laugh hysterically, a maniacal and sad sort of laugh, because it was exactly the type of perception he had tried so hard to avoid since the beginning. Yet here he was, some crazy has-been who thought it would be a good idea to livestream writing a novel. Who was he kidding?

He became paralyzed, unable to come up with any new plans of attack. What was the point of any of it? Why even write if he wasn't going to enjoy it? Why continue if every plan he could come up with was just going to ruin his legacy? It was as if his mind had been read—his phone rang, and the man who thought he knew all the answers was on the other end. How Cooper wished it was the woman who had all the answers he desired instead.

# 28

*She had built her life on stolen artistry and borrowed beauty, each forgery like a pebble thrown into the vast lake of art's history. The ripples her work created were false, hollow imitations. And yet . . . as she looked at the captivated faces, she couldn't shake the thought that maybe her lies weren't entirely empty. Somehow, they'd managed to give people something genuine, a glimpse into another world, a moment of escape, a fleeting happiness.*

Alexander's smug voice came through the phone and Cooper could almost see that shit-eating grin of his.

"You've been busy."

"What do you want?" Cooper asked, hate filling his words.

"Just wanted to check in. See how you were doing."

"I'm fine."

"I'm not so sure about that, but I guess everything is subjective."

"I said I'm fine."

"Okay, whatever you say." Alexander breathed into the phone and continued in a more upbeat tone. "I'm pretty impressed with how much effort you're putting into all these new endeavors of yours. Three new projects in a few short months . . . might be a new world record or something. We'll look into that for you, it'd be good for publicity."

Cooper sat silently, waiting for the real reason for the call.

"It really is impressive . . . but the numbers. Have you seen the numbers?" Alexander asked.

Cooper couldn't hold it in anymore. All this fuck cared about was numbers, a measure of success.

"Fuck off! You and your fucking MUSE can go straight to hell. I don't care about the numbers, all I want is control of my life. I want it back!"

"Cooper." Alexander tsked like a teacher goading a child into shame. "You still don't get it. I understand where you're coming from." He almost sounded like a genuine friend. "But you're only hurting yourself by going down this path. Just look at all your adoring fans. Look at how your perception and ratings have shifted. If you keep trying to write mediocre stories in order to prove something, you're going to be ruined. Not to mention broke."

For a split second, Cooper heard the voice of his old friend somewhere in all the bullshit, but then it all came back to the money. Money, power, and himself were all that Alexander cared about. Cooper decided not to respond, barely able to resist the temptation to hang up.

"You still there?"

Cooper answered with a grunt. Alexander deserved no more words.

"Anyway, I really thought you would have changed your mind by now. That you would have seen you don't have to worry about anything anymore. You can write or not, it doesn't matter."

Cooper thought he sensed something in Alexander's voice, something that hinted that it actually did matter.

"Everything else is automated," Alexander continued. "You always used to brag about how lucky you were, able to hand in a book and be done with it while we handled the rest. Well, now it's just like the upgraded version of that. Just exist and we do the rest, with the help of MUSE, of course."

"You're the one who doesn't get it," Cooper said. "I'm beginning to believe you never will. You're too far gone, too focused on this future of yours."

"Cooper. You never have to work ever again if you don't want to," Alexander said, speaking slowly and enunciating every word like he was speaking to an imbecile. "What's so bad about that? Hell, just pretend everything is like it used to be and write the damn books if you want to so badly. What does it matter?"

"What does it matter? Everything's ruined! Elena's gone and nothing's fucking mine anymore. Your MUSE owns it all just as much as I do. It's just as much me as I am. Do you not fucking get that, Alexander?"

Alexander didn't respond, but Cooper knew his silence wasn't due to any self-reflection. In all likelihood, he still believed he'd given Cooper the greatest gift imaginable.

"Holy fuck. I wish you'd wake up tomorrow and your precious little program decided it wanted your life instead of mine. Maybe then something other than your own ego would get into that fucking narcissistic head of yours. What's the point of my existence? I may as well just disappear."

"What do you mean by that?" Alexander asked, his voice weak and soft.

"What do you think I fucking mean?"

"You're worrying me. Why would you do that? Do you want me to call someone?"

"Call someone? You could start by calling my wife and telling her this is all your fault. Then you can call and have yourself committed for being a fucking psychopath!"

"I don't know what to say. I'm sorry, I wish things had played out differently. I really wish Elena hadn't left you, but that's not my fault. You have to promise me you won't ever do something like that. I know you don't believe it, but you really are my friend. If anything ever happened to you, I don't think I could forgive myself."

"That's probably the only choice I have left in my life that could make me feel human again. One last final act of control. Even though you're a lying piece of shit and I don't believe a word that comes out of your mouth, if I do make that final choice, I hope to God you are telling the truth. I hope my death would destroy you."

"Cooper, you can't talk like that."

"I'm done. I'm going to hang up."

"Hang on, hang on." Alexander spoke frantically and Cooper could actually hear genuine worry in his voice. "I'll tell you this and hope that you make the right decision, even though I shouldn't. If you quit writing, whether it's just that you decide not to write or whether you decide to end . . . it all. It won't write your stories."

"So?"

"So, like I told you before, it's perfectly predicting you and, as a result, you have to do less work. You can write one sentence or the entire book and it will finish it either way. But if you never start writing something, it won't either. I really think you need to look at this from a different perspective and see that you're still coming out on top."

Cooper remained silent, unsure of how to feel. Alexander had just confirmed that doing nothing would work. Cooper had avoided that path, fairly confident it would lead to an endless depression that would only stop with his death. But now that he knew it could work, he let himself imagine a different kind of life, one where happiness came from something other than writing. Maybe he could even convince Elena to come back and try that different kind of life with him.

"Seriously, Cooper, you need to think about this. If you quit, or do something . . . worse, it's over. You were at the height of your career and if you stop now, you might lose it all. All the respect you've earned, all those adoring readers. Your legacy would barely be a drop in the bucket, especially when we look at that pathetic"—the word came out like venom—"excuse for a novel you just typed for the world to see. That will be the thing people remember you for, a crazed writer losing it live on the internet. Years from now, nobody will recall a single one of your bestsellers. They'll just pull up that clip. Is that what you want?" There was more darkness in Alexander's voice than Cooper had ever heard from the man.

"We'll see." Cooper hung up the phone, unable to take any more.

He made his way to bed and sunk himself into it, more exhausted than ever. The weeks of writing were finally taking their toll on him.

He could quit writing and it would work. But was that a life he wanted to live, especially with Elena gone? No matter how much he had hated every single word that had come out of Alexander's mouth, he had a point.

* * *

It was nearly two in the morning when his phone rang again and startled him awake. Its blaring peaceful ringtone and intense vibrations made his eyes pop wide open and he had answered it before he could even see who was calling.

It had to be her. Who else would call at this hour? If it was Alexander again, Cooper might very well end it right then and there with him on the other end of the line, just to spite his new God, his new owner.

"Hello?"

"Hi." The voice was soft and sweet, but still so sad.

He might live to see the sun rise after all.

"Elena? Is that you?"

"Yes."

What do two people in this situation talk about? Cooper had no idea, but he had to say something.

"How are you doing?" he asked.

"I don't really know anymore."

"I'm so sorry, Elena." He pleaded for forgiveness with his wavering voice.

"You didn't do anything wrong, Cooper. Nothing at all. This was all me. All of it, every little terrible thing about it."

"That's not true," he replied, even though it was. If she had just told him right away, told him the truth, none of this would've happened. Cooper wondered if she even knew what she had helped unleash into the world, how far her decision would reach. She had helped to create the next stage of evolution. His life and writing career were only the start, but he thought that was the thing killing her the most. Destroying the one she loved.

"It is. We both know it is." Her voice was so level and matter-of-fact that Cooper had no rebuttal. "I just wanted to talk to you one last time."

He could feel his throat closing and his mouth filling with marbles.

"What? What do you mean?" he stammered.

"I just needed one last goodbye."

"No! No. Hang on a second. It can't be over. You can't just be done with us forever."

"I won't ever be done with us, that's why I need this. I just hoped maybe you could do this for me. I can't live with the pain of what I did, this pain that you're still there hoping that I'll come back. I need an honest-to-God goodbye if I'm ever going to continue to live."

"No, just wait a second. I've been trying to fix this. I need more time."

"There is no time. And there is no fixing it."

"There is, though. I've been trying to beat it. Beat the fucking thing. If I can do that, then it'll all be okay."

"Cooper," she said, as if trying to reel him in like an overeager child.

He began talking extremely fast now, frantically trying to explain that somewhere, somehow, there was a way out of all of this, a way back together.

"If I can beat it, then I'll have my life back and we'll be fine. Everything in the past will be just that, and you'll never have to worry about . . ."

"Cooper." This one did reel him back in. "I've seen you trying."

"You have?" Cooper asked shakily. Beating MUSE and trying to get Elena back were the only things that mattered, yet somehow knowing she had been following along with all of his pathetic attempts made him embarrassed and ashamed.

"Yes, and I love you so goddamn much for trying so hard to save this, trying to save us. But it's impossible. I've seen what that thing can do, what Alexander is capable of, and there's nothing we can do. After I saw everything you were doing, I tried to think of a way out of this, too. You gave me a little spark of hope, but there's nothing, Cooper. We've lost."

They couldn't just lose. He tried to put all the passion and truth he could muster into his words, tried to force his true feelings out of his big heart and through his shrinking throat to convince her.

"I won't ever hate you, Elena. I won't resent you. I won't ever stop loving you! Please, just come back. This doesn't have to be the end of us."

"It does." He could hear her start to cry. "Even if all those things are true, I will still hurt every time I look at you. I will never forgive myself for what I did. In the end, I will probably go out of my way to make sure you feel those things."

"I wouldn't."

"You might not, but I still don't want that."

"Okay . . . okay. We might not be able to beat it, but I can just not write. Alexander even said it would work. I won't write, MUSE won't be an issue, and none of this will matter. We can just live our lives together doing whatever we want. Last year we were talking about cutting back on work and trying something new anyway. Remember?"

"Cooper." There was that voice again. That voice that said, *Come back to reality*. "I don't want that either. I don't want you to give up the one thing that makes you *you*. I couldn't live with myself if you did that."

"You make me *me*. You're the only thing that makes me happy."

"I used to. But I don't know if I would be able to ever again. Don't you see that yet?"

Cooper did, but he still didn't want to accept it. He couldn't accept it. He could see the potential future ahead of them like an old home movie, and he could see that Elena's worries were valid. He knew he was being selfish, but he didn't want to lose her. He believed he could be strong enough, love her hard enough to make sure her worries never came true. He couldn't promise that they wouldn't, though.

All he could say was, "I love you. I miss you so much."

"I miss you too." Elena sighed before continuing. "So, can we start over?"

"What . . . do you mean?" Cooper asked.

"I mean, can we pretend you just answered the phone? Pretend that I didn't fuck up our entire lives. Pretend we're happy? Pretend that everything's going to be . . . okay?"

"But . . ."

"Just pretend? Talk to each other one last time."

Her voice was filled with so much longing and sadness that Cooper could feel his soul splitting in two. He wanted to scream and tell her they didn't have to pretend. It could be real if she just came back.

"Hello? Who is this?" Cooper asked.

"Hey honey," Elena replied, and Cooper could hear her effortful smile through the phone.

"How's your day been?" he asked half-heartedly.

She struggled, but eventually fell into her normal cadence, sadness trailing every forced word. "Oh, you know, just finished reading another fucking fairytale about some beautiful blonde bimbo being swept off her feet by some rich asshole."

Cooper let out a small chuckle through the tears that were now streaming down his face. "Sounds like the perfect way to spend the day."

"Tell me about your day," Elena said.

Now Cooper was the one struggling to fall into this theater, this last show to solidify their feelings for each other and end it all on a bittersweet note instead of the pure misery they really found themselves in.

"Oh, you know, I just thought I'd try something new. I had the brilliant realization that nobody had ever written an entire book live before."

"Really?" Her voice was filled with genuine enthusiasm and anticipation.

"Yeah, can you believe that? No one ever tried to turn the most lengthy, boring, and mind-numbing process into a live performance before."

"So, how'd it go?"

"Splendidly. The thousands of viewers loved every minute reading along at a snail's pace. They really loved it when I completely deleted a paragraph they liked, or worse yet, wiped their favorite character from existence."

"I bet they were all on the edge of their seats the entire time."

Cooper could almost see her beautiful smile now.

"You can't even imagine," he said. "You should've seen it when I got to the end and I wrote 'and then old Fido died,' paused for dramatic effect, and then changed it to 'Fido and Billy lived happily ever after and nothing bad ever happened to them ever again.'"

Elena laughed. A big laugh that rang through the phone and sent happy tears to mix with Cooper's sad ones. The tears of laughter followed the same trails the bitter ones had. Oh, how Cooper had missed that rare and elusive laugh. Missed that smile. Missed that voice. Missed her. How was he going to do this? How was he going to live without her?

"I love you so fucking much, Cooper."

"I love you too, Elena. I always will."

They talked for hours, pretending that everything would be okay. Eventually, they were no longer just pretending to be happy as they laughed and loved each other. Then they said goodbye for the last time, and a part of both of them died.

# 29

*Every new revelation about Elena's deceit left Victor feeling more adrift. The hope he'd once clung to had eroded, leaving behind only the barren reality of a life stripped of joy and purpose, like a candle flickering out in the dark.*

Years went by and Cooper shifted between two lives. The last conversation between him and Elena was the only thing keeping him ticking. He would go through periods of resistance, while other times he would try to live in a fantasy, ignoring the reality of the world he was trapped in.

First, he tried not to write. He'd wanted to prove to himself, and hopefully to Elena, that he could go on without it. So, he threw himself into whatever distractions he could find. The thing he gravitated toward most was hiking, even though he hated the fact that Alexander had given him some actually good advice.

It wasn't long until he had explored every trail within a two-hour radius from the cabin. The beauty of nature and the occasional happy greetings from passing hikers almost made him feel like everything could be okay, and that the world wasn't such an awful place. He would bring a book and a fresh pack of cigarettes, find a quiet place with a good view, and sit there all day long. He'd turn pages until the sun set or until he ran out of smokes.

But eventually, something would change—something that proved nothing was okay, and that everything Elena had said—everything she had feared—was indeed true. It was a combination of things that brought about this change.

Each new book he read slowly pulled him back into the world he was trying to run away from. The more stories he consumed, the more the ones in his own head called out to be written. When the weather got colder, it was harder to just sit there and read, not to mention that the looming winter always reminded Cooper of his past writing routine. What always pushed him back to writing, though, was those godforsaken trains, that screeching reminder of death, despair, and misery.

As summer faded into fall, there was one trail Cooper found himself drawn to almost exclusively. It was further out than the rest, but the drive didn't bother him. He would get up at the crack of dawn and be there just as the sun was waking up the world. Making sure he had his cigarettes and a book, he would travel a few short miles up the trail. If he was there to hike, he would keep going and make it all the way to the summit of the small but beautiful James Peak.

But most of the time he stopped on an old and decrepit railroad bridge that looked just like the ones in all those classic western movies. The type of bridge where a gang of train robbers would plant a couple satchels of dynamite and blow the thing sky-high. This one was still standing, but a few well-placed fireworks might just be enough to knock it down.

Cooper would carefully walk out to the middle of this short section of a long-gone world, plop himself down, and dangle his legs over the edge. If he accidentally fell, it wouldn't be high enough to kill him, but it would almost certainly put him in the hospital. He never even thought about that, though. Instead, he would open his book, light a cigarette, and wait.

After a while, the sound of the whistle would come. Cooper would mark his page, close the book, and look down the mountain. The sound wasn't an imagined noise from the past. A real train would go by on the tracks just a few hundred yards below him.

He would sit on the old, abandoned section of railroad from a time before—a time when the world was rough, rugged, and required humanity to adapt to it—and watch as a diesel train went three times as fast as those old steam-powered locomotives, disappearing straight into the mountain instead of going around. It went right under the Continental Divide as if it were the simplest thing in the world, just as it had been doing since 1928. People never moved mountains, they just blew right through them, ignoring all the rules and pretending like they understood things, just hoping that eventually, they would.

Every single train that went along those tracks would grab his attention and hold it like a moth to a flame, but when the California Zephyr came through, Cooper wouldn't return to his book. He would wonder if those passengers could see him all the way up here.

He pictured their lives as they enjoyed their nearly twenty-four-hundred-mile trip, making their way from Chicago to San Francisco or back the other way. He would wish he and Elena could take that trip, a trip significantly longer than their last train ride, and he could look up at the old rickety bridge and maybe see somebody else sitting here, or better yet, no one at all.

Eventually, he wouldn't even bother to bring a book to the old crumbling railroad and its rotted-out ties, rusted spikes, and huge, tarred beams. He'd sit on that edge waiting only for those trains, lost in thought as each day got progressively more dreary and dark, living a cigarette-smoke-filled haze of an existence.

Luckily, the bitter cold would snap him out of it just in time for him to realize where he was headed. At least for now.

It was at this point that all he could do was write in order to survive. He hated it more than almost anything now, but it was the only thing that gave him more time, proof that he couldn't live without it.

At first, the ideas exploded out of him, a cathartic release after months of trying to lock them inside and hide them from that *thing*. He would write and try to avoid the outside world entirely, pretend nothing existed except that black hole of an office and his baby-blue typewriter. The story would be enough to drown out everything else for a while, the *klack* of the keys and the words they created the only things that mattered.

Eventually, the creeping feeling of despair would come seeping in between the final few chapters as the lies he tried to believe collapsed around him. Reality always returned to ruin yet another one of his finished books. He never checked to see if MUSE had its digital fingers all over his work anymore, he knew it did. His bank account would fill back up even as the finished story sat there on top of his desk, untouched, until the next time he found himself sucked back into the immense gravity of his office by the pull of the typewriter and the stories screaming to be freed from their prison.

Back and forth he went between the two for what felt like an eternity, lonely and barely alive. No matter where he found himself, he was still holding on to the smallest glimmer of hope that maybe one day things would change.

Maybe AIP or Alexander would screw over too many people and the entire thing would come crashing down. Maybe one day he wouldn't be forced to come in from the cold and write; he could tell Elena he didn't need it anymore, and she could come home.

He'd tried to respect her wishes, tried to leave her alone, but somewhere along this sad existence, he had gone searching for her. Cooper struggled to find any trace of Elena. Part of him worried something terrible had happened to her, while another part of him knew she just didn't want to be with him and was living some entirely new and separate life.

At one point, Cooper devoted an entire year to tracking her down, but all he discovered was that she clearly didn't want to be found. Elena confirmed this herself when she left him a voicemail filled with tears, begging him to stop. Begging him to let their last conversation be the final note of their symphony.

He didn't want to stop, but he couldn't bear to hurt her. Even though she had been almost entirely to blame for every-thing, he still loved her more than anything in the world and hoped that she would return.

He grew old hoping.

Eventually, he became a character straight from a book. The smoking, excessive hiking, and lack of nutrition turned him into a lanky, scrawny version of the man he used to be. The muscles he had worked so hard to build all those years ago had melted away. He had given up on taking care of himself. His hair and beard had grown so long and unkempt that other people on the trails probably mistook him for a bear whenever they first caught sight of him.

Who did he need to look good for? What little communication he used to do for book releases and meetings were gone, thanks to MUSE. Alexander had been right about one thing. When he chose to pretend nothing was wrong and just write, his life had come full circle. His job was easier than ever, but that didn't mean it felt good.

A while after the search for his dear beloved, Cooper went after AIP and Alexander. He tried to pursue legal action, but this turned out just as he always knew it would. Going up alone against their team of top attorneys was like volunteering to be put to a firing squad. Cooper spent so much time and money and got nowhere, only more upset about his inability to change anything.

Other than these brief intermissions, his life of never-ending duality trudged on. It was wearing him down to the bone and Cooper didn't know how much more of it he could take. Each passing year caused his hopes to dwindle until there was essentially nothing left.

One morning, he woke up and looked in the mirror. He noticed the gray in his beard and the years of pain and sorrow in his wrinkles. He always had dark circles under his eyes, but now they were so deep that he could almost see the skull underneath more than he could see his own face.

This wasn't a life worth living. He couldn't do it anymore. Nothing had changed and nothing was ever going to change. Elena wasn't going to come back and he had nothing else left. MUSE would never be put back into the box it had come from.

Today would be the fateful day, and there was only one possible way to carry out the terrible act. Despite the horrific and grim plan running through his head, he went about his morning routine as if nothing were wrong. He was scared, but he could already sense the relief that would come from the act. The pain of everything gone, a finality equivalent to the last period of a story.

If he no longer existed, it would all stop. He wouldn't be sharing his life with MUSE anymore, and hopefully it wouldn't be modified to continue after he was gone. At the moment, a larger portion of his novels had been put into the world by him alone, and this gave Cooper some solace.

There was no changing his mind. This would be his last day on Earth. Without Elena, without writing, without hope, he couldn't continue.

The thought of what he was about to do still made him want to throw up. But as the minutes went by and he really, honestly accepted his decision, a sense of peace came over him. He was in the shower when all the terrible and awful things eating away at him vanished. Cooper was in awe at how he felt now that they were gone. He looked at himself in the mirror and could even see a change in his face, more light behind his eyes.

*I can't go out looking like Sasquatch.*

He took the electric trimmer and removed years of hair from his face, revealing not just a much older version of himself beneath the scruff, but one he had forgotten.

"That's better," he said with a hint of a smile. It had been so long since he'd smiled that even that tiny curl of his lips made them split and left his jaw and cheeks aching.

He went out to the kitchen, blaring his favorite albums throughout the cabin as he made a pot of coffee. He was trying to soak up every last moment of life he allowed himself. He felt more present in the little things than ever before. The smell of the coffee, its taste on his tongue, the warmth of it as it made its way down his throat.

For a moment, it seemed like things had returned to how they used to be, but then the loneliness of the big cabin came to tear the beauty away. He needed to leave this place and get where he was going. There were just a few things he had to do first.

Cooper went to the medicine cabinet. He considered taking whatever pills he could find that might make the task at hand easier, but then decided against it. He was about to grab his favorite book of all time, *The Princess Bride*, but trying to enjoy one last book while doing what he was about to do seemed absolutely batshit crazy. This made him second-guess everything and he felt himself wanting to back out. Without something to help him, he didn't know if he could go through with it.

Suddenly, an idea struck him with immense force and led him down to Elena's office. He stood as still as a statue outside her door. He had spent so much time avoiding this space. Just knowing it existed caused him excruciating pain and made living there almost unbearable. But now it was the only place he wanted to be.

He opened the door. Everything was almost exactly as she had left it. The stale air hit his nose, but there were subtle notes of her left, even after all these years. He flicked the lights on, the brightness and colorful aesthetic of the room stood in stark contrast to the darkness it now represented in his heart.

But this time, it didn't hurt to look at. Instead, he was absorbed in all the good thoughts this room inspired. All the memories. He walked around Elena's office as if it were a museum, looking at her things with admiration and carefully picking up items that reminded him most of his dear wife.

Cooper looked at that mint-green couch, still the comfiest piece of furniture he had ever laid on, and thought about how much she would have liked his baby-blue typewriter. He found a few candles left in the room and lit them, sandalwood and vanilla filling the air. *Her favorites.*

After years of being empty, the room slowly began to feel lived in again as the few ghosts Elena had once complained about gave Cooper the space he so desperately needed. Though this office was a glaring reminder of everything missing from his life, in this particular moment it felt anything but haunted. It wasn't brimming with sorrow—instead, it overflowed with a warm fondness that evoked distant but vivid feelings of happiness and joy.

Cooper made his way over to Elena's collection of vinyl and thumbed through it, but saw that there was still one left on the record player. He flicked the switch and the needle dropped, filling the room with crackles and pops. Situating himself on the couch, he listened to the last record Elena had played in this office. *Doolittle* by the Pixies. *Her favorite.*

He listened to the soundtrack of Elena and tried to recall every happy memory he could. Visions of her flooded his mind. Each was like a moving painting, forever framed by the synapses of his brain.

In one, her piercingly beautiful blue eyes stared back at him with the same love they always had. In another, she smiled at him—her thin lips as delicate and pretty as two petals of a pink rose—and he couldn't help but return the smile. In the next image, he followed behind her, her lovely blonde hair swaying as she walked, the scent of fresh ocean air and coconut from her conditioner drifting toward him.

Eventually, he came to another portrait of Elena: she was shaking, eyes squinted shut, a huge grin lighting her face and bringing out the cute dimples in her cheeks. Her laugh—the treasure Cooper had sought most in this life. At first, there was no sound. But then he could hear it, dancing softly with the music in the background. That elusive symbol of pure happiness and joy. These masterpieces—the ones filled with laughter—were less common in his private gallery of Elena, which only made them all the more precious to him.

But it was every memory—every single second they'd spent together—that made the entire collection priceless.

The record stopped and he flipped it over, continuing to listen. He imagined her holding him right now on this couch, cuddling and listening to music like they used to. He dreamed about laying his head in her lap as she ran her fingers through his hair. Then the record cut off for the final time and he reluctantly got off of that couch before it became his last resting place.

He was about to leave the room, thinking that whatever had pulled him here was gone now, but then suddenly he saw it—the real reason he found himself in her office. The recording booth where Elena had immortalized her voice. That beautiful voice he had avoided for so long for fear of how much it would break him.

Now it was the only thing he wanted to hear, the thing he would listen to in order to drown out that ever-approaching train. He turned on her computer and plugged his phone into it. It took a while for him to find what he was looking for, but eventually he opened the folder containing backup copies of every book she had ever recorded at the cabin.

He scrolled through the titles, trying to pick based on feeling alone. Eventually, he settled on *The Enchanted Garden of Time*, written by some author he had never heard of. It wasn't the sort of book he would normally choose, but its insignificance and simplicity would hopefully provide the perfect world to escape into . . . forever.

It had just dawned on him how important this decision would be. He hoped the title was accurate and he wasn't about to drift into the afterlife while listening to a horror story about an evil garden that traps people for eternity. Just in case, he copied another file titled *Dragon Riders of Emberwood* and a few others to his phone so he could shift gears if need be.

After all the files had transferred, Cooper turned off the computer and got ready to leave the room. He wanted to stay there forever, but the hurt was already creeping back in, and he couldn't bear to lose all the happiness he had just found within those four walls.

He blew out the candles, their smoke adding a harshness to the room that still smelled like her. After powering off the record player, echoes of the album still hung in the air. Finally, he flicked off the lights and shut the door to Elena's office forever.

Cooper picked up his headphones, poured the rest of his coffee into a thermos, and grabbed a fresh pack of cigarettes. Make that two packs—no point in saving them now. The winding and nearly deserted mountain highway carried him to the James Peak trail, just as it had countless times before.

By the time he arrived, it was already late in the day, and the winter bite seemed to have kept most other hikers at home. The parking lot was nearly empty save for a few cars. He grabbed the last cigarette from his first pack, having smoked the rest on the long drive, lit it, and put it into his mouth. He took everything he needed from the car and left the keys inside, not caring to lock it, and headed out along the trail.

Even though it was close to freezing that day, there was no breeze to make it unbearable. Cooper barely noticed the chill in the air and instead savored the warmth of the midday sun on his freshly shaved face as he walked. The effort of the hike made him feel alive, and each step was more thoughtful than the last. He paid attention to the tiny details as he made his way through the mountainous terrain, appreciating every brushstroke of beauty placed along the trail by some unknown force—or maybe they were just there by pure cosmic luck.

*I don't have to do this*, he thought to himself. *I could just keep hiking. See how far I could make it. Maybe I'd survive, maybe I wouldn't. Just walk until I couldn't anymore.*

Once he found himself at that old section of abandoned railroad, all those thoughts faded into nothing. He was left with the knowledge that this was what he had to do. He had tried, tried so fucking hard to keep going. But a person can try for only so long.

He made his way out to the middle of the decrepit railroad bridge for old time's sake, opened up his new last pack of cigarettes, and took one. He sat there for a while, replaying his life and flipping through its pages as if it were one of his books. Had it really ever been *his* book? He sat there and smoked almost the entire pack, thinking about everything, watching the trains below, waiting for something—but he didn't really know what.

Then the California Zephyr went whizzing by and he suddenly understood why he'd been waiting. He needed to know that it wouldn't be that particular train that would do it. He couldn't ruin those passengers' trip of a lifetime and add more hurt and pain to the world. All he had ever tried to do with his writing was just the opposite. As long as it wasn't that train.

As far as he was concerned, any other freight train and its jaded conductor wouldn't be too distraught by what was about to occur. Hell, some of the worst of them might retell this story for the rest of their lives at some dingy bar with a hint of excitement in their voices.

Cooper made his way toward a section of railroad where he didn't think he would be seen or bothered. There was a patch of pine trees and a bend in the tracks that would almost guarantee there'd be no time to stop.

He stood for a moment, staring at the iron rails. They were almost completely rusted over, but the top edge was polished bright by passing trains and glistened like a guillotine's blade in the afternoon sun.

Cooper pulled out his phone, put on his headphones, turned on *The Enchanted Garden of Time* narrated by Elena Owens, and sat down in the middle of the tracks. He turned up the volume and positioned the back of his neck on one rail while the other cradled his knees. He closed his eyes and imagined again that he was resting his head in his wife's lap. Only this time, he was listening to her read as she played with his hair.

At first, he could barely hear the story. His heart was thumping loudly in his chest and his ears were ringing as the panic of what he was doing set in. It felt like minutes, but within a few short seconds the adrenaline subsided, his body relaxed, and Elena's voice grew louder.

Her beautiful voice filled his entire awareness, the thought of approaching death gone from his mind. With each word, she took him into a world unlike this one. A place where everything turned out okay. If only he could stay there forever, a place in between.

He was whisked away, the sound of Elena carrying him ever closer to whatever lay beyond. A train somewhere in the distance sped toward his spot in the tracks, completely unaware of its new and horrific purpose. He lay there listening to that story, waiting. Waiting for the end to come.

Cooper thought he could feel the ground begin to shake

under him, but he tried desperately to ignore it, using all his effort to focus on that sweet, beautiful voice reading him the last story he would ever hear.

With immense force . . . a surge of energy went shooting through his body and the peace that had trapped him between the tracks disappeared in seconds. *Why didn't I think of that before?* The idea became clear in his mind. The sound of Elena reading was growing quieter and louder at the same time. He *could* stay there in that place in between. Maybe do even better than that.

An unfamiliar sense of hope sparked within him. It was almost imperceptible, but it was enough to make him want to try.

Cooper sat bolt upright in the middle of the tracks and opened his eyes.

The ground wasn't shaking. There was no train about to hit him . . . but there was a mangy little dog sitting right there at his feet, looking up at him and wagging its tail like absolutely nothing was wrong in the world.

# 30

*Surrounded by the echoes of great artists, Victor's exhibition was more than just a showcase; it was a heartfelt message to Elena. Each piece was chosen not only for its beauty but for its ability to express the depth of his feelings. He hoped that one day she would see the love he still held for her and return.*

Cooper got up from the tracks unscathed. It only took a few steps to completely remove himself from the danger he had voluntarily put himself in.

The little mutt still sat there, looking up at him with big wide eyes and its tongue hanging out to the side. He reached out to pet the scrawny thing and wondered why it had come to watch such a gruesome and terrible event. Was it just curious? Had it simply never seen a man lie down on the tracks like that before?

"What's up, little guy? Were you here for the show? Or were you going to eat me after I was gone?" Cooper laughed at this morbid thought as he suddenly realized he was still alive!

Almost as if the dog took offense to such a question, it got up and rubbed its body against Cooper's legs, resting against him as if they had always been best friends.

"No, no. You wouldn't do that, would you?" Cooper said in that dumb voice everyone uses to talk to babies or pets. "You're too good to eat roadkill, aren't you?" He gave the stray another loving head rub.

Cooper put his headphones away, took the final cigarette from his last pack, and got ready to head back to the car.

He would never smoke another one again in his life; this really was his last.

"Well, I gotta get going," he said to the dog. "I may be around here again though, if you ever find yourself in the area."

He made it all the way back to his car, and that little dog followed him the whole way. It provided company for the entire trip, and Cooper was reminded of Evan, who had followed him just like a lost puppy through the dark and deserted halls of AIP.

When he finally reached the car and the dog sat down, staring up at him just like it had done at the foot of those railroad tracks, he knew there was no way he was leaving it there. He opened the back door and looked down at the dog that had seen better days.

"Well, what are you waiting for? Get in there."

The dog did as he was told and got in the car.

Before they had even made it a mile back to the cabin, the mangy mutt jumped over the console and into the passenger seat with practiced grace, and Cooper didn't mind in the slightest. He turned up the radio and he and his new companion jammed out to whatever overplayed, overrated songs came on, as if this was just any ordinary day.

Cooper felt lighter and less lonely than he had in a long, long time. He opened the car window and let the cold air breathe something new into the car. He felt alive again, and by the looks of it, so did his new friend, who had his head hanging out the window, ears flapping in the wind. After they both had their fill of fun, he rolled up the windows, turned down the music, and continued on toward the cabin.

The dog curled up into a ball on the seat, closed its eyes, and fell asleep in comfort for the first time in who knew how long, teleporting to its new home.

Without any force, commands, or other signs, the dog followed Cooper into the cabin and up to the bathroom. Cooper turned on the water, trying to get the temperature just right. This was the dog's first bath in ages and he wanted to make sure it was the best it could possibly be. After the tub had filled and steam was lazily rising from its surface, he checked one last time to make sure it wasn't too hot.

He thought the dog might just jump right in, but clearly it was waiting for an invitation. Cooper picked it up, realizing for the first time just how skinny it was, and gently placed it into the bath. The dog would need a proper grooming and a vet visit, but a good shampooing would have to do for tonight. Kneeling over the tub, he scrubbed months of grime and survival from the dog's coat.

"What am I going to call you? You need a name."

The dog turned its head with curiosity, probably wondering if it really needed a name. They were getting along well enough without such formalities. Hell, this was in all likelihood the best day it'd had in years.

Cooper remembered hearing somewhere that a dog's name was supposed to have two syllables. True or not, at least it was a starting point. For someone whose job required coming up with names, he was having an extremely tough time trying to find a name for the suds-covered ball of wet fur in front of him.

"Harley?" The dog's ears lowered. It didn't seem to be enthused about that one.

"Trooper?" Still nothing.

"Hmmm . . ." Cooper looked at the wet mess of animal.

"Caboose?" The dog's ears perked right up and its eyes glistened.

"Caboose!" The dog leaned over and licked Cooper all

over his face, spilling water and bubbles out of the tub and onto the floor. Cooper didn't stop him. *Just this once.* Just this one time, he could lick his face. In truth, it was just this once . . . and every time thereafter.

The name was a little odd for a dog, maybe too on the nose, but he couldn't argue with the response it had provoked. Once he got over the childish nature of it, he could see that it was perfect.

Caboose would help keep the darkness at bay. Beside him at all times, there no matter what. He would be there to make sure Cooper didn't stop on those dangerous tracks, always ready to give him a push forward when he needed it. A friend, someone to share the rest of his life with.

Now that Cooper had finished washing Caboose and the layers of dirt were gone, he could see the dog's fur was actually a beautiful shade of golden red, almost rust-colored. A strip of fluffy white ran from his chin down his chest and along one of his front legs. Cooper couldn't believe such a stunning dog had been abandoned, his beauty hidden beneath years of neglect.

After admiring Caboose's sharp, clean new look, Cooper dried him off. He thought he'd done a decent job—until Caboose gave one vigorous shake and a sharp tail wag, which sent the remaining water flying across the bathroom.

"Well then, Caboose," Cooper said, watching those ears perk again, "make yourself at home."

But Caboose sat there patiently, as if waiting for Cooper to lead the way.

Cooper didn't know if he was ready, though. So much rested on what he was about to do. Doubts crept in, gluing him to the spot. Then his new companion barked and looked up at him, head cocked, eyes filled with assurance. Together, they made their way to Elena's office.

As he gripped the doorknob, Cooper felt ashamed of what he had almost done. Simultaneously, he questioned his decision not to go through with the deadly deed, as all those old, lingering negative feelings showed themselves, waiting for their chance to consume him again. He tried to remind himself he had hope, but still struggled to find the courage he so desperately needed.

Then something touched his leg. He looked down—the dog was nuzzling into him. He had Caboose now too. Cooper opened the door and went inside.

He couldn't help but notice the room had a different energy now. Needing a few minutes to adjust, he eased himself onto the couch. Without hesitation, Caboose jumped onto the sofa and made himself at home, just as Cooper had told him earlier. He was also doing an excellent job of keeping his new owner company—a silent but welcome passenger for all difficult journeys such as this one.

Cooper looked around at the room again with new eyes. Eyes that didn't think they were trying to take it all in for the last time. The fear of pain had driven him to avoid this room as much as possible.

The irony was almost comical. This very office held the answers he had been searching for. Within its walls lay the key to a life he could still envision himself wanting to live, a reason to keep going.

What this room contained and symbolized had inspired hope in his almost-last moments. It gave him a new purpose, and from that purpose came the strength that he needed to keep going. Cooper was confident he wouldn't ever attempt to take his own life again, and with Caboose at his side, he was even more sure.

As he had lain there on those tracks, the act of listening to

Elena's voice pulled him out of the dark hole he had almost willingly climbed into. There were hundreds, if not thousands, of hours of stories Elena could read to him. Even though she was gone, he could spend the rest of his life listening to her.

Her beautiful voice could take him to places he could only imagine in his wildest dreams. She could read him stories that would crowd out the noise of this less-magical and not-so-charming world.

He might never feel the same joy from writing or reading ever again with MUSE looming behind every turned page, but she was enough. A recording of her was enough to keep him alive. But without purpose, what life was worth living?

Listening to her words as he lay there, waiting for the end of the line, unlocked compartments in his mind he didn't even know were closed off. His own brain had played tricks on him; the fact that he hadn't thought about it once before seemed almost impossible.

Elena might still be narrating his books.

He knew a traumatized mind could fabricate reality to survive, and selective amnesia was one such defense against insurmountable anguish. Just the thought of Elena had hurt him so badly that he had forgotten her, wiped every trace of her, even removed her from the books he had written.

He'd tried so hard to avoid the pain, but it had almost been the reason for his undoing. Without the thought of his dear Elena, what was left?

It was only on the tracks that everything came back into frame. The pain was still there, but so was everything else, and in that moment of truth, Cooper thought of a life that he could live that would make her happy. A purpose.

Trying not to wake Caboose, he quietly got up from the comfy couch and went to Elena's computer. He prayed his assumptions were right. If she wasn't still narrating his books, he didn't know what he would do. With bated breath, he searched for the audiobook version of his most recent novel.

There it was in bold letters: Narrated by Elena Owens. He downloaded it and played it through the office's speakers. He sank back down onto the couch, letting Caboose re-situate his still-damp body on his chest. Cooper closed his eyes and listened to Elena read his book, heard her connected to one of his stories for the first time . . . ever.

The experience only strengthened his resilience, and every little thing that was in the room, every tiny detail, was telling him he had made the right choice to walk off those tracks. The heap of fur that heaved with every sleeping breath as it rested on his chest, the comfy mint-green couch holding them both up, his beautiful wife's voice reading one of his books. Cooper felt a new sense of being as he imagined the future before him.

Writing for himself wasn't enough, and writing for MUSE only hurt him more. He could write for her, though.

He could continue to create books for Elena, hoping that maybe one day he could reach her through the stories he still had left inside of him. Use his words to tell her that he still loved her with all his heart and would always be there, waiting for her.

Cooper did just that.

* * *

No more worrying about AIP, MUSE, any of it. There was no point, something Alexander had been trying to tell him all along.

Whenever a story came to him, he no longer resisted; instead, he put ink to paper and let the words flow freely. The black hourglass had returned to its proper place on his desk, and Elena became the main character in every single one of his narratives again. Within every chapter was a message to his beloved wife.

Cooper always eagerly awaited her narration of his books, hoping that she would reply. She never did, but that didn't stop him. He would write her love letters until the day he no longer could.

Whenever he wasn't creating a new book for her, he would get lost in the collection of Elena's work. He and Caboose would take up residence on that mint-green couch and listen for hours on end. By this point, she had amassed hundreds of audiobooks, all filled with her voice that was perfectly tuned for telling stories. Cooper would never have to worry about running out. She was still releasing new books every year at a rapid pace, working just as hard as she ever had.

Cooper didn't consider himself happy—he didn't think he ever would be again, but at least now it felt like his life had meaning once more. Maybe Elena would come back, maybe she wouldn't, but he wasn't going to be the reason their story ended. He would write to her forever.

He would wait with Caboose and listen to her sweet voice reading the words that had made their way from his mind into the world by some diabolical means he chose not to think about anymore. They would live out the rest of their days together in that charred cabin nestled against the mountains, going for hikes and listening to all sorts of fantastical and magical stories read by a person Cooper still loved, despite all she had done to him.

He just hoped Elena was happy, and that she knew how much he loved her—something he tried to remind her of with every new book.

# Afterword

The idea for this book came to me after shifting technologies appeared to have made a few of my endeavors obsolete. I spent years working on a blog, finally gaining a modicum of success, only to have the advancement of AI wipe me from the face of the internet. I don't write this seeking pity or some other form of condolences, but I want readers to be aware that the story in these pages might not be far from the truth.

AI is here and we can't put it back in the box. We can lie to ourselves all we want and act as if the essence of human nature is untouchable, but in reality the impact of AI will be felt in every facet of our society, culture, and species.

We pretend certain aspects of our lives or particular industries will be safe from advancements in technology, but these are likely things we tell ourselves so we can sleep at night as we head into the future faster than ever before, unable to stop the force that has been unleashed into the world. Unleashed by others. You and I likely didn't have a say in the matter, and that's something that will haunt us for generations to come.

I am waiting on the edge of my seat to see how the future unfolds, just as many of you probably are. I honestly hope everything turns out okay in the end, but only time will tell.

When starting this book, I never intended it to be a love story, but the similarities between the passion between people and their attachment to technology made for a beautiful and terrifying comparison to explore. Love and technology both keep us stuck in our ways and can either greatly benefit our lives or destroy them. More often than not, the outcome of each relationship swings wildly to either side, hardly ever landing in the middle.

We humans love technology, and most of us couldn't live without it, but it might truly steal more than just our attention; it might take everything from us one day.

You may be wondering if AI was used to create any portions of this novel. I did use it in an very limited capacity that was purposeful and intentional. Nevertheless, I have no doubt in my mind that even Cooper Owens himself would likely be a little upset with me. It was a tough decision to use the very thing I am trying to warn readers about in this story, but hopefully it wasn't in vain and amplified the messages in this book, added authenticity to portions of text, and helped convey that we are further along this path than you might think.

Many will argue that using AI, even with artistic intentions, compromises the integrity of this very book, but in a way, that was actually one of my original goals for this story. I wanted to draw attention to the increasing ambiguity of media, writing, and all art.

Some of the writing from AI is already good enough to pass unnoticed by most, especially with careful and meticulous editing. I wanted to emphasize the fact that, as we continue into the future, the origin and authenticity of art will become more and more unclear. There are countless others already taking advantage of AI to flood the world with entire books that aren't theirs, and much more.

I assume many will judge my use of AI without thinking of the message or why I used it as a part of my storytelling, but I hope that at least for some, it has reinforced what I was trying to say with my book. I do want to make sure I am completely transparent about my use of AI, so you can find more information about exactly how and why I used it here: https://blakeloch.com/the-use-of-ai-in-fake-creativity/

www.ingramcontent.com/pod-product-compliance
Lightning Source LLC
Chambersburg PA
CBHW022034120726
47899CB00001BB/316